THE
MOSAIC LEGACY

BOOK ONE
OUT OF LINE

m.b. myka

Amaku

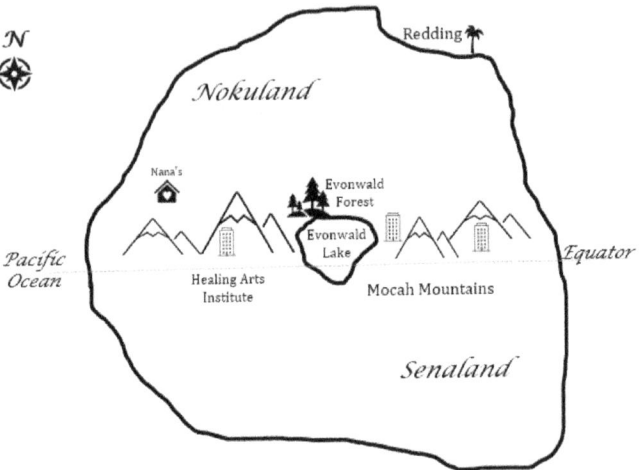

THE MOSAIC LEGACY

BOOK ONE
OUT OF LINE

m.b. myka

MOSAIC LEGACY
Out of Line

Copyright © 2022 m.b. myka
All rights reserved. This is the sole work of the author, and no portion of this publication may be copied or re-published in any publication without express permission of the publisher or author.

Edited by George Verongos
Cover by George Verongos

This is a work of fiction. All the names, characters, businesses, places, events, and incidents in this book are either the product of the author's imagination or used in a fictitious manner. Any resemblance to actual persons, living or dead, or actual events is purely coincidental.

ISBN: 979-8-9869316-1-6

To Chris and Ryan

CONTENTS

Prologue 1
Academic Testing 5
Confirmation 23
Institutionalized 31
Pathology 57
Elder Gift 71
The Nightmare 83
Holiday break 97
Revalidation 129
Helping Annette 137
Not So Fun Spring Break 149
Life's a Beach 163
A Ring, An Aunt, and A First Kiss 179
Surfing Under Siege 193
Bracelet From Glenn 209
The Yacht 233
Bur$t 251
Midsummer Proposition 267
The Parade 273
Another Trial 285
Grandmother 297
Definition of Insanity 311
In the Cards 317
Gang Activity 331
Home on the Ranch 345

PROLOGUE

A SILENT SCREAM howled through my head. My own horror woke me. Witnessing the burning car carrying my parent's bodies being pushed over the cliff felt like my heart was being ripped from my chest. My lungs released the breath I'd been holding with a loud "Ooof." Why this dream, again? Why now? Damp sheets peeled off my trembling legs as I stood to get a drink of water. Slowly, feeling my way in the dark, trying to avoid waking Nana, was engrained in my ritual.

This nightmare is always so real. It plays like a movie, never changing any details. When I try to explain that it might be part of my past, Nana fervently dismisses it. "Yes, your parents died in a car crash, but they were not pushed over a cliff." Nana assures me. "It's your mind mixing up the details of the past. There is no report or record of you having a younger sister. It must be a make-believe friend."

The nightmare and memories of my sister's abduction are so real to me. After eight years, they are starting to fade from my consciousness. Maybe that's why my subconscious isn't letting them go.

"You had the nightmare," Nana stated.

She held out a glass of water to me. She hadn't turned on a light even though there was no one else to wake up, but that was Nana, always trying to save the planet in every way she could.

With moonlight spilling through the window above the sink, it didn't take long for my eyes to adjust to the darkness.

"Yes, I'm sorry it woke you." I took the glass and drank the cool artesian water greedily. Leaving the empty glass in the clean sink, unwashed, to reuse at breakfast was just prudence to Nana. Turning from the sink, Nana hands me a clean, folded, fitted sheet. She's always two steps ahead. Nana followed me to the bedroom and helped with replacing the damp bedding. It would be pinned and drying on the clothesline before breakfast.

My damp T-shirt joined the discarded sheet on the room's only chair. Slipping into a dry nightshirt cooled my skin.

Nana tucked me in like a child and kissed my forehead. Some threads of color swirled lightly around her as she used a spell on me to make me feel drowsy. Aura colors activate when people use magic. Few people can see the colors. From my earlier years, it was entrenched in my habits to not mention seeing them. Nana is subtle and sparing with her magic. I had to focus hard to catch her using it. One very strange thing was I couldn't pick up her thoughts like other people I've touched.

Here in the foothills, folks don't use magic much, and when they do, they try to make it look like normal nonmagical life. They're modest, very unlike the northern cities where the amount of power you have dictates your social standing. Wanting to fit in and remembering to keep my yellow magic secret, I practice often but at very subtle levels.

"Your yellow magic is rare and special," my mother always told me, "Touching someone, skin to skin, allows your mind magic to hear, see, and feel other's thoughts."

Of course, not every thought they ever had, just the current or most vivid ones. Observing every thought in someone else's head is exhausting. Many people are much meaner in their thoughts. Some minds are so consumed with sex, filters are needed to make sense of the rest of their world. It's unbelievable how much some males think about procreating.

You have to ask the right questions to get the information you want. Often, people don't even know their own mind, and they certainly don't want me knowing more than they want to share. Humans lie to themselves more than they lie to each other in order to avoid any truths that threaten their beliefs or fragile egos. It can take time to figure out which thoughts can be trusted from which people.

Humans really like to believe the reality their mind creates is factual.

Even though Nana had used a spell to make me drowsy, all my thoughts and memories from the nightmare kept me awake.

ACADEMIC TESTING

"TODAY IS THE big day, Sera," Nana said, with forced enthusiasm, while she sat sipping her morning tea at breakfast. She was smiling, but overall, she looked sad. It was audition day at the community center, the Nokuland High Council hosted the testing event at many locations. Anyone in their thirteenth year of life could participate if they had preregistered. Teenagers were given color challenges for red, green, and blue magic. A few teens that showed promise or earned high enough scores would be given scholarships to training institutes.

Magical people typically don't get to use their powers until their teens. Magic is passed down through your parentage, and it has a unique code, just like DNA. It needs to be activated, and puberty is the main catalyst. My yellow mind magic was fully activated by my parents' deaths. Mom's warnings about not letting anyone know that we could talk to each other without voices still echoes in my memories.

"Nana, their brochure says they don't rely on scan scores to give out the boarding school admissions. I can still qualify." My protest sounded weak. There had been no sign of me developing any magic other than yellow, even though I was pubescent. They didn't even bother to test for yellow because of its rarity.

Nana isn't my grandmother; that's what most people call her. But she is my foster family, my protector and mentor. People that don't know Nana find her intimidating at first. Without a doubt, there's some mama bear in her. She is a big woman. Not fat but tall, broad, and strong. Her red hair is always securely braided with the tail tucked under, except at night. Not one thing about her shows any vanity. Minimalists could learn from her. Most every day, she wears a long-sleeved shirt with coveralls and sturdy boots for outside or slippers for in the house. If she owns more than lip balm for makeup, its hidden well. Even without makeup, she is a striking woman in her early sixties. We both use homemade lotions to keep our hands and faces protected from sun damage. A peculiar thing about her was if you looked at her in certain circumstances, you'd see elegance.

This small house was built for a hired hand. Nana rents out the main ranch house to the Bensons. If it wasn't for them, I'd most likely not know how non-minimalists lived. We mostly ate what Nana could grow or raise. With that type of diet and keeping up with chores, it was nearly impossible to build any fat.

We don't shop very much. Mostly we use the Bensons' castoffs. My wardrobe is from clothes Lysa has outgrown. Our sheets, towels, and blankets are worn thin, some have stains and a few even have patches in places. With no one to impress, these softly used items are perfect for ranch life. Nana taught me to sew by hand, and we use any scrap of material we get our hands on to make aprons, bags, pouches, purses, and hair coverings. We use the over-the-neck pouches to gather eggs, fruit, vegetables, and nuts, especially during chore time. On any given day, working around the ranch, a gathering bag or two is hooked over my neck and shoulders. Around my waist are pouches for smaller items. One small pouch hangs around my neck like a necklace but is always tucked into the front of my shirt. For trips to town, the bags are left at home. Even from a young age, I realized that our ranch clothes and gear seemed strange to others.

"Mrs. Benson wants you to stop by before leaving for testing. She'll help with your hair before you go." Nana said. She did the same before registration. For ranch life, my light brown hair was kept in neat braids tied with twine. Before going to town, Mrs. Benson liked to fuss over my appearance.

"One day soon, you'll grow into those big dreamy hazel eyes and long legs. You'll be the prettiest one around if you learn to fix your hair," Mrs. Benson would tell me while trimming and curling my hair. She liked bangs on me, and always cut a bit of the sides to frame my face. She unbraids the back and puts it in a high ponytail. "There's no doubt there is something special about you." It was nice to hear her say this, but she told her kids that same thing.

She always had a nice outfit for me, saved from Lysa's outgrown clothes, for town visits. "You have two completely different looks, one for the ranch and one for town," Neal commented. When Mrs. Benson took me and Neal in for registration, she'd warned us before entering the examination room, "Keep your expectations realistic. Scholarships are rare and it's a competitive process. City residents get the largest percentile."

"That might be because most of the population lives in cities," Neal said, with a bit of attitude.

Waiting for the scan results, we heard, "I've never seen anyone register *no* magic. Everyone has at least a little," said the confused lady, reading the results on the screen. She showed the results to her colleagues, to Mrs. Benson, then to Neal, and finally to me. *Double zero.* This stupid camera must not see yellow, but there still should've been a magical score. Everyone in Amaku has *some* magic.

Neal and Mrs. Benson were frozen in shock. Both looked so concerned for me. I was getting anxious about not being allowed to test. I'd touched the examiner when she showed me my score, and I was prepared to use some mind magic on this woman if she didn't put me on the list.

Magic is a little bit like a voice, just because you have vocal cords doesn't mean you can sing or have perfect pitch. The younger your training starts, and the better the teacher is, contribute to how eloquent you are with your powers. There is no wand, per se, to channel its use, but objects and runes assist. Many people have signs like a poker tell. The less expression you show, the greater advantage you have. My tell is that my lips purse like I'm playing the flute. It isn't necessary, it just happens from concentrating so hard. For some, their hand will mimic the action they want the power to take.

Trial and error became my teacher, and there always seemed to be some consequences. Using mind manipulation to make Lysa play dolls with me, even though she had outgrown them, just made her resentful. When shopping with Mrs. Benson, I would get the clerks to give me free candy, but they started to think I was stealing even though they offered me the sweets. With several years of practice, I'm good at getting people to do and think most anything. Manipulating others is too much like playing with paper dolls, and that makes people boring.

One technique I've perfected that's useful is to smudge a person's thought or memory. The first time it was successful, I asked Mrs. Benson about her first husband, and she became distressed.

"Who told you I had a first husband?"

Trying to cover up my mistake, I asked a question.

"You had a first husband?" I asked with raised eyebrows. Her mind had a tiny moment of distraction.

"That's not the point, I want to know who told you?"

"I don't remember anyone telling me you had a first husband. Were you married before?" Then as her mind replayed my words about her husband, I interrupted the electricity of thought. It worked sort of like an old-fashioned radio where you turn the dial to get a station. Twisting the thought ever so slightly muddled her memory, just enough to confuse her. Then I asked why she didn't want people to know, and her thoughts betrayed her, telling me that she hadn't told Lysa that Mr. Benson wasn't her biological father.

Another mind trick was to stimulate someone's brain to release hormones and chemicals to soothe anxiety or fear. I use that several times a day, starting with the day my parents were killed. Overuse causes headaches when you stop, like caffeine. As my grief became less intense, there wasn't much of a need to use it.

I could get others to calm down by stimulating their brains. A few times I was able to experiment on acquaintances that had touched me. It wasn't ethical but necessary to find meaning and value. Using strangers as my test subjects, I would stimulate very tiny amounts of brain chemicals to induce paranoia, panic, or even fear, and then return them to a calm state.

After some discussion, the clerk decided that I could take the tests, much in the same way some adults humor special needs children. She typed a note to the judges, stating that they should be understanding and compassionate.

"Sera, just remember, it is not the end of the world if you don't get offered a scholarship. You can stay here as long as you like and help me on the ranch." Nana assured me while clearing the table.

Being raised lovingly by Nana on this environmentally-friendly ranch offered stability I never had with my parents. We would move from place to place all the time. Just when we'd get comfortable, it would be time to move. It was enjoyable at the time because I didn't know anything different, but now, this was my home. Even though this ranch was homebase to me, I longed to see and do more. Wanting to find out who killed my parents and finding my sister, spurred my restlessness.

"Did you get your chores done?"

Nana asked this every morning. It was habit in the same way some people ask, "Did you sleep well?" but not as sensitive.

"Sure did. Eggs are gathered. Cats and dogs are fed. Garden is watered. Chris is out feeding the livestock."

Nana homeschooled me. She taught me to read, write, do math, and have knowledge of everything on the ranch. She didn't advertise it, but she had magic. Not once did she teach me anything to do with the supernatural.

If I didn't have the nightmare about what happened to my family, I would've been completely oblivious to the cruelty of humans. My little sister was out in that cruel world facing who knew what. Years of looking for Tatiana's face at every gathering left me wondering what she would look like now.

On the day of the test, Mrs. Benson rode with Neal and me to the community center in their self-driving vehicle. She had errands to run while we were being tested. The Benson family included me in everything they could. In a way, they were my surrogate family. I was a few years younger than their daughter, Lysa. Nearly all my clothes were once hers. Being slimmer than her, each item hung a little big on me.

Their son, Neal, was my age. He was a skinny, brainy nerd. He was a chip off the old block, his dad, the absent-minded professor who taught chemistry at the local university. Neal was going to be tested today as well. His scans showed magic but not enough in any color to qualify for a scholarship. Based on his registration scores, there was little chance of a high score on the exams. Luckily, he wasn't really interested in boarding school but just wanted to make sure he wasn't missing something.

"Sera, before you go in, can I have a minute?" Mrs. Benson asked. She was in her late thirties and was always neat and tidy. In a way, she was probably my best friend. Neal had jumped out of the car as soon as we stopped and was halfway to the community center entrance.

"Sure," I said warmly, but I was impatient to get inside and kept looking toward the door.

We both got out of the car, and she pulled a necklace from her purse. My eyes widened. I instantly recognized my mom's pendant of six stones set around a nearly see-through gem that reflected all the colors. It looked a bit like a flower. One stone for each petal of black, white, yellow, green, red, and blue. She motioned for me to turn around so she could put it on me. Tears welled up at the memory. This was the only link to my family. It came off my mom's dead body. Losing it had added another void to my life. This was part of the horrible nightmare. My happiness of its return was sullied by the memory of my parents' deaths.

"You were probably too young to remember, but when you first came to live with Nana, you had this pendant in your hand, and you wouldn't put it down for one moment. I had the broken chain repaired. When I took it to your house, Nana asked me to keep it until there was a suitable time to give it to you."

"I lost it the first time Lysa had me sleep over." Holding the pendant up and twisting it from side to side confirmed it still had the mosaic kaleidoscope effect.

"Yes, and when we opened the vent to clean, this was sitting right there. I have held onto it until you were old enough not to lose it again. Today felt like the perfect day to return it. It'll be like your mother watching over you, bringing you good luck."

Now a single set of tears did escape. Holding my eyes shut, I tilted my head toward the sky to keep more tears from forming. The stones rested on my chest like it was magnetically drawn to me. As I turned around, my voice sounded husky when I said, "You can't imagine how much this means to me."

"It looks radiant on you," she said with a smile, wiping the tears from my cheeks with her thumbs.

I thanked her with a quick hug and turned to sprint to the entrance. At the registration table, my name was last on the list shown on the touch screen monitor embedded in the desk's surface. Amaku was heavily managed through technology and magic, but Nana didn't like it. On the ranch, it was easy to have a life without constantly looking into screens.

At Nana's, there was no television, radio, or phone. The Bensons let me spend a couple of hours each evening with them so I wouldn't be completely ignorant of the outside world. Nana used a computer sparingly, but she believed that face-to-face was the most effective way for her to conduct business.

Our main entertainment was reading from actual paper books. Nana would exchange them, bartering with vendors at the markets. She'd barter them back when we were done reading them. I would stack the unread ones on my dresser, and when read, they were returned back into the bag.

One bag had a book that changed my life, and I kept it in my drawer rather than trading it back. It was a small, tan, leather-bound book on yellow magic. It was titled *Legati Magicum Flavus*. It isn't a youth book like the others, and it is quite hard to read, but the most important lesson I found was how to shield my mind and brain from magic. If you compared my gift to someone who had gold bricks that they had to always carry around, and then one day, they learned how to turn the bricks into a thin jumpsuit with a hood and a veil for the face. Imagine how much easier it would be to carry the gold.

Learning to make a shield was valuable to everyone, but what was great for me was that I could channel the energy so that the buildup didn't overwhelm me. Headaches were rare once I learned this skill. Even though the book taught me about the usefulness of shielding, there wasn't any opportunities to test if it worked. Meeting someone with yellow above intuition level wasn't something that happened in the country. Combining the protective shield with a chant or spell, one day, I'll be able to feel when someone tries to use magic on me.

Looking on as they checked me in, it was easy to deduce that they'd been testing a group every hour since nine o'clock this morning. A girl, maybe sixteen years old, guided me to a waiting room, but just as I was ready to go in, she stopped me.

"You should probably hide that necklace," she said as she pointed to my neck. "I know it has been debunked that those stones enhance magic, but the judges might think you're trying to cheat." Before I could say anything, she was returning to the registration table.

I put the necklace under my T-shirt. The instructions said to wear comfortable clothing, but once inside the room, I saw that only Neal and I had followed that suggestion. In the room sat four other kids all in their dress clothes. The only adult in the room motioned for me to take a seat as he stood by the door.

"You will be called one at a time. You will stand at the middle of the stage and wait for your testing to begin. The test is broken into three parts, red, green, and blue. Each test will only take a few minutes. When the judges determine you have completed your challenges, you will be dismissed to go home. First up is Neal Benson. The rest of you wait here, quietly." He guided Neal out the door.

It seemed like all the other occupants knew each other and started talking as soon as he shut the door. Closing my eyes helped to concentrate on Neal. His thoughts resonated even through the walls and with some distance between us. Through the years, we had touched skin to skin many times, mostly watching movies with him and his family. He was a bit nervous and was doing math in his head to keep his thoughts from stirring up any more emotions. From his thoughts, I could tell the auditorium only had three judges and a few helpers. A male judge asked for his name and then told him the red test was about to begin.

"OOF," his brain projected huge surprise and then they told him the red test was over. "What the frick?" Neal was irritated that someone grabbed at him. But before he could think anything else, they announced the next test.

For the second test, green, one of the helpers wheeled a small cart in front of him with seedling crates on it. Neal looked at the green judge for instruction, but all she said was, "Go." He seemed confused, he looked around the cart and found a spray bottle that held clear liquid. He sprayed it on the dry dirt and then just stood there.

After about thirty seconds of nothing, the green judge said, "I've seen enough."

Next, they wheeled over a lady on a hospital gurney. She was very still, breathing on her own but had a feeding tube. Neal looked at the healing judge and she did give a bit of instruction.

"See if you can tell us what is wrong with her."

After looking for a few moments, he said, "I think she's in a coma," My eyes rolled back at the obvious answer.

"Okay, that will be all." The blue judge dismissed him.

One by one, the occupants of the waiting room were led to the stage; I wasn't picking anything up from any of them. I was the very last out of the room and last for the day. Neal's last name being Benson and mine being Webster, it was easy to see we were being called alphabetically.

From the stage, I could see the judges were bored and getting ready to leave; after all, it was just the *special* kid left. Clearing my throat reminded them that the day wasn't over. They stopped what they were doing and sat down. A guy in a red shirt asked me to introduce myself.

"Hi, I'm Sera Webster." Even though I was only Nana's foster child, I was using her last name because no one in the foster system knew mine. All they got from me was my first name.

Each judge wore a shirt the same color of the magic they were testing. The man in the red shirt informed me the physical test was about to begin.

"The council doesn't test for yellow?" I asked without thinking.

They all chuckled. "Anyone with yellow is registered from birth," the green judge said dismissively.

Seconds later, someone grabbed me roughly from behind. Without a thought, a force from within me thrust the person all the way back into the stage curtain. The necklace felt warm against my chest. *Holy Smokes, what was that?* I turned to see if the grabber was all right, and fortunately, the person was dressed in padded clothes and a helmet. OMGosh! Red magic! And it was strong. My skin was tingling from the excitement. My hands fisted at my sides in an effort to steady my nerves.

When I turned back around, the man in the red shirt was typing vigorously on his tablet. The other two judges were definitely paying attention to me now. A cart was wheeled in front of me. "This is your green challenge; you can begin when you're ready."

I held my hand out, palm down over what looked like the bottom half of an egg carton with dirt in each compartment. There were seeds buried in the dry soil. All but two were familiar, even without seeing them. I found the spray bottle and made sure each patch of dirt received some moisture. Holding my hands over the cart and closing my eyes to concentrate, my magic stimulated the seeds, encouraging them to grow. The necklace was radiating something through my body and down to the plants. A gasp came from somewhere, and I felt a tickle on my palm at the same time. My eyes popped open. Each seed had grown a few inches above the top of the soil. Giddiness returned, sending tingles up and down my extremities, again. This necklace really was something. Now the nature judge was typing and scrolling rapidly. The plant cart was wheeled away, and the patient on the gurney was brought to center stage.

"Tell us what you can ascertain about this patient," the lady in blue said while looking very alert.

The red judge leaned toward the green judge and said, "Her scores are double zero, this isn't possible."

This patient wasn't emitting any readings. A stool was wheeled over and placed near the patient's head. Strangely, her face seemed vaguely familiar. I sat down on the stool and placed my hands on either side of her head, my palms covering each ear. The yellow stone shot out a bolt of energy through my hands, and I spoke to her with my mind.

"Hello, is anyone in there?" I mentally asked.

"Go away and leave me alone." She may have been comatose, but her brain was functioning.

"Why?"

"I have no need for that ugly cruel world out there, leave me in peace." Without her permission, I poked around her memories, and she had suffered torture at the hands of someone she knew as Annette. In my nightmare, a lady named Annette found me trapped between my parent's bodies.

"Mandy, is that you?"

"Who are you?"

"You might not remember me, but when I was young, Annette took me to a doctor's house. You signed a contract the morning we left." I told her, amazed that my memory was so clear now. How could I ever have doubted that terrible day didn't happen?

"That contract," she hissed. "I never wanted to sign it. That is why Annette was there, to force me. That whole hospital leadership keeps people bound to their employer. You'd be sick if you knew how many of us were forced to sign contracts without free will."

Mandy went on to tell me about how badly the doctor treated her. She was her indentured servant, and when she refused to work eighteen hours a day, Annette was brought back to change her mind. When gentle persuasion didn't work, she started using stronger and stronger magic until Mandy's mind broke, and she fell into a coma. Several people had already healed her brain, but she didn't want to wake up and face life with the doctor again.

"How about we have you wake up, then you could claim you don't remember anything but your name and that you grew up in Senaland. They'd have to return you there, and then you could reunite with your family."

"What? And the doctor just gets to go on without punishment, continuing to bind people into servitude?"

"Well, as far as we know, she is not being punished right now, but I can promise you that if I ever get the chance, she will pay for what she has done to you."

"Fine, but if I get stuck here in Nokuland again, I will find a way to have you cursed."

Pulling on the yellow stone's magic, a huge pulse burst through Mandy's mind. The strength of the energy released my hands from her head. My eyes opened when I heard her gagging. The healing judge was standing next to me. It was apparent that she had been trying to get my attention for some time.

"OH, MY WORD," she spurted out when Mandy's eyes opened.

The assistants and the blue magic judge started fussing over Mandy, holding her hands down so that she couldn't yank out the feeding tube. From what I could pick up from their conversation and activity, they were requesting transport to a local hospital.

The judge returned to the table and informed the other two. "She has to be given a scholarship to the Healing Arts Institute." A heated discussion broke out. It was confounding to realize that all three were fighting over me, the *special* kid. Without realizing it, my right hand clutched the pendant through my shirt.

CONFIRMATION

ONE OF THE helpers motioned me toward the exit. On the way out, I noticed the sprouted plants just sitting off to the side with all the other cartons. "Can I take the carton home?"

"Sure, they're just going to be tossed out," they said and handed me the one I'd sprouted.

When I got outside, Mrs. Benson and Neal were waiting in the car.

"What do you have there?" Mrs. Benson asked, as I slid into the back seat.

"That looks like the carton from the green nature test." Neal eyed me suspiciously from the front passenger seat. "You didn't make them grow, did you?" When I nodded, he turned back toward the front and slumped deep into his seat. "Mom, forget everything I said about how good I did on the tests."

"So, you've got some green in you." Mrs. Benson caught my eye in the rearview mirror. "Did you know before today?" She was curious.

"Absolutely, no idea!" I said shaking my head side to side. With the mindset of keeping my magic a secret, there was no talk of the activated red, but it was hard holding in the excitement. Mrs. Benson kept checking on me in the mirror all the way home.

All my focus was on keeping the new magic from spilling out. I thanked Mrs. Benson for the ride when we got to Nana's house. Nana was sitting on the front porch swing shelling peas. I sat beside her and rested the carton on my lap.

"What do we have here?" Nana finished what was in her hand. She reached over and inspected each plant.

"It's my nature test, they let me bring it home."

"These two are rather rare," she said, pointing to the ones I didn't recognize.

"Do you know what they are?" I asked.

"I can't say for certain, but this one appears to be a relative of parsley, and this one may be a type of basil." Her primness suggested she knew more about the plants.

"Would it be all right if I grew those two in my room just to see how they look fully grown?"

"I suppose, but you better not let them get into the garden or fields," she warned.

"I promise."

"It looks like your green test went mighty fine. I imagine they will offer you at least a partial scholarship to the Agricultural Institute." She seemed concerned at the last thought.

For the next thirty minutes or so, we shelled the peas without talking. I had done it so many times over the years that my mind could wander. Nana was minimalist in her conversation, too.

This ranch was so safe and comforting for me. I hadn't realized that traveling around with Mom and Dad had made me an anxious child. Once I recovered from the initial grief, I realized how much calmer it was living here. This ranch, Nana, the Bensons, and Chris were my comfort zone.

"How did you do on your big test?" Chris asked, pulling me out of my thoughts. He was standing on the porch and holding three freshly caught and gutted trout. Nana stood to open the door for him.

Chris was Nana's hired all-around ranch hand. His main job was to run the pellet mill. There was a large barn just for the manufacturing and a silo to store what wasn't picked up right away. Local farmers and lumber operations would drop off any unwanted wood chips, sawdust, plant stalks, and other biological material to be pressed into tiny pellets they used for feeding into clean-burning furnaces and stoves. That is what Nana used in our stove for cooking. We rarely ever needed to heat the house.

Chris also took care of the ranch. He was ageless in his worn coveralls and straw hat. He was quite shy and didn't want much to do with people, but he was comfortable with Nana, me, the Bensons, and the locals. A small pack of dogs and sometimes a few barn cats followed him everywhere. Watching him work with animals made me think he was the kindest person on the planet.

Animals are interesting but don't use language at the same level as humans. Some are clearly smarter than others. Staying safe, getting out of extreme weather, protecting what they believe is theirs, and having a food supply are high on their priorities, much like humans. Most animals like to play and respond to intellectual stimulus. They know who the leader is, and any member challenging that creates a struggle. Mating season brings on lots of confrontations.

All the animal behaviors are similar to human conduct. We're part of the animal kingdom. We just have a lot of social rules imposed on us, and necessarily so—otherwise, we would behave much differently. We rely on our families and communities like an animal relies on their herd or pack. Our law system has become our leader, letting us know what is allowed and what is punishable. It's important to have a rule enforcer at home, too. Nothing works better than having consistent rules as well as catching and correcting bad behavior right as it happens.

Chris's question wasn't to be taken lightly because he rarely spoke, except to Nana, and mostly about ranch business.

"It activated my magic."

He slipped out of his untied work boots using the wooden bootjack by the door. "About time," was all he said with a nod. His mouth was upturned as he went into the house with Nana to drop off the fish. The animals knew better than to follow him into the house, and they settled down, all curling around my feet.

He lived in the livestock barn in an apartment on the second floor. Most evenings, he ate with us or the Bensons. This man worked tirelessly for Nana and seemed to enjoy all of it. We had chickens for laying eggs, a milk cow, a few cattle, some horses, and even a pig pen. There were a few beehives for honey and wax. Fruit and nut trees, as well as several types of berry bushes, lined the yard. We ground our own flour from wheat berries, corn, and nearly every type of grain. Chris worked in partnership with Nana, ensuring every creature was healthy and every plant was fruitful.

This ranch produced wholesome foods, and nearly everything we consumed was organic. Fresh air was my favorite; even with the animals away from the house by some distance, it still beat town air. What little girl didn't want to grow up riding horses and swimming?

We were in the foothills, and the mountains stretched all along the south of us as far as you could see. A creek rushed past our ranch and emptied into a huge lake. We could snatch fresh trout from the stream with a few flicks of our fly-fishing rods. The lake was like liquid glass and reflected every sunrise and sunset. God's country, people would say. We were compared to the Amish, but we were not associated with any groups that kept us in this peaceful life. Nana just wanted to be good to the Earth and good to our bodies.

Interestingly, she was quite rich, in land, money, and heart, but you would never guess it from all her minimalist ways. From Chris's and Mrs. Benson's thoughts, I learned Nana was quite wealthy, enough to be an elite. I didn't know exactly what she owned, but it impressed people that worked with her. Nana's whole world was efficient, and she never used fossil fuels. Even the ranch equipment had to run on renewable energy. She was a country woman through and through. Outsiders thought she was gruff, snappy, and a bit mean, but with me, she was encouraging and supportive. I witnessed many of her donations to the community. No one within Nana's long reach went hungry or lacked a comfortable place to rest their head.

Even though this place would always be home, in my heart, I wanted more. The yellow magic energy in me was growing hungrier and more powerful with every passing year. Getting away from here might enable me to find someone to train me. The mind magic was rare, and with Mom warning me to not let anyone know I could use it, I was scared to talk about it.

The only way to get accepted into a magical institute was through a talent scholarship, no amount of money, power, or influence could get someone's child admitted. It would be a real honor for anyone to be allowed to attend. A high percentage of the students were from rich and powerful families because having a lot of magic could make you rich and powerful.

Now that my red and green magic was activated, I began to practice every free moment. It even worked without wearing the necklace. Neal practiced with me a few days, but when he couldn't keep up, he quit. At first, we moved dead leaves around, then gradually, I could move heavier objects. It paralleled a physical training program. The more I practiced, the stronger I became. Using red too much would leave me tired and sore. Green could make vegetables grow very fast, but they had no flavor. If a flower bloom was rushed, it died quickly. Practicing on plants always left me thirsty.

My new windowsill plants were nurtured and pampered. Using a light energy of green was like singing to them. Vibrations on the roots and leaves gave stimulation without forcing them to grow.

The next week, when I was returning from the Bensons', there was a car parked on the side of our house. It was a short walking distance between the two homes, allowing me to spend plenty of time at their house.

In the kitchen, Nana and a smartly dressed lady were huddled together over our simple table, discussing something on a tablet.

"Here she is," Nana informed the lady. When the visitor lifted her head, I recognized her from the testing day. She was an attractive woman in her forties, looking capable of running any business. "Sera, this is Ms. Mason from the Healing Arts Institute; she tells me she was the judge for your blue test and that you are being given a full-ride scholarship. There must be some mistake. You made the plants grow." Nana spoke, looking bemused.

"Hello, Sera, I've been telling Nana there is no mistake. You didn't tell her about bringing Mandy out of a coma?" she asked, incredulously. Nana looked a little hurt and proud.

"Well, I didn't want to take credit for something that might have happened without my help," I said, trying to downplay my actions. I used yellow magic on Mandy, not blue, but no one could know.

"Speaking of making sure," Ms. Mason pulled a small blade from Nana's knife block and sliced between her thumb and index finger. She thrust the bleeding hand towards me and said, "Let's see what you can do."

Grabbing a dish towel from near the sink, I wrapped it around her hand. Blue magic sprang to life as soon as I touched her arm. Very quickly, her hand was back to normal, with no visible scar. Leaving me holding the only evidence of her wound, the now bloody towel which she used a corner of to wipe the blade clean and then place it in the sink.

"I'm sure my bit of blue magic helped that along," Ms. Mason said, but it came out husky. "No mistake, we definitely want Sera to join us as soon as possible."

INSTITUTIONALIZED

PEOPLE SAY I'M lucky to be here, and I am, but not just for the reasons they think. They think I'm lucky to be living on Nana's ranch. Most children without relations to take them in are in orphanages until they are adults. It is incredible to be with this wonderful woman, living on the most beautiful place on Earth, but the thing is, my yellow mind magic is what makes me blessed. And it is driving my longing to explore the rest of the island.

Mrs. Benson threw a going away party for me in conjunction with Lysa's sixteenth birthday. Needless to say, Lysa wasn't thrilled. Not that I had any friends to invite, she didn't like that one present was mine, even though I opened it before her guests arrived.

"Oh wow, that's the newest TeleCom." Neal marveled at my tablet before it was even completely unwrapped. "I can help you set it up."

Knowing that Nana shunned anything to do with technology, Mrs. Benson jumped a big hurdle and was able to talk her into giving me a communications tablet so I could keep in touch while away at school. It included a subscription for social media and internet access. Neal helped me set up my account, though, I didn't have anyone to add as a contact except the Bensons and Nana.

In Nokuland, we only have a government-run social media platform that you have to pay a monthly fee to use. They saw how crazy the news outlets and social media sites made people in the rest of the world. Here, there are no advertisements, and our network doesn't use software to get people addicted. There are separate tabs for different venues. A tab each for news, videos, pictures, email, and messaging. There are measures in place to make sure the news is factual. People or organizations posting false information will lose the ability to publish. Penalties include fines or imprisonment, depending on the severity of the offense. Opinions can be included if they are clearly labeled as such. It isn't allowed to incite feelings of anger and negativity on purpose. Without personalized algorithms and opinions to induce rage, looking at a screen wasn't remarkably interesting. Generally, if you were looking at a screen, it meant your life was dull.

Lysa and Neal attend the local schools. Being homeschooled by Nana left me hungry for more and missing a sense of belonging among peers. There are so few people in my life that I take extra care to not upset anyone. But that backfired a little when Lysa became annoyed that I didn't irritate people. At first, being on the ranch, I spent a lot of time in people's minds but realized that life was easier not knowing their every thought. Now, I limit the use of yellow to when I really want or need something.

The Bensons hosted the combined party outside on their car pad. Mr. Benson was grilling burgers and hotdogs throughout the day. Mrs. Benson and her adult friends were keeping the other food and snacks replenished on a long folding table along one side, while speakers and the music were on the other. It was a large group, nearly everyone from Lysa's high school class attended. Some lawn games are set up, but the main activity is on the water. A few guests were just sitting on the bank of the lake, some swimming and jumping off an old tire swing, others were in kayaks. Neal had a few of his friends out windsurfing. It was exciting to use my healing magic when someone sliced their toe on a rock.

At dusk, everyone came off the water to watch the sunset, and then the dancing started. Only a few partygoers were dancing as couples. Mostly, we just danced in a big group and enjoyed the music. During one song, I was having so much fun that my magic colors fluttered out like the ribbons a rhythmic gymnast would use. The dancers stepped in and out of the colors without even noticing. At the end of the song, I twirled several times, and in one of the rotations, I noticed Nana was watching me with an enthralled look of pride on her face, but by the next turn, she was no longer watching me. Now that my magic was increasing in color and energy, I decided to use most of it for my protective shield.

On the morning I left, Nana gave me a hug goodbye.

"I'm here for anything you need. Use your tablet to keep in touch." Her face showed concern as she waved until we were out of sight. Mrs. Benson cried when she hugged me goodbye at the train station. She struggled with guilt over enjoying my company more than her own daughter's. Of course, she didn't know I was reading her thoughts and could keep from annoying her. If we all were watching a movie and she was too tired to make popcorn, my offering to make some before she even asked one of her children helped to get into her affections. When she was baking, whatever ingredients she needed, I had measured and waiting. Lysa didn't help in the kitchen without an argument or sass. Of course, Mrs. Benson loved her children and would give them anything they needed, but me, she liked.

On the train ride to the institute, the window seat offered the best view of the passing scenery. It could have been a national park in any country of the world, it was that breathtaking. Watching, it struck me that I had only ever lived near these mountains that divided our continent between Nokuland and Senaland. The most magical people live on the northernmost coast of Nokuland. The continental divide crossings are strongly monitored, in order to protect the non-magical from risk of abuse.

Centuries ago, when families had more children, the youngest ended up having very little power. When they were shunned from matches, powerful people started hiring them for mundane and menial tasks. This change led to abuses and the less magical moved south to Senaland to protect themselves.

These mountains were thought to provide sanctuary for the elder magicians who wish to live as hermits. It's possible for magic to morph and become unpredictable, especially with age. Out of respect and wanting to protect loved ones they isolated themselves in the sparsely populated mountains. One article I read said that a majority of the hermits had yellow magic. If you weren't trained properly or if you misused the legacy, it could drive you a bit crazy. Nokuland had a few mentally handicapped. They simply were normal people who hadn't been properly trained to use their powers, which was a shame because when used properly, it could be helpful.

Helping people was what I wanted to do with my magic. Like when Neal was sad about his dad not wanting to talk sports with him. Sports is a big part of their relationship, but Mr. Benson was cutting Neal short when he tried to start a conversation. From Mr. Benson's thoughts, I found he wanted to have more in-depth conversations, but Neal only wanted to talk about his favorite players and teams.

"Neal, you only see what you want to see in sports. How come you can't give credit to a player for a good play when they aren't on your favorite team?" I asked him just as his dad was about to tune him out. That question spurred on a good debate between them.

Helping people felt so good that it had to be what magic was meant for, but everything I'd seen about the big city elites was that they used it to build money, power, and popularity.

Both of my parents grew up in the flat land of the north coast, I remember my mother telling me, but I don't remember ever being there. It meant they were part of the elite or at least close to the powerful. With no memories of grandparents, aunts, uncles, or cousins; Nana, Chris, and the Bensons felt more like family than even my little sister, Tatiana.

The whole continent of Amaku was amazing. *Who wouldn't want to see it all?* ran through my thoughts to calm any doubts about leaving Nana and the ranch.

Amaku had been magically created. A kind of magic utopia. It's located in the middle of the Pacific Ocean on the equator and roughly split down the middle by our Mocah Mountains. The altitude and ocean breezes provide nearly idyllic weather year-round. The mountains provide a natural barrier between two very different countries. They intentionally keep Amaku hidden from the rest of the world. Some like to quote a classic novel and say, "It is not down on any map; true places never are."

As the train carried me further away from the ranch, it felt like spells and wards were being eroded, and I wondered how much stuff Nana had used to protect me. Maybe that's why she looked so concerned about me leaving the ranch.

At one of the stops, I watched as a family said goodbye to a boy about my age. It was so beautiful and sad at the same time. It was easy to see they loved him and were going to miss him. There were lots of hugs and kisses. Watching this family's farewell left me hollow like I'd missed out on something special. They all wore green T-shirts, so it was easy to see he'd gotten a scholarship to the Agricultural Institute.

Starting this new life wasn't overly daunting. If needed, my gift of duplicating others information and skills would make the learning easier.

Copying skills from others happened by accident. One day, I overheard Lysa telling her mom, "Sera always wants to play dolls. Mom, I've outgrown them. She has no interest in makeup or boys. Don't make me play with her just because she's lonely. I have my own friends." Feeling embarrassed and hurt, I stayed away from their house.

After three days, Lysa was bored. "Do you want to go horseback riding?" she asked with her chin slightly tucked in.

"I don't know how." Staring at my boot while kicking at the dirt, provided a reason to avoid looking at her.

"I can teach you," she offered.

After teaching me to bridle and saddle the horse, she helped me mount. I envied her experience, but on its own, my magic found the key elements and copied her horsemanship into my brain. Things like how to hold the reins, use my legs, and to feel the horse as well as watching the ears.

"See! Trying something new isn't scary. You're enjoying it and you look so happy. You must have natural ability to learn so fast," Lysa praised.

After that, I copied everything interesting from the few people in my life, except Nana. Her mind was solidly protected.

Disembarking at the Healing Arts Station, per my acceptance package instructions, I towed one suitcase and carried a backpack. We were told to only bring necessities. Not knowing what they thought was necessary, I brought a little of everything. Just a short walk from the train station was a cable car with the words Healing Arts Institute on it. I had a flashback to the worst day of my life. This was the same cable train that Annette and I rode to the doctor's home. My memory was reinforced when we reached the top, and I recognized the front doors of the massive stone building. A chill of apprehension ran down my spine.

Stopping at the front desk for directions to the female dormitory, the receptionist told me, "Enjoy the lobby and shops before reporting in. You won't get many chances to visit them anytime soon." There was a gift shop, hair salon, a food court, and a convenience store near the lobby. Without getting completely familiar with my surroundings, I headed toward the back of the building, following signs to the east wing. Once I was buzzed into the dormitory, there was another reception desk. First, my luggage was taken behind the desk and searched by two female guards. The only thing they confiscated was homemade protein bars from Mrs. Benson, and they didn't even ask if I wanted to eat one before they trashed them. Now my clothes and toiletries were tossed together.

"We're going to need you to log onto your digital devices," the guard at the desk informed me.

Holding up the tablet, I logged in using my face and voice. They directed me to a portal to download software that limited the usage to only evenings and weekends while on school grounds.

One of the guards gave an orientation tour with a couple other students that showed up at the same time I did. We went down a flight of stairs to where they pointed out the cafeteria, a small retail store, a laundry area, an auditorium, and the classroom areas.

"Down here, we're directly below the garden area, and all this space is also shared with the west wing, but every effort is made to keep you separated from the males. Although some interaction is unavoidable." We stopped at classroom number six. "You will need to be in this classroom tomorrow morning at eight o'clock, in uniform. Breakfast is served from six-thirty to seven-thirty, so you have plenty of time to eat before then." We then climbed back up one flight of stairs at the opposite end from where we started.

"This is the first-year students' floor, every year you advance, you get to move up a floor. Stay off the other floors unless you're invited." She pointed to a door near the guard's station. "Each level has a dayroom with a large screen at the end of the corridor." We stopped at a door on the west side of the hall.

To enter my room, I was given a code to use on the number pad and she had me enter my fingerprint as well. The room had white walls, two dressers, two beds, two wardrobe closets, and a sink with a mirror. A windowed door at the far side led to a small fenced-in patio that was only just large enough for one chair and a small table. We were at garden level, all the other years we would have balconies. She pointed out the male dormitories on the west wing. "Do not ever go over there."

She gave me a small book and said, "Make sure you read this handbook. Follow the rules, and you won't get in any trouble." Then she led the others to their rooms.

After she left, I explored the room more closely. A door near the sink led to the bathroom that had a shower and toilet. A second door in the bathroom led to another dorm room that was a mirror image of the one I was assigned. So, four of us were sharing one shower and toilet.

Clearly the first to arrive, I chose the left side of the room to unpack. For bedding and my uniforms, I walked back to the laundry. Our school uniforms were light blue scrubs and white cotton T-shirts. The clerk issued me pants, pull over shirts, button up tunics with pockets, and white clogs that were very liquid proof. I was also given a towel, a hand towel, a washcloth, and bedding.

"None of the uniforms or bedding are personal, once they are dirty, you exchange them one-for-one. When you turn in something dirty, you'll receive clean replacements. Laundering issued items are free; you have to pay for personal items, or you can use the machines in that room over there." The male attendant pointed to a room directly across the hall as he looked me over. He was dressed in the school uniform and looked to be around seventeen. Other than being around Neal, I didn't have much experience with the opposite sex. My cheeks blushed from his expression.

"Are you a student?" I asked.

"Yes, I didn't earn a full scholarship this year, so I'm on a work-study schedule. My family can't afford to pay the remaining balance, so I have to work in order to stay a student. I put in about twenty hours a week. I'm usually here, but they can assign me anywhere."

"Thanks," I said and headed back to my room with my large bundle. Back at the room, the door was open, and a girl about my size and age with light hair with several pastel highlights was unpacking her luggage.

"Hey roomie, I'm Caly Pollin, what's your name?" She greeted me over her shoulder.

"Sera Webster," I answered, dropping the bundle on my bed. I put my uniforms away, hung the towels up, and started making the bed.

"Oh, good, you didn't bring your own linens. I was afraid I'd be the only one," said Caly.

"Why would we bring our own?"

"Nicer colors and softer towels."

"Oh, it didn't even cross my mind," I replied.

"This place seems kind of like a prison, huh?" she muttered.

"I don't know, I've never been to prison," I said and gave her a half smile.

"Me either," she laughed, "You should have waited for me before getting your bedding and uniforms, now you're going to have to go back again, so I don't have to go alone." The words sounded matter-of-fact, but her eyes were pleading. Clearly, she was more social than me, which was a plus.

She was cute in her jeans and T-shirt, and even though I was in a dress, she was more glamorous. Her big blue eyes, button nose, and sparkling grin with straight white teeth were mesmerizing. She talked nonstop. She was from a northeast city, and she knew of at least one other girl who would be attending the academy with us.

"Her name is Sharlyn Horton, and you're going to love her, NOT. Her family is super-rich and powerful. The rest of the people in the world are just their minions," she rolled her eyes on the last word, but I was stuck on the fact that she used the word "super" a lot. "Her only redeeming quality is her brother. Tifton is a few years older than us, and he is super-cute, but he is attending the Protection Institute. His red is super-strong," now her eyes looked a little dreamy. "Though, don't get your hopes up, word on the street is that his family has an arranged marriage in mind."

"That seems a bit old-fashioned, I had no idea that type of thinking was still around."

"In the power classes, it is definitely still a thing. Families want to make certain their children stay in the good graces of the lawmakers while getting the strongest match possible. The council killed the last couple that defied the rules and then took their child to be raised in a different family. If you don't follow the rules, you pay the price, and your family does too. The relatives protested about not getting the child, but their request was turned down by the council. That kid will grow up to be the most powerful magician that ever lived. Both parents had extremely high scores. The mom had strong yellow and even the dad had some. Can you imagine? Yellow is so rare, and then to be firstborn from that combination. They should have known they would never get approval. That's off-the-charts powerful." Caly looked and sounded wistful at the last comment.

My jaw dropped. "How long ago was this? Do you know anything about the child?" I asked. My intuition was thinking this might be about my parents and Tatiana. I remember my mom telling me, using her yellow magic, that I would be powerful, especially since I was firstborn.

"It was a girl about two years old. This was about eight or nine years ago, I think, so it was fairly recent. You haven't heard this story?" she asked. "The Crystal and Justin Kendler assassinations?" When I shook my head no, she said, "Back home, everyone knows it. Every time someone breaks a dating rule, we hear it all over again."

I wanted to ask more about the girl. This really might be Tatiana, but I didn't want to draw too much attention to my interest. "What are the dating rules?" I asked.

"Well, most important is that two powerful magic-holders can't have children together, or at least not without council approval. This couple put their request to the council, but they were turned down, so they went into hiding. It was believed that they were already expecting a baby when they asked for permission to marry, but when they were found, the child was much younger than everyone expected. So, it's kind of weird that they went into hiding without being pregnant. I mean, they could've just lived together without marriage. It's a mystery. You've really never heard of this?" she repeated.

"I grew up in the foothills, magic is not really a big deal there."

"Probably not a big deal when you don't have much power," Caly said and then looked apologetic when she realized how it could be an insult to me. "You obviously have a lot of power, or you wouldn't be here," she said, trying to reassure me. "What's your blue score?"

Oh great, why hadn't I thought of a response to this question. No way I was going to tell her mine was a double zero. "You tell me yours first."

"Well, it doesn't matter," she shrugged, "It's okay if you don't want to tell me. We're all over twenty-nine. Some kids from Redding didn't get accepted, and they had scores above twenty-nine but just barely. It's going to be down to very small increments between us. I'm twenty-nine point seventy-six. Sharlyn is twenty-nine point seventy-seven. You'd think she was ten points higher by her attitude. Her mom called the institute to find out everyone's standings, but the only thing they would tell her is that Sharlyn has the highest score. Her head was so big before she heard, but now she's more of a total pompous ass, if that's even possible. But you know what? I saw both of our scores at the preregistration. She was twenty-nine point seven-six-five, and I was the *exact* same, but somehow her number got rounded up, and mine got rounded down, so you can't tell me this selection process isn't without outside influence."

Thankfully, she didn't ask again about my score. It's not easy telling someone you received the lowest score ever in the history of magic, especially someone who tied with the highest in our grade.

At the laundry, Caly flirted relentlessly with the attendant. He was blushing from all the attention she was giving him. I just watched in awe. He didn't even notice me this time. It wouldn't have even crossed my mind to flirt; he wasn't that good-looking.

Back at the room, Caly had just finished putting away her uniforms and making her bed when we heard some rumbling coming down the hall. We both poked our heads out to see the escort guard pulling two large matching suitcases. Walking right behind her was a very stylish thirteen-year-old who also pulled a suitcase. Disdain dripped from the little princess's face. She was bigger than average. She had long, smooth, dark brown hair and was wearing sunglasses indoors. Her clothes were immaculate. The white button shirt complimented her figure, and the blue jeans that hugged her hips were tucked into high-heeled, black leather boots. She was our age but looked so grown up.

They stopped at the east-facing corner room. On the other end of the hallway was the dayroom and the guard station, so those two corners were not bedrooms. Leaving these two corners available, and she was the first to move into one. With a mixture of awe and curiosity, I followed the tiny parade. Peeking in the doorway, I could see that this corner room had more windows than our room, and you could see breathtaking views of the mountains.

"What are you looking at? You nosy slaveborn nitwit," the princess scowled, and then she slammed the door in my face, using red magic that shot out and even looked like a snake biting right through the door. Without any thought, my red magic responded, shattering her bedroom door with its protective response. My head snapped back, just as her force grazed my shield. My magic blocked her energy from pummeling me into the wall behind me. I looked at Caly with blinking squinted eyes, my forehead scrunched, and an eyebrow raised. My heart was racing. It was frightening and oddly comforting that there was an automatic response to her attack.

"Rude." I said, turning to stare straight at the new arrival.

"That's Sharlyn," Caly said, just loud enough for me to hear.

The demolished door stunned Sharlyn. She gawked confused at the shattered pieces. She even lifted her sunglasses to get a better look.

"You'll be paying for that," the escort informed Sharlyn.

"Let's get out of here. You don't want to be around a Horton when they are mad." Caly warned, as she pulled me toward our room.

"You were right, I'm not going to like her. Why would she call me slaveborn?" I asked when we reached our room.

"It's just the elitists' way of insulting someone. If you don't have enough yellow or red magic, you're going to be someone's bitch, sort of thing. Though it's not really acceptable to call anyone that, she believes her family is above everyone else, and she is mostly right. She probably called you that because you're with me, and if you were someone of importance, she'd already know you."

After a pause, I asked Caly, "Why is she here when her red magic is so strong?"

"I'm not sure, but it is probably some the elites old-fashioned thinking. Blue is daintier. Red is rough and tumble, suitable for men. She's picked up a lot of training from Tifton. Still, it'd have to be that her blue registered stronger."

"Sheesh, her healing powers should wake the dead then." I joked.

"No one can do that." Caly responded, making me think she thought I wasn't very bright. "Blue takes a while to get the hang of it. I haven't even healed a bug bite."

Time to change the subject before I let it slip that my healing already worked. "Do you want to visit the retail store with me?"

"Sure, but I don't have any money to spend," she offered self-consciously.

"Oh, that isn't right, didn't your scholarship include some spending money?"

"Nope, I'm only just barely covered for one year. I'll have to really impress them if I'm to have another year. Definitely no spending money."

"Wow, that's messed up." According to the documents, a small stipend was included in my scholarship, but no instructions on how to receive it. Fortunately, Nana made sure I had a fund account that was beyond generous, bordering on obscene. "Come to think of it, let's try the garden first. Maybe we can find two pots for some plants I brought with me."

"You brought plants, and they didn't confiscate them when you were searched?" Caly asked.

Pulling one of the sprouts out of my dress pocket, I said, "Well they're pretty easy to miss."

"Those don't look like any plants I've seen before," Caly commented.

"Nana thinks they might be related to parsley and basil."

"You don't know what they are, but you want to grow them? You've got a little strange in you, Sera," she said and gave me a happy smile.

We were just stepping into the courtyard when a gardener stopped us. "You kids aren't supposed to be in this area without an escort." In a vague sort of way, she reminded me of Nana, but she was in her forties rather than her sixties.

"Our patio needs some foliage," I said, pointing over to the barren space, all the while looking around for anything useful. "That aloe plant could use some nurturing," I pointed at a small neglected potted plant.

She picked up the wilted plant and inspected it. "I guess that would be all right," she said hesitantly, chewing on the inside of her lip.

"We will need some extra pots to grow the babies." Caly pointed at a few tiny aloe sprouts. I gave her a thankful glance.

"Plants can really help in the healing arts if one takes the initiative to learn," said the gardener. She did seem earnest about getting us interested. "Well, if you kids clean up this area here you can have two extra pots." The pots she referred to were just very plain cheap starter planters, but they would do for now.

It only took us about ten minutes to tidy up the shelves, and we also earned a small watering can. I scooped up some soil into each pot. When we arrived back at the room, I put the supplies on the patio table. I planted my two sprouts, watered them, and then washed up for supper.

When we got to the cafeteria, a guard stopped us from entering. "I see that you two haven't read the handbook. Students will be in uniform until after the evening meal. You will need to get into the proper clothes before being allowed to enter."

"Today, isn't a school day," Caly said.

"Look inside the cafeteria. Do you see anyone in street clothes?" We did peek in, and everyone was in uniform.

"See, I told you this was like a prison," Caly whispered near my ear, as we headed back.

When we returned to the cafeteria, we were directed through a typical food line. We could choose our meal from what was available. Most of it looked a bit overcooked. I opted for the salad bar. Looking around the table area for the east wing, we could see that the long tables were marked one through six. The tables were arranged in neat rows with one table in the center labeled "faculty." On the opposite side of the food line were seven matching tables for the west wing. We could see glimpses of the boys.

At table six were the girls we had seen in our hallway, but when we got close, I could see a red force bubble surrounding the entire table and stopped. It was obvious that Caly didn't see it because she walked right into it and bounced back a step, spilling some of her food onto the tray she was holding. All the girls at the table laughed, some harder than others. The face with the most smugness was, of course, Sharlyn. I could see the red streaming from her. It made sense that she had strong physical magic if she had a brother at the Protection Institute.

Table five was a bit messy with food and still had three girls sitting there. I caught the eye of the closest. She motioned for us to come sit with them.

"Here, you can sit with us, but you will have to wipe down the whole table when you're done," she said with a shrug. I was beginning to think cleaning was a type of currency in this place.

Caly and I looked at each other with a sigh and sat down. My salad was disappointing, the vegetables were so much blander than anything on the ranch, and the dressing was mass produced. I took a quick glance at table six and noticed the red shield was gone. It figured that the show of force was just for Caly and me. Caly wasn't near as bothered as me by this stunt, and it made me sad to think she was used to this kind of treatment.

Later, back in our room, when helping Caly put a few music posters on her side of the room, I asked, "How come that bubble stunt didn't piss you off?"

"It did, but you can't show people like Sharlyn that it bothers you or it will encourage them to do more of it. She will try more stuff because she finds pleasure in upsetting people. Her mom is exactly the same way, so mean. You have to feign boredom with her antics, and the best you can hope for is that she will find someone else to pick on. They always have to have a target."

"How do you know about her mother?"

"I sort of grew up with Sharlyn. My mom works for her mom. We stay in their house in the servants' rooms. As kids, we used to be best friends. Everyone that works for that lady is miserable until you figure out the game. You must be one hundred percent supportive of everything she suggests. Nothing is ever her fault. You will be sacrificed for anything, especially if something will make her look bad. As the saying goes. They were abused children."

"Sharlyn looks totally spoiled; how could she be abused?" I asked, questioning the logic of her last sentence.

"Yes, she is! She gets everything she ever wants, but her mom is super self-absorbed, so she doesn't know how to give love or attention. Sharlyn is just an object to help glorify her mother. With nothing to stop the cycle, it will continue. It's really quite sad if you think about it."

"So, you're saying you feel sorry for her and buy into the poor-little-rich-kid excuse?"

"No, just that I understand the game rules better than you." She gave me a wink.

"Her bratty behavior is already getting on my last nerve," I said.

"Well then, she is winning the game and you're playing right into her sweet spot. A country girl like you is going to have to toughen up if you want to survive." She eyed my communications tablet. "Can I use that for a minute to let my mom know I made it here?"

"Sure, if you first teach me how to send a message." With Caly's help, I let Nana and the Bensons know I had made it safely, and then Caly used the tablet until she went to sleep. It was hurtful to be less interesting than my tablet. She could've at least showed me some of what was so captivating.

Lying in bed that night, I read the handbook. *Any infraction of the rules and you will be sent to the detention room with further restrictions up to dismissal.*

No student is allowed outside the dormitory or school areas without an escort.

No leaving your suite after 9 pm or before 6 am.

Rooms need to be clean, neat, and tidy. There are random inspections.

Shirts are to be worn tucked in, tunics excluded.

No food or drink in the dorm rooms.

No alcohol consumption while in residence.

No drugs or medicine. Not even aspirin.

No misuse of magic is allowed. (Interesting how no one stopped Sharlyn.)

All devices need to be muted. You can listen to music and sound only through earbuds or headphones.

It continued in giving instructions on the wear of accessories. No large or distracting jewelry was allowed.

Courtesy to instructors and fellow students was required. (Again, except Sharlyn.)

It explained restricted areas. Fitness requirements. Hair regulations.

I started questioning being here. This wasn't at all like I had imagined. I didn't expect the uniforms, all the rules, the unimaginative food, or the hostile fellow students. It *was* a little like a prison. We were mostly limited to the classroom, cafeteria, bedroom, and dayroom; it was all so confining compared to the vast expanse of the great outdoors I had at the ranch. I'd never had to follow a schedule before. Caly was the best thing about this place, but in her eyes, I was just a naïve country bumpkin, and apparently, my tablet was more intriguing.

My thoughts were causing feelings of loneliness and despair. First like a kick to the stomach, then my throat tightened with a silent cry of despair, and my nose started to run. For the first time in my life, I was homesick. Curling into a fetal position and hugging my pillow, a couple of tears slipped out of my eyes.

PATHOLOGY

THE NEXT MORNING, we realized we should have worked out a bathroom schedule with our suitemates. Everyone wanted the shower about the same time. Taking a quick shower without getting my hair wet, I ended up waiting for Caly while she dried and curled her hair, then she applied eye makeup and lip gloss.

"Aren't you going to put on makeup?"

"I don't have any, my neighbor would experiment on me once in a while, but on the ranch, it didn't impress the cows, horses, or vegetables," I said with a wry smile, feeling more out of place. She applied a bit of liner to my eyes and some of the lip gloss.

"Good thing you don't need much." Caly unbraided my hair and used one of her hair accessories to put it in a quick bun. "Don't wear your hair in braids around the others unless you're going to do it up nice." Her words stung, but she was only trying to help me fit in.

We walked to the classroom, pausing at the door. This was my first time ever in a school setting. At least I didn't have to worry about fashion with everyone in scrubs. However, it was easy to see why Caly spent so much time on her hair and makeup. Each desk had a computer to one side, and several students were already seated. Sharlyn and her suitemates were giggling. Strange how coming from a rich and powerful family made you popular. Other students were hanging on their every word. All four of Sharlyn's group had blue diamonds on their right ring fingers and moved their hands to catch the light and show off.

"Typically, the rings are presents from parents at graduation. At least they didn't get the tattoo," Caly murmured near my ear.

As Caly sat, her chair was pulled out from under her by a red claw coming from Sharlyn. Hurrying to get off the floor and into her seat, she looked at me through misty eyes. As I took the chair from the desk next to her, a red streak came from the same group. Without a conscious thought, my magic blocked it before it reached its target. It wiped the smile right off Sharlyn's face, and her mob was asking if she had sent the magic. Their questions reminded me that they couldn't see the magic, nor could their brains give credence to the possibility that I might be capable of blocking.

Anger shone in her eyes. There was a shift of circumstances. Sharlyn was zeroing her hostile intentions on me.

In the first-year classroom, we learned that the first term would be spent on learning and testing our basic knowledge. Language and math skills had to be at a certain proficiency before we could move on with healing lessons. Class was held five days a week, Monday through Friday, eight o'clock until four. In the evenings, they wanted us to participate in physical training on our own, but if we couldn't keep up during Sunday group sports, we would be forced to follow a monitored workout plan. We would be mostly working at our own pace, but if we fell behind, we would be spending our evenings or Saturdays with a tutor from one of the higher levels.

Our instructor was Ms. Fine, who really didn't live up to her name. She was a very average-looking laboratory technician type. For her first lesson, she explained the school structure. For the first six years, we would be living in the dormitory with our cafeteria table, our classroom, and our floor all matching our year number. Those few selected for the next level would be moved to the hospital.

Year	Grade	Age	Achievement
1	Freshman	13-14	
2	Sophomore	14-15	
3	Junior	15-16	Emergency Technician
4	Senior	17-18	Nurse
5	Level 1	18-19	Physician's Assistant
6	Level 2	19-20	Intern
7	Level 3	21-22	Resident
8	Level 4	22-23	Doctorate

On the second day, I made the mistake of showing knowledge far above a basic education. I zoomed through the self-paced modules and reached the end, thanks to the pretests. If you had a passing grade on the test, the program skipped the content in that section and moved to the next pretest.

Ms. Fine was amazed. The other fifteen students just gaped at me when she said, "Ms. Webster has completed all the advanced sections." My success was in great thanks to my ability to copy from other's minds. The Bensons were highly educated, especially Mr. Benson. He had a doctorate in chemistry as it was required to be a professor at university, and I'd copied his knowledge and skills. All I had to do was touch a person once, even very lightly, and my magic held the keys to their brain.

The Healing Arts Institute wasn't an adequate school for me, but there weren't enough yellow carriers to have a school. Each child with more than five percent would apprentice under someone with years of experience controlling its use. Annette was the only person I knew who had a good grasp on how to use the yellow magic, and I certainly didn't want to study under someone who used her powers to enslave people to servitude.

First priority was to get inside some of my classmates' heads, so I could stay in the average range and not bring attention to myself. Which meant I'd need to start touching people, and that could be considered rude in the magical community, especially if you didn't ask first. I had yet to find a non-creepy way to ask to touch someone. Before hatching a plan, on day three, I was escorted to Dean Harrison's office. Fortunately, she didn't have time for me, and her office manager delivered the message.

"Since, your training level was now out of line, you're to report to the morgue," his voice was sympathetic. "The dean says that is the only place in the institute that can take on your schooling, at this time."

It's amazing how fast your world can change with just a few sentences. One moment you're a normal healing arts student; the next, you're going to work in a place where they cut on dead bodies. Nothing had prepared me for this new assignment.

By eight-thirty, I was in the morgue. My security escort introduced me to the pathologist, Dr. Corona. He was tall, thin, and wore a headband with a light and magnifying glass attached. His white lab coat had seen better days.

"Dr. Corona, this is Sera Webster, she will be assisting you until further notice."

The doctor seemed taken aback. "This is the help they send me?" He asked indignantly. The escort just shrugged and walked away.

The doctor wasn't any happier than I was being in the morgue, but he politely gave me a tour of a small laboratory, the cold storage area, and his office, then told me his rules. "Never touch anything I haven't asked you to touch, and never do anything without my permission. Don't touch any equipment until you're fully trained. No personal electronic devices are allowed in this area. Once you're trained, you can use the intercom system if you need to communicate." It seemed like everything was white or made of metal.

"I've never had an assistant look as young as you. How old are you?"

"Thirteen."

A low whistle escaped his lips. "Dang, that's just..." His voice trailed off. "I'd like to take it easy on you, being as it's your first day, but I'm in the middle of an autopsy and could really use an extra set of hands."

Biting my tongue hard kept me from groaning. Another thing about this place I didn't even consider was dead bodies. Definitely hadn't thought about cutting into dead bodies. Vaguely, I knew about medical anatomy courses that used cadavers, but foolishly, I believed it wouldn't be for several years. Basically, my imagination had us sitting in class or learning to heal sick people. Not actually dealing with the deceased. He guided me to a small room he had not included in the tour. There were two big, deep sinks with foot pedals to start and stop the water.

We put on shoe covers and masks, then he showed me how to scrub my hands very thoroughly with disinfectant, even using a small brush under my fingernails. Next came the gowns that closed in the back, a hair net, and gloves, which we helped each other put on. Even the smallest size of glove was loose on me. He explained this gear was similar to the operating room, but the difference was that we were more concerned with protecting us, not the patient.

The smell of blood, bone, and decay of a dead body hit me as soon as we entered the back room. The cadaver was in the center of the room on a table. I swayed quite a bit and needed to grab Dr. Corona's arm for stability. When we reached the body, Dr. Corona had to pull from my grasp and use his arm to support me. I was weaving and bobbing much like a boxer going down in slow motion. Grabbing onto the table to steady myself, my eyes squeezed shut, and dry heaving replaced what had been steady breaths. Finally, a pulse of magic helped to calm me. Oh my, why hadn't I thought of that earlier?

"I must apologize, just yesterday, I insisted that Dean Harrison send me a helper. Usually, things are quiet around here, and I can handle everything myself, but in addition to my morgue duties, I'm working on some research. I demanded an assistant to get caught up, thinking she would send me an intern. No one could've foreseen that she'd take her frustrations out on a first-year student. Do you think this is something you can do? You don't have to stay if you can't handle it."

"I'll be all right," I said, pulsing more magic just for good measure. When I opened my eyes, Dr. Corona was studying me.

"That was a quick recovery. For a moment you looked faint, and now you're as calm as can be."

Thankfully, the initial cutting and the bone sawing were already done. I couldn't have handled that without copious amounts of magic. Not having any idea what was expected, I simply did what the doctor asked of me. He kept his instructions basic. "Grab that vial." "Write down this weight." "Get a slide from over there." "Hold this."

The doctor and I had not touched skin to skin, due to the protective gear, but when we were finished for the day, he put his hand on my shoulder and told me, "You did great." His index finger rested on my neck and that was all that was needed. Boom. I now had access to his mind. Without understanding my magic completely, I knew my yellow powers were stronger than most. My magic took advantage whenever it could to find a way into someone's mind.

"Tomorrow morning have your escort take you back up to the dean's office," my heart dropped, I guessed this was it for me in the morgue. "Matt can get you a badge, so you can have unescorted access to the hospital, I've put in a request, and it was approved. I'll need you to be running specimens to the hospital's main laboratory, mail room, and other departments as needed," the doctor continued.

Well, that was much nicer than being fired after the first day. Free reign to roam outside the dorm area was like giving a golden ticket to a first-year student.

Back at my room, Caly was grumpy. "I hate that you aren't in the classroom, but I understand it. What I don't understand is why you left me alone for lunch. I felt like chum in shark-infested water," she accused.

"Oh, I'm so sorry. We didn't stop for lunch, but really, there was no way I could've eaten anything. Dean Harrison sent me to assist in the morgue, and I had to help with an autopsy," I said defensively.

"That can't be right, what was the dean thinking?" Caly asked, as her mouth gaped open.

"Dr. Corona, the pathologist doing the autopsy, thinks it was his fault for insisting that Harrison assign him an assistant by today. He even apologized to me."

"How was it?" she asked.

"Gross and interesting. He kept me busy, and he is meticulous about explaining everything. I'm sure he was mostly trying to keep my mind off the corpse. At the beginning, I almost fainted and then almost threw up."

"I'm pretty sure I would've done both," Caly commented.

"So, what happened at lunch?" I asked.

"Sharlyn and her ever-eager-to-please minions threw food at me, and the guards made *me* clean up. They all said it was me throwing it, but how stupid do you have to be to believe that when all the food was on or around me?" Her eyes looked misty, and without thinking, I pulled her into a hug. She hugged me back. My magic jumped with excitement, two new brains to explore in less than an hour. Caly stepped back and asked, "What was that?"

Luckily, I didn't answer right away. She reached for my chain and pulled out the flower pendant. "Oh, I thought I felt something hard."

I let out the breath I was holding. Whew, for a second there, I thought she had felt my magic.

"It looks valuable," I could see her lie, she thought it was plain rocks. The blue stone glimmered a little while she held it in her hand, but she had no clue.

"Umm, thanks," I said, quickly putting it back under my shirt.

After supper, I took a long hot shower. When I was done, Caly had her headphones on and was rocking out in her own world, looking up at a poster of her favorite rock idol. We could've spent some time watching a mini-series or a movie in the dayroom, but we didn't want to be around Sharlyn and her sycophants. Which was super-fine with me because I had a mind to sort through.

Even without any formal training, I had invaded many minds; the Bensons', random strangers, and acquaintances I'd bumped into. Through trial and error, I learned some techniques. My own mind needed to be as quiet as possible. You really didn't want to let the person know you were rifling around their personal business, especially if you had not asked for permission. I probed gently and slid in easily. This room, this situation was ideal. It was just the two of us, and she had the music to occupy her conscious thoughts.

Pulling on my yellow, I focused straight on her brain, sending tiny pulses in her direction. Staying aware of everything around me and rummaging around in her thoughts and memories was simple. The music was so loud that I nearly stopped. Instead, I imagined splitting the curtain of sound and pushing it to the sides. She was listening to her favorite band to help block out her thoughts. Wow, right at the top of her thoughts, Caly had a huge anxiety problem that she hid from the world. It came mostly from the Hortons. Sharlyn and Caly were best friends when they were younger, until Mrs. Horton told Sharlyn, "Stop hanging around the peons or they will drag you down." This was said right in front of Caly. Since then, Sharlyn has had nothing to do with her.

Using soothing pulses, I muted her threads of anxiety. It was like calming a frayed piece of yarn. Over the years, I realized you shouldn't make substantial changes, or you might be changing personalities, and that felt wrong. Things I looked for in people's minds was anything worth copying. High on my list were skills or talents, knowledge libraries, and any event that taught life-changing lessons. Of course, I always wanted to know what people really thought of me.

Caly thought I looked like Katie Holmes in *Dawson's Creek*. I had no idea what that meant, but she had been forced to stream watch some old episodes of the series with her mother, so she would know. She was jealous of me testing out of the basic courses and angry that it left her with no buffer against Sharlyn and her entourage. She believed I was her best option to hang out with, and then Jamyla and Kya, the two girls next-door who shared our bathroom. Seems like all four of us came from lower-class families, or at least that was what Caly thought. No way did I consider any of us lower.

Kya and Jamyla were both tall and trim, and though they came from very different backgrounds, they could've been related. They had honey-colored skin, large dark brown eyes, and slightly larger noses. Kya wore her straight hair chin-length with bangs combed over to give the top lift.

Jamyla's was in a crew cut, and when it was humid, it was extra curly.

More things Caly worried about—she had no money, and she was using all her toiletries sparingly. She was planning to wash her clothes without detergent. She was embarrassed that her entire wardrobe had once belonged to Sharlyn. Secretly, she longed to be Sharlyn's friend again. She believed her magic wasn't activated, she worried it might never happen.

Magic needed an event to activate. Puberty was the most common trigger. My yellow started with my parents' deaths and the kiss I gave Mom. Though Caly's was active, she wasn't tapping into all the power. I broke down the barrier for her so she could now draw on the magic. She was given the scholarship on her scans showing a high percentile of blue, not because she performed well on any test. Thirty percent in any color was the maximum, and she registered well above twenty-nine, enough for a scholarship. Her scholarship was conditional since she hadn't actually used any blue, yet. Maybe some people never access their real powers and potential. Her anxiety was at the root of the blocked ability. After today, she should be able to call on the healing because I tamped down her self-doubt.

I slipped out as quietly as I had slipped in and decided to just go to sleep. My meddling in Caly's brain felt like a good deed. Hopefully, it'd make her future more promising.

ELDER GIFT

WHEN I ARRIVED at the morgue the next day, there were no bodies. My new badge gave me a sense of freedom. After being assigned a corner desk with what the doctor called a fluorescence microscope, he talked me through the basics of setting it up. He pointed out he had a camera attachment that was connected to a computer. His instructions included how to handle the slides and use the attachment clips. He had me wear cotton gloves over latex ones. I was to count the number of red squiggly shapes on each slide. There was a box of about one hundred of them. Reading from his mind, I learned it was for a research project he was working on, and that he already knew the numbers. This was to verify his numbers and, thus, test the trustworthiness of my attention to detail.

While my conscious brain was counting and recording the squiggles, my mind's eye used the yellow magic on Dr. Corona. His knowledge of anatomy and physiology was extensive, but the most amazing thing was his self-made three-dimensional model of the human body. Every part was labeled as well as color coded, and it allowed you to zoom in or out. I copied that into my brain. Luckily, we were in the same vicinity all day, and the magic could use a slower rate of transfer for more detail. What took him years to build, I easily acquired in a day.

The next day, he gave me some documents to proofread. He just wanted me to fix any grammar and spelling that my thirteen-year-old brain would find. While doing that, I dug around all his amazing findings. He had even helped solve some criminal cases. I could've dug into his personal life, but it was depressing. He was divorced and only had a few friends. He thought I was smart but felt sorry for his part in me assisting in the morgue. He was truly angry at Dean Harrison, and it was apparent they didn't get along.

My badge wasn't intended for me to visit the shops in the lobby or the hospital wards, just mainly running Dr. Corona's errands. I chose to spend my lunches in the hospital food court, much to Caly's disappointment. It was closer to the morgue and had better food choices. It included a pizza place, Asian food, fried chicken, and a sandwich shop. Sitting in a corner allowed for practicing my magic on total strangers. I would bump into people to read their minds, then have them change their mind about what to eat or drink. So many hospital guests were worried about loved ones. It felt good to sooth their anxieties. I was getting very competent at these simple tricks.

From the institute, the only people I was getting to know were Caly, Jamyla, and Kya. Being my roommate, I spent more time with Caly. Without her knowledge, I soothed her anxieties and helped her with math. We bartered with laundry duty. I'd wash her clothes with mine, so she didn't have to worry about detergent; in exchange, she would fold and put mine away.

Four months under Dr. Corona's supervision went fast. Cutting and sawing bones became natural. He'd never had a more valued assistant, but then none of the others read his thoughts. During my last week there, something strange happened. I returned from a lunch break to find a body covered by a plastic blanket on the metal autopsy table.

"We have some important visitors coming down, I need you to sit in the corner and be as quiet as a mouse. They usually don't linger long." Dr. Corona pointed to my work corner and then headed to the visitor entrance.

When I passed the table, the body's wrinkled old hand had slipped out from the plastic cover. When I grabbed the hand to tuck it back under, a huge rush of magic blasted into me. "Use it wisely," I heard an old man's voice in my head. It reminded me of similar magic exchanges with my mom and dad's bodies. Not wanting to disappoint Dr. Corona, I scurried to my desk. My body was all tingly and full of magic. Before, I had a balloon without air; now, it was completely inflated. No, not a balloon, more solid like an orange, and each wedge was a different color. If using my magic was like riding a horse, until now, it had been a tame pony. This was a huge wild stallion with wings. If Mom's magic felt like warm cocoa, this felt like the whiskey Chris distilled in the barn. Turning off the desk lamps, I hunkered down in the chair and pushed it back into the corner as far as the walls would allow.

Dr. Corona returned with a group of seven adults. They varied in age, shape, size, color, and gender. The only thing they seemed to have in common was an obscene wear of gemstones. Every one of them was strong in magic and had multicolored auras surrounding them. Wow. This was new. Before, I could see magic when someone used it. This was different. The auras only flared out a few inches from their outlines, but some showed two or three colors, and all of them had a tiny bit of yellow. Even the doctor had a blue aura with thin layers of red and green surrounding him. My new gift must be picking this up.

It was apparent they were here to see the body. They gathered around the table. Without having touched any of them, their thoughts were broadcasting into my brain, making the quiet room sound like a party. Many voices talking at once and over each other. Each one of them was hoping they would be chosen as the recipient of this elder's magical spirit.

The doctor carefully removed the plastic sheet. Under it was the body of a man that could easily be over one hundred years old. The visitor's joined hands, making a closed circle. They raised and held their clasped hands about a foot over the body.

"On the count of three," said a lady, who looked to be the oldest. "One, two, three." They all lowered their hands and touched the body. Disappointment replaced their excitement. Each was wondering who received the spirit gift. *What the heck was a spirit gift?* I wondered, *It must be related to the changes in my magic when I moved the elder's hand.*

A few even spoke their disappointment, "Nothing changed for me," one said.

"Me either," another said.

One by one, they all touched the body again to make sure nothing was missed.

Most remained quiet, but the lady who had counted asked the doctor, "No one was allowed to touch the body, right?"

"Definitely, not. Your delivery team gave us very clear instructions," he told her, as they headed to the exit as a group. Many were taking off the excess of jewelry as they walked out.

Their voices quieted as they exited, leaving me with a headache from all the noise they emitted.

"Do you know who they are?" the doctor asked when he returned.

"No."

"They're the Nokuland Council. What a bunch of goofballs, wanting to touch a dead body. They do that ritual every time one of the elders dies. Elders hold incredible amounts of magic. Though this time they seemed extra disappointed," he mused. "They believe the dead can pass on some magical energy or power; they call it a spirit gift. Personally, I think that is simply crazy. I have dealt with many bodies, and not one has passed me any magic. They hold hands to make sure everyone gets an equal chance." He shook his head in disbelief.

For the rest of the day, I kept hearing every thought in Dr. Corona's head, and it was irritating and distracting. Spending most of the afternoon in the bathroom holding my hands over my ears didn't really help, but from this distance, the doctor's thoughts were quieter. I practiced blocking it out and had some success, but it was draining. Back at the lab, his aura was constantly moving, making me dizzy if I stared too long.

"Are you feeling all right?" he asked me several times.

"I'm fine," I lied. No way was I going to see a nurse and be exposed to all the minds in the hallways and waiting room.

At four o'clock, I couldn't get back to my room fast enough. I planned to take a shower and go to bed with a pillow over my ears. Caly refused to let me miss dinner.

"You have to eat with me," she pleaded. "When you're around, Sharlyn doesn't mess with me as much." I wasn't going to be much of a buffer for her tonight. Dinner was excruciating, with so many people in one place. Everyone was excited about the end of first term and going home for the holiday break. Layers of voices from conversations and thoughts bombard my head. I kept blasting soothing pulses to stop me from screaming and running out of the cafeteria like a lunatic.

During the week break between semesters, students could travel home. Nana sent word in a care package that I wouldn't be allowed to travel to the ranch. The institute didn't consider her my real family. Normally, a foster parent would be allowed to have a child home for the holidays. It was puzzling. She assured me that she had filed paperwork to officially adopt me, but that could take some time. Spending a week alone didn't sound so bad if Nana was going to be my forever family.

Nana typically spent the first part of the holiday season giving out care packages to local people in need. Otherwise, she would've come here to spend time with me. We both understood without words that her community support and her charity came first. My situation wasn't dire, just uncomfortable.

The last line of her note read, "Sera, you are part of my heart and will always be my family. I'm going to get this fixed." She and the Bensons sent a genuinely nice food package with lots of farm goodness and homemade treats. Since the cafeteria wasn't open over the break, the food would be allowed in my room. Even though it was a dormitory rule, no one had received any punishment for breaking it.

"You haven't listened to a word I've said," Caly accused at supper when I didn't respond to one of her questions. Looking at her, the blue glow of her aura burned into my brain as if I were staring into a neon sign, and that didn't help the pain one bit.

"Sorry, this migraine is crushing my brain. I'm not listening to anyone." I almost choked from the irony since just the opposite was true. "Let's go back to the room."

Caly followed me up to the room and decided to stay rather than spend time in the dayroom watching television. Dang. It would've been nice to have a quiet evening. Her music wasn't my favorite, and it was loud enough to hear even though she had her headphones on. Escaping onto the patio with an excuse to water the plants, the noise in my head dimmed. There had to be a way to control this new magic. Each page of my *Legati Magicum Flavus* book was slowly flashing through my mind. This gift had only been with me a few hours, and already jumping off a cliff seemed like a good option.

Outside, it was much quieter. As I leaned back to rest my head on the top of the chair, one of the plants caught my attention. The parsley one seemed to be giving off extra vibrations, so I leaned in and took a closer look. Nothing different in its appearance, just the buzzing. I lightly pinched at the small green petals to see if that would make it stop, and they crumbled to dust. Wow, that was new. Touching the powder to my tongue sent an immediate calm and the stones in my necklace tugged at me. When the black stone glowed, the noise wavered, going quieter at times. This plant dust had activated the stone, but there was no black magic. Was there?

I touched another leaf on the same plant, nothing happened this time. Touching the aloe or the basil didn't do anything. Concentrating on the black stone, and after about an hour of trial and error, the new magic flipped on and off with concentration. With more practice, the black stone was no longer needed, just like the other magic colors. The black stone seemed to teach control of this noisy painful gift, enabling me to turn it on and off at will. OH, THANK GOD! Bouncing with excitement, I kissed the pendant. No psychiatric care would be needed, nor being locked in a padded room.

The aloe plant still looked a bit wilted. With my mind calmer, the green and blue of my magic wanted to reach out to the plant. Approaching the plant, the two colors merged into one. Turquoise pulsed toward the plant and the gel leaves plumped up. Helping this tiny plant left an aftermath of warm vibrations tingling through my body.

After staying outside until every vibe subsided, entering the room was peaceful. Caly's music and aura were undetectable. Her air guitar performance told me she was still listening. Oh wow, was this ever a relief. Laying down on my bed to enjoy the peaceful quiet, I cradled the rock pendant in my palm, holding it near my chest. Concentrating on the stones, I could light them up one at a time, then even in combinations. Turning my palm to look at the new magic, the pendant projected an image into my hand. It was globe-shaped, and the colors were rolling around like a kaleidoscope. Focusing on yellow made it glow like a miniature sun in my hands. One hundred percent golden, not a dot of any other color. Concentrating on red, it became red. When all the colors of the necklace were considered equally, it changed into wedges of light. Without using my magic to control the colors, they blended into a jumbled mosaic, making me think of a kaleidoscope. Thinking of only red and yellow, it shone orange. I could add black to make darker shades of the color and adding white made different tints and highlights. Red with blue could meld into purple. I was trying to imagine what that combination could do. Force plus healing, maybe it could heal someone without touching them. So many possibilities mixing colors.

Massive power and control were making me giddy. The yearning for the magic to be set free was so potent. It felt like I was learning to ride this huge powerful chameleon, and I longed to show it off in a parade. The power swirling inside me was seductive, and I wanted to dance with the ribbons waving around me in a look-at-me-look-what-I-can-do pirouette.

Doing something rash, could easily ruin my freedom. A strong moral compass was needed to keep this from corrupting me. A very clear understanding of right and wrong was easy in theory, desires and emotion muddled the crisp separation. People often found ways to believe crossing the line was justified. Thankfully, my time with Nana had supplied me with a solid, humble foundation. Now, if only walking this thin tightrope without falling could be copied from someone.

There was a great advantage to keeping this all hidden. Not being controlled and making my own choices were my top contenders. Being in the public limelight wasn't appealing to me. If the council knew or even suspected, I would be strictly monitored and controlled. Realizing there was no one I could share this with dampened my excitement. There was a vast separation between me and the rest of humanity.

All alone in a desert oasis. While my world was spinning faster, everything and everyone else was in slow motion. One thing that felt duty-bound would be to use this legacy to turn wrongs into rights. This power had to be used for the betterment of Amaku. First on the agenda was getting Mandy some justice.

THE NIGHTMARE

MY EYES SNAPPED open to a quickly fading bright light. Outside the room, my two-year-old sister was half sobbing and half shrieking, "Mommy! Mommy! Mommy!" Each time it sounded farther away.

"Shut up, you little brat," boomed a gruff unfamiliar voice. Heavy footsteps faded with Tatiana's voice as she was carried away. First, the front door slammed shut hard enough for the bed to tremble, followed by a couple of car doors opening and closing. In between, I heard one more shriek for Mommy. Eerie beams of the headlights circled the walls of the bedroom as gravel crunched, then the sound of the engine slowly dwindling until there was only silence.

Lying in the quiet darkness, I whimpered, "Mommy? Daddy?" and even though I was snuggled between them, neither replied. Over and over, I tried to get them to talk to me. Neither responded. Frantically trying to move only increased my panic. My tiny body was pinned tight between both their bodies and held down by the blankets. Earlier in the night, after a bad dream, Mommy allowed me to crawl under the covers between them. Sometime after that, they both must have tossed and turned enough to trap me between them, held in place much like a fly trapped in a spider's web.

Wiggling, I tried to use my body to push free, first from Daddy and then from Mommy. Neither moved even a tiny bit. Tears were streaming down the sides of my face. My sobbing pleas for them to wake up went unanswered. Eventually, exhaustion took over, and I dozed off for a while.

When the sunlight began streaming through the curtains, I woke. Nothing had improved. The panic started again. My breathing was rapid.

"Help me, Mommy, Daddy, please help me," I begged into the stillness.

My bladder was full, adding to my discomfort. To keep my mind off that, I started to look around the room. The cabin ceiling had a fan with a light, the blades turning slowly and quietly. There wasn't much else to see, just the upper parts of the curtains and doors. When I turned my head to the left, Mommy's face was quite close to mine. Her eyes were partly opened.

"Mommy, please talk to me," I pleaded.

Trying to get closer to her, I tensed my legs and tried to scooch up the bed. No progress was made. I stretched my neck out and puckered out my lips as far as I could. Finally, I was able to lightly kiss her on the nose.

A wave of electric fuzz surfed from Mommy's body through mine, and I heard her voice inside my head, "Sera, Mommy loves you." I felt warm and full like eating a freshly baked chocolate chip cookie on a cold day. In the powerful rush, my body forgot to hold my pee, and I wet myself. Being five years old and not wetting myself in years, tears streamed down, again.

After several more kisses, nothing else happened. I tried to reach out to my dad as well, but too many layers of blankets kept me from touching him. All I could see of him was the back of his head and shoulders.

Remembering how Mommy calmed me down, her soothing words played out in my head.

"Concentrate on your mind's eye, right in the middle of your head. Talk to your brain and ask it to release the good stuff that calms you. Take a deep breath and hold it for as long as you can." IT WORKED! The roaring panic stopped. My yellow magic did that! I did it all by myself, but the loneliness and helplessness stayed.

What else could help? My parents always told me how important concentration and focus were when using magic. I rolled my tongue, bit my lower lip, closed my eyes tight, and tried to force the blankets or bodies to move. After many, many attempts of nothing moving, I gave up trying.

With nothing else to do, I looked at the ceiling. It was white and bumpy. Scrunching my eyes, I could see shapes in the bumps. At first, I could see a stick, a ball, and a face, but as time wore on, the images became scary things like snakes, spiders, and angry faces. So, I stopped doing that. I continually pinched the bedding and my pajamas trying to pull anything loose. I rolled my tongue around in my mouth, working up enough moisture to swallow. With a little bit of maneuvering, I was able to trap the sheet in my mouth and I sucked on that for comfort.

My throat was dry, and my stomach grumbled several times. Being wet, hungry, thirsty, and stuck between my motionless parents created a huge sense of helplessness. Several times, I had to reuse the calming spell. I sung favorite songs over and over.

Both my parents had told me repeatedly how special I was and how I would be one of the most powerful wizards that ever lived. Now, I questioned if that were true since I couldn't even move a blanket.

Sometime later, after the shadows of the curtain tops had moved to the other side, a car pulled up in front of the cabin, crunching the gravel. Several people came inside, and just when I was going to call out for help, a woman's voice gave out instructions.

"Gather up all personal items and pack them into their bags," she commanded.

Clicking heels on the floor warned of someone's approach. That someone walked in the room and was coming closer to the bed. Some of the blankets were yanked from me. I WAS FREE. I scrambled to reach my dad. Another wave of energy rushed into me as wonderful as a hug, but Dad hadn't moved. "Be a good girl," his voice echoed in my head for the last time.

Looking at the stranger, I thought she was my mom for a split second but quickly realized Mommy was right beside me. This lady had very blonde hair neatly pulled back into a bun. Her blue suit was out of place up here in a mountain cabin. She was grabbing Mommy's arm. "Damn," she cursed. Then grabbed at Dad as well. "Damn it," she swore again.

"Who are you?" she demanded, looking straight at me.

"Sera," I answered, shaking. The warm hug feeling had already gone.

She started toward me, and I began scooting away from her. A burly man dived on top of me, pinning me down on top of my mom's body. Something hard under my palm vibrated energy and my hand closed around it. It was the necklace that was always around her neck.

"Gross, she smells like piss," he said near my ear.

"I've got her, you take care of the bodies. GET UP!" the lady barked, and both of us got off the bed and stood up. Mom's necklace was now in my hand, it was strange that the chain broke free so easily.

As two men moved my dad's body out of the room, the woman took a hold of my forearm and told me to follow her. I felt a weight press down on my mind like a heavy wet blanket. I saw her use the yellow mind magic just as much as I could feel it. She propelled me toward the bathroom and told me to get into the tub. Once seated in the tub, she turned the shower on, jetting cold water over me. I tried to let out a scream in protest, but no sound came out. My thirst pulled the refreshing wetness down my throat instead.

"Get out of your pajamas," she ordered crisply.

I stood up and struggled out of the soaked material, making sure to not let go of the pendant, and tossed the soggy garments toward the back of the tub. She shampooed my hair and used a soapy washcloth to clean my body. After I rinsed off, she draped a towel around my shoulders and used another smaller towel on my hair. She grabbed Mom's comb from near the sink and pulled it through my tangled strands.

From the other room, one of the guys asked, "Do you need anything for the girl?"

"Bring me a set of clean clothes, put the rest of her stuff in the suitcase, and put it the car. While you're out there, bring me my bag."

He brought the clothes for me. The top was a colorful pink tunic with kittens, some underwear, and black tights. After she finished drying me, she helped me get dressed. She had just finished with drying my hair when the guy came back with a large, blue purse that matched her suit and shoes. When she was turned away from me, I slipped the necklace into my pocket.

"She needs shoes."

"Yes, ma'am," he nodded, and then he left again.

From her bag, she pulled out what looked like a small camera and took a picture of me. I was nervous. Mommy never let anyone take a picture of me. When the man came back with my pink sneakers, he looked over her shoulder at the device.

"What's that?"

She scrunched her face like she was going to snap at him but decided to explain. "It's a spectrometer that measures magic, like an infrared camera measures heat."

"I don't see anything."

"Apparently, she has less magic than you," she said, as she snapped a picture of him.

"All I see are a few, thin colored lines," he said, looking at the display again.

"Yes, that is showing me how much and what kind of magic you hold in your body. You are less than ten percent, but hers is nothing. See these double zeros at the bottom of her image? Nothing! I've never seen that before, so now I'm wondering what she was doing between those two powerful wizards." She looked puzzled, and I could feel her disappointment. Why didn't that camera see my magic? She had touched me before the shower, skin to skin. Some magical strangers didn't like to touch, she did it without concern. Now, she was able to keep me silent. I reached out with my new magic and found brown slime in her brain. YUCK. I pulled back quickly because that oozy stuff was making my stomach hurt. She narrowed her eyes and gave me a quizzical look.

I was put into the back seat of their car. One of the men drove my parent's car while we followed. From their conversation, I knew my parent's bodies were in our car. The road had sharp curves in several places. We were coming down off a mountain. I wanted to ask what was going to happen to me, but I still could not speak.

We made a brief stop where the road was a bit wider. I watched with my palm on the window, my chin resting on my thumb. I was staring at them between my fingers. The two men dumped gas all over the inside of our car, lit it on fire, and then pushed it over the cliff. As the car rolled out of sight, my chest sunk, and my head slid down the pane. I used my mind magic to ease this new pain, but still, it felt like someone was stabbing me and then twisting the blade right into my heart.

The lady moved me and my suitcase to another car that was parked off to the side of the road. This car was much shinier and softer. She had me sit in the front passenger seat. I was nervous without a booster. Any other day, I would've been excited to be in the front and without my car seat.

She drove through the mountains that seemed to play hide and seek through the trees until after dark. We stopped, got out, and then got into a cabled train that took us much higher into the mountains. We were the only ones on board, not even a driver. When it stopped, we were near a huge stone building. I'd never seen anything so big. I started to count the windows from the bottom to the top but couldn't finish before we entered the building through glass doors that opened automatically for us. In the lobby, a young receptionist sprang up from her chair into an attentive stance.

"Good evening," she said, nervously.

The lady didn't even give the girl a glance, as we walked straight to a long hallway of elevators. We stopped at the furthest one. She pressed some numbers on a pad, the doors sprang open, and we stepped inside. The doors closed, and the lift lurched upward, making my stomach flip a little.

Just outside the elevator, she pressed a button near a door. I heard a buzzing sound on the inside. After a few moments, a security guard opened the door and let us in.

His, "Good evening, ma'am," was also ignored.

This whole place smelled of the nasty stuff Dad would wash his hands with, and I was sure we had gone into a hospital, but right now, I was surprised to see that we were in someone's home. The lady I was with was about my mom's size and age. The lady that came into the living room where we were standing, was shorter, rounder, had black hair and was older. She was in a garment that could have been pajamas or a dress. She gave me a brief questioning glance.

"Annette, so glad to see you came so quickly, let's talk in my study." We both followed her. I was still on autopilot mode.

"You wait here." Annette pointed to a chair right outside the study door.

I sat down, let my head rest against the wall, and closed my eyes. I'm not sure why she had me wait outside; I could hear everything they said.

"Always glad to help out friends, but this time I need a favor in return. I picked up that stray while sanitizing the council's assassination," said Annette.

"Rumor has it that they had acquired the Kendler child," said the lady.

"Indeed, they did, this one was found trapped between the fugitive's bodies, but before you get excited, she doesn't have any magical readings." I heard some shuffling. "Look here, double zeros. I know how much you like the magically challenged working for you. If you take her off my hands, then I'll make up your assistant's mind free of charge."

"I don't really see how taking on a child will help me." The lady sounded irritated.

"You would be solving my problem, and you could raise her to be your perfect helper. Someone who could visit Senaland for you. She will never be a true citizen of Nokuland with no magic. We could put it in Mandy's contract so that she can be responsible for the brat," suggested Annette.

"Tempting, but then she would be in Mandy's office all day, and I'm not sure that would be a good situation."

"She is in obedience mode right now; we could just leave that in place. A child her age could run quick errands like getting your lunches and so many other possibilities. Anyway, we need a place to sleep, and you can think about it overnight and let me know in the morning."

The lady whose house we were in poked her head out the door.

"Kent, get these two settled for the night."

"Yes, Dr. Gobel, right away."

"We will need something to eat," Annette said, still inside the room.

"And Kent, make sure Margaret gets them some dinner."

"Yes, ma'am."

"So did you get their spirit gifts," the doctor asked Annette.

"No, not from either body. It was the strangest thing. The girl they collected had strong readings but not nearly as much as a firstborn of two powerful wizards should have. The bodies didn't transfer their spirit to me and could not have given them to the girl. If the woman didn't look so much like me, I would think we had gotten the wrong couple," said Annette.

"Surely the magical imprint they received matched the fugitives or the kill bomb wouldn't have worked."

"I agree, but it's all so strange."

"Perhaps, the child you have with you is the firstborn, but maybe her DNA mutated. Sort of like an albino. At high levels, maybe magic moderates itself. That would explain the double zeroes," suggested Dr. Gobel.

Over breakfast the next morning, I watched as Annette worked mind magic on the doctor's assistant, Mandy. Mandy was signing papers while Annette simply rested her hands on Mandy's shoulders in a friendly manner. I could feel Annette's mind goo thicken, and I could see in my mind's eye it was like tar. Right before she released the Mandy, Annette erased her memory of being forced to sign. Alarm bells went off in my head, and I stilled them quickly when Annette looked my way. Even at five years old, I knew that the brown goo was bad news, but the erasing, especially after having someone do something against their will, could get you in big trouble.

The doctor had decided not to place me under Mandy's care but sent me off to be entered into the Nokuland's foster system.

HOLIDAY BREAK

FRIDAY AFTERNOON, AFTER semester finals, the dormitory fluttered with activity. In the hallway, I hugged Caly, said goodbye to Jamyla and Kya, wishing them a fun week at home. Each expressed sadness for me staying.

"I'll bring something back for your birthday," Caly promised.

Knowing how little money she and her mom had, I assured her, "No present is necessary." Just like a rotten cherry on top of my holiday alone, I was going to turn fourteen with no one to help me celebrate.

After they were gone, I headed to the administration offices in search of Ms. Fine. Not only was she our teacher, but she was the first-year student counselor as well. She was seated at her desk, finishing our grades before she left. I gave the door a light knock.

"Sera, what can I do for you?" she asked.

"Well, since I'm stuck here all week alone, I was hoping for a pass to allow me into the hospital areas."

"I'm not sure that is something I can arrange. Don't you already have a badge from Dr. Corona?"

"That badge expired today. It was only good until the end of the term. I can no longer swipe out. Who would be able to give me permission?" I asked.

"We would have to go as high as the Dean of Students, Ms. Harrison."

"Let's go," I encouraged her. With only a little magic, but intense concentration, a compliance signal negated her resistance. She didn't have a mind shield to resist my request. When I released the energy in her direction, she agreed to escort me. It really was like using my mind to slingshot some magic to her brain to make her obey me. Interfering with people's decisions was walking in a dark gray area between right and wrong, but I assured myself it was justified. This would only take a few minutes of her time.

When we arrived at Dean Harrison's outer office, her assistant was going to say she was busy, so I released a pulse at him, too. He was a lean efficient man in his late twenties, and something felt off about him. My first guess was a spell, hex, or ward, but my senses didn't feel any of those things.

"Let me check to see if she will see you without an appointment," he said, walking toward her office. Staying right on his heels, my yellow energy was now directed at the dean. The assistant announced, "Sera Webster would like to see you."

"Come in, Miss Webster," the dean said, even before the assistant finished speaking. "That will be all, Matt," she said. She walked around her desk and motioned for the open-mouthed assistant to leave.

Once the door was shut, she returned to her seat and motioned for me to sit. "What can I do for you?" she asked. She too, looked efficient and professional. No one would accuse her of being kind and gentle. Her bleached blond hair was styled in a curly helmet. She looked to be in her forties, but the way her skin stretched over her cheek bones hinted that she was pushing sixty.

"As you might know, I wasn't allowed to go home this week," I stopped, and she nodded for me to continue. "Ms. Fine informed me that I'd need your permission to be allowed outside the school areas. I would like to be able to make visits to patients to help pass the time." All the while I was sending pulses of magical energy to ensure she agreed with my request. She needed more pulses than Ms. Fine to agree to the hospital pass.

"That seems like a simple enough request, I'll have Matt print you an access badge. It will only be good for the week, and I better not get any complaints about you," she warned.

"Thank you, I appreciate your support on this." I gave her a friendly smile.

"Make sure you check with the floor nurses before approaching any patients. You will need both the nurses and the patient's approval. And thank you for not being bitter about the morgue assignment," she said with fake sweetness that left a bitter taste in my mouth. I really didn't like this woman, and I was sure it wasn't just because I picked up on Dr. Corona's negativity.

Back out at Matt's desk, he took my picture and input my information for the badge. Ms. Fine headed back to her office in the dormitory, shaking her head as if in complete amazement.

"We haven't formally met." When I put out my hand for a handshake, Matt engaged, giving me access to his mind. "I'm Sera Webster, and you are?"

"Matt, Dean Harrison's personal assistant." How odd of him not to give his last name. Trekking through his mind, it was clear to see he was under the influence of mind control. Yellow threads reached out into the world connecting him to other members of Dean Harrison's office and household staff. Even more strands connected their group to other clusters. Dr. Gobel's staff was the most closely linked. This had to be the work of Annette. It was identical to what she had done to Mandy, confirming her comment about the leadership at the hospital. Disgust and anger rose from my core. It wasn't anything Matt had done. Forcing my face to stay neutral was a struggle, but he didn't need to think he was doing anything wrong.

I made sure Matt dated the pass effective to the end of next term, not just one week. Reaching for the badge, my shaking hand reflected a tattletale tremor of my emotions.

"Are you feeling okay?" Matt asked.

"Sure. As good as can be expected."

Slipping my new "explorer" badge lanyard over my head, I exited the office. First destination was the shops and beauty salon located on the entrance level. Before I got to the elevator, an office door sign for scholarships pulled my attention. It was a very small office, Ms. Mason at a desk with two chairs for clients. I rapped lightly on her door.

"Come in, how can I help you?" Ms. Mason asked, looking puzzled. I could see she wasn't expecting anyone on the last day of the semester, but then she smiled when she recognized me.

"Well, I saw the plaque on your door."

"Sera, it's so good to see you. I heard about them sending you to assist in the morgue. I did lodge a complaint, but it was ignored." She was holding something back, not by her choice, there were traces of mind magic. A pulse let me see what she was forced to hide without leaving a trail of my meddling. Covered behind the magic was a finance scandal. Part of her job was to give out funds, so that the students could buy toiletries and have some spending money. What was interesting was that only a few of the students actually received access to the money. Students weren't even told they had money. All the leftover was transferred to an account controlled by Dean Harrison. That money was intended for every student at the institute. All the way up to the residents in the doctorate program, and Ms. Mason suspected the skimming enterprise expanded beyond scholarship funds.

"Well, thanks for trying to protect me, Dr. Corona made sure my time there was very educational. I gained a lot of good experience. I stopped in to ask you a question."

"About what?" she asked.

"Students access to spending money."

"Oh yes, I open bank accounts for first-year students at the beginning of the year and deposits are made monthly until they leave our program."

"I didn't receive any. Could you please check to see what the holdup might be?"

She typed while looking at her screen. "This is strange, many of the students haven't been given access codes and cards."

"Would it be possible to get mine now?"

"Sure." She was frightened of Dean Harrison, but she typed a bit more and told me to put my thumb on a scanner. The printer behind me spit out a page. She collected the printout and put it in front of me. Then she sat in the chair beside me and talked me through the paperwork. "With this pin number and your thumb print, you can purchase up to this amount per month." She pointed at the number. It wasn't as generous as Nana's allowance, but Caly, Jamyla, and Kya would be pleased with the funds.

"Please sign on the screen and use your thumbprint to accept receipt."

"So, my friends can come and get signed up for access when they get back, right?" I asked.

She checked her computer for each of my suite mates and said, "They just need to be escorted here during office hours." It was interesting that her office hours were the same as class time. I'd have to get them a pass and be escorted by Ms. Fine. I was thinking a class field trip might be in order.

"Great, thanks."

While I was waiting for the elevator, Ms. Mason scurried from her office to the dean's.

Instead of continuing to the shops, I returned to the dormitory. First, to make sure Ms. Fine knew she needed to escort the class to get their accounts activated. Second, I wanted to change clothes, wearing my school scrubs in the hospital made me stand out like a broken thumb.

After changing into jeans, a lightweight hoodie, and canvas shoes, I went to explore the hospital. Once I left the dormitory wearing regular clothes, it was unnecessary to display the badge. Not many people would know I was a student without the scrubs, I simply looked like a visitor. Teachers and staff were also leaving for the holiday break, so not many people remaining would recognize me. Mainly, the badge gave me permission to leave the dormitory. So, I tucked the badge under my hoodie. After exploring and finding my way around with ease, I spent the remainder of the day planning my week.

Saturday morning, after sending Nana and the Bensons a thank you note, I went to the beauty parlor the minute it opened. I wanted something to celebrate my fourteenth birthday. At the salon reception desk, a very nice-looking guy in his twenties informed me they only took reservations and that there were no openings unless someone canceled.

"Would you like me to put you on the waiting list?" he asked.

"No, my schedule is not very flexible." As I turned to leave, I bumped into an immaculately dressed lady carrying a purse that cost more than a year's wages for the average worker.

"What's wrong with you? Don't you look where you're going?" she snapped. I could see from her thoughts that she was here for a haircut and highlights, as well as her nails. With a few spikes of yellow sent her way, instantly, she was too upset to keep her appointment. She left huffing her irritation.

"Do you have an opening now?" I asked sweetly.

"Well, we have a waiting list we usually call when we have openings. But with so little notice, no one will be able to make it in time. With that client canceling without twenty-four hours' notice, she will get charged the full appointment price. So, sweetie, it looks like your first appointment will be free."

He gave me an incredibly pleased smile and indicated I should follow him. He talked while we walked to his station. That lady was one of his clients and one he dearly hated. She had made several derisive comments about gay people. Even to me, a hick from the country, it was easy to see Chaz was gay. It felt like a display of honor upsetting her. Hours of luxurious treatments sped by quickly. Chaz and a very pleasant nail technician took turns pampering me. He even threw in sculpting my eyebrows and loaded me up with free samples. I made a reoccurring appointment with him for the first Saturday of every month. Chaz's Saturday openings were nearly nonexistent, due to his loyal clients. But he pointed out that his angry client had forgotten to book any future appointments. I insisted he let me pay a tip amounting to twenty percent of her total bill.

My next stop was the gift store, which was quite large and sold much more than just gifts. My purchases included a large scenic poster of the mountains and an exceptionally soft, fluffy teddy bear for Caly. It had a headband with the name of her favorite group, Bur$t, and held a miniature bright red electric guitar. Lingering over the jewelry section to see if any of the gems were giving off energy didn't produce any results.

Studying the hospital map in the lobby, made it clear that many of the staff lived in residence. Dr. Gobel, the hospital administrator who bound Mandy with the help of Annette's yellow magic, was listed in the penthouse. The top three floors were for doctors, and then the next five floors were for support staff like nurses, physician assistants, and those in training to be physicians. Nonprofessional staff most likely rode the trains in from nearby towns.

Back at the dorm room, I found a video on my tablet from the Bensons and Nana, wishing me happy birthday. My reply included a picture of me with my new hair style.

Caly's teddy bear needed some personal touches. Taking a few items from the giveaway table in the dayroom, I hand-sewed him a pair of jeans and a T-shirt that somewhat resembled the poster above her bed. I left the gift resting on her pillow.

The next day, visiting some of the wards, it became apparent to me that most patients had visitors, being as it was Sunday. The few that didn't were sleeping. So, I explored the basement levels of the hospital and found a gymnasium with a pool. At the sign-in desk, there was a list of classes available ranging from yoga, martial arts, aerobics, and body sculpting. Many were booked up for weeks. There was a Krav Maga class starting in a few minutes. It was completely booked, but I only wanted to meet the instructor.

When I found Gideon, he was stretching and getting prepared for class. His name was stitched into his workout jacket.

"Hi, are you the Krav Maga instructor?" I asked.

"Yes, we're booked, but what can I do for you?"

"Oh yeah, the sign-up list made that clear. Plus, you're teaching advanced, I wouldn't be qualified." I extended my hand and was pleased he shook it.

"I'm Sera."

"Nice to meet you, Sera. I'm Gideon."

"I just have a few quick questions. How old does one need to be to start training? And would you allow me to just watch this class to see if it would be something I would be interested in learning?" I asked. Mind pulses were sent to ensure he didn't turn me down.

"Really any age, as long as you can find an instructor willing to take you on as a student. And, of course, you can watch, but I'll need you to stay quiet over on the bleachers."

"Thank you, I'll be so quiet you might forget I'm here." Flashing a thankful smile, I headed to where he had pointed. By the time I was seated, he was ready to start the class. It was amazing to see every one of his students had a black belt. Switching on party mode for just a second, made it obvious every student had a red aura. From their thoughts, it was easy to figure these were the hospital's security guards. Remarkable. While watching, I transferred a copy of Gideon's proficiency. My skills wouldn't match his. Our reach, body strength, muscle mass, and flexibility were all different. It was useful, even without matching characteristics. His exercise routines, and his motivation for staying fit were also captured.

When class ended, I thanked him. "I really did forget you were there," he said, amazed.

An aikido class was coming up. The gentleness of this style was much more in line with the philosophy Nana instilled in me. So, I stayed, met the instructor, and copied it as well.

Whenever my magic energy starts to leak, I experiment with different ways to expel the excess. Using magic at an accelerated rate increased my accuracy, proficiency, and overall sense of well-being. The patio was a good place to hone my green nature potential. Concentrating on the garden roots, urging them to grow deeper and thicker, I released enough to stop any leakage. Seeking out sickly roots provided the opportunity to use turquoise to heal them. Afterward, the garden smelled sweeter and looked healthier.

Behind the Healing Arts Institute was a gorge with a variety of terrain. It transitioned from soft slopes to some sharp cliffs. I decided to explore the hiking trails. They were marked like ski slopes; easy, intermediate, and difficult. This was a restricted area during the semesters. Instructors would bring us out here for Sunday activities. Being my first time alone, I took an easy path. There were a few plateaus with huge boulders on the way to the bottom, making natural resting points. When I stumbled on an uneven point in a path, I used red to flatten the area into wider, longer steps to make the area safer.

When using green on scan mode, every living creature in the area became visible. Squirrels, ants, rodents, deer, birds, and many more. Even the nocturnal animals. I found a sleeping raccoon family, some coyotes, and even a mountain lion. This area made me feel more at home.

Monday, with permission to spend the whole day in the children's ward, my magic was again eager for release. The first patient I came across was a little seven-year-old girl. She was hospitalized and undergoing tests. She had continuous stomach aches, dizziness, and headaches. She was scheduled for a brain scan in the afternoon.

"Navy, will you hold my hand while you tell me about what kind of puppy you think is the best?" I asked, glancing at her mom to make sure she was comfortable with me. She was just thankful for any distraction. Navy had just been talking about wanting a puppy that she would love so much. While she talked, I flooded her body with a blue scan. There was a mass in her brain that, when compared to Dr. Corona's anatomy module, should not have been there.

Sending in a stream of focused magic to the tumor, the magic broke down the mass into infinitesimally small pieces. Not knowing what to do with these particles, the magic pulled them out and brought the particles into my body. Instantly, I knew that wasn't correct. Excusing myself, I sped to the nearest rest room barely making it in time to vomit everything out of my stomach. In the toilet bowl was slimy dark goo, and it smelled very disgusting. It took several flushes before the water was clear again. I needed time to recover, so I just sat on the bathroom floor and rested my head on the cool metal stall. Then I rinsed my mouth several times and stopped at a vending machine to get some mint gum.

Peeking into Navy's room, I saw she was pleading with her mom. "Mommy my tummy is all better. I don't need the test anymore." Clearly, her mom wasn't believing a word of it.

In the next room, there was a ten-year-old boy who had broken his leg jumping on his friend's trampoline. His leg was elevated and was being gently stretched. His parents would be in later. After talking with him for a few minutes, I challenged him to an arm-wrestling match, which I let him win. I sent pulses to his leg, careful not to completely heal the bones and pull the broken ends in a much better healing position while easing the inflammation and swelling. "See! I'm stronger than you," he said as I was leaving.

I smiled and waved. "You sure are."

That afternoon, passing the nurse's station to return to the dorm, I heard, "Is it just me or has this been the easiest day we've had in a long time?"

And the response was, "I think it's been the easiest day I've ever had on this floor."

Lying in bed that night, my magic was calm. It wasn't realistic to think of healing every patient, after all, the plan was to go undetected. Tomorrow's focus would be on getting some justice for Mandy.

No food was being served in the dining hall during break. Most meals I just snacked on items from the farm package or ate something nutritious in the hospital food court. This morning, while eating oatmeal, I was plotting my objectives for the week. Find access to Dr. Gobel to release any staff under Annette's contracts and figure out some reparations.

It turned out that Dr. Gobel's office was on the same floor as Dean Harrison's, directly across from the administrators' private elevator. On either side of the door to the doctor's office suite hung matching square stones; one was black, and one was white. I tried to enter the suite, but a multicolored magic net that stretched between the two stones held me back. It seemed to be a ward that required anyone with magic to need permission to enter. Grasping my necklace to call on my stones was puzzling, only the black gave any response. It pulled my magical energy deep inside my body. Trying again to enter, it felt like I was walking into a room where the air was thick like pudding, and the pressure brought on queasiness. A metallic taste coated my tongue. Regretting my forced entry, I made it to the administrative assistant's desk, only to lean on it for support.

"Can I help you," the attractive young woman behind the desk asked, looking concerned.

Before I could get anything out of my mouth, Dr. Gobel came out of her office and magic pulled down on me like a sliding switch lowers light to darkness. Coming through the door barrier must have triggered a silent alarm in her office. Squeezing my eyes shut didn't save me from the darkness. The next time I opened my eyes, I was sitting crumpled next to the desk.

"What business do you have with this office," the doctor demanded.

No response formed with this heavy electricity pressing down on me. The doctor slowly lightened the weight, and some of the pressure eased. Her body was emitting anger and pleasure. She was firing dark blue pulses at me that hurt. What?? I thought blue was supposed to make you feel better; this was painful. Each pulse made me quiver and whimper involuntarily. Trying desperately to escape the pain, a part of me was leaving my body. My own whimpers seemed far away. With every groan, plea, or sob, she cackled. She was getting pleasure from my pain. Just as consciousness was slipping away a second time, she stopped the sharp pulses and released the pressure a tiny bit.

My breath was almost back to normal now.

"What are you doing here?" she repeated. With everything still scrambled, I couldn't answer. "I'm going to stop the pressure, but if you make one move to call on your energy, I'll slam it back down and leave it there. Do you hear me?" she demanded. A weak nod of agreement satisfied her.

When she took the pressure off, I reached up to clutch the pendant still under my shirt. The movement looked the same as grabbing at my chest in pain. The stones gave me strength. I concentrated on wanting her mind and body locked in place. In an instant, a huge spike of orange blasted out in all directions, freezing Dr. Gobel and the assistant in place. It took me a few moments to stand up. On wobbly legs and using the desk for support, I reached over and touched the assistant, sending instructions to forget this encounter. Working my way over to the doctor to touch her took willpower. Releasing the mind freeze but sending fear into her created the desired effect. She could talk but not move.

"What do you fear most?" I asked. It was easier if they were thinking and talking about what I wanted to know. It was much more effective than digging for information.

"Dying slowly and painfully," she said.

Sending more fear to heighten the emotion of that thought, I warned, "It could happen right now, unless you cooperate. If you want to live, you will need to answer all my questions honestly and completely. Let's start with your darkest secrets." I had no intention of killing her, but she didn't need to know that.

"I keep staff under mind control contracts. I've embezzled millions from the institute, along with Dean Harrison and the help of Annette. I use my blue magic to inflict pain and torture for my own pleasure." She spoke of her horrid crimes as easy as a grocery list.

"How do you use blue to hurt someone?" I asked, still surprised that this was possible.

"You combine it with dark magic, using a black stone."

"How do you have dark magic? I don't see it," I said.

"Do you see magic?" she asked, looking at me very closely.

Oh crap! I was going to have to smudge her after this conversation.

"How do you use black?" I asked again, this time slow and firm.

"I was given the ability to use it by my friend Annette Teufel. I have a rock pendant that I wear at all times." I picked up her necklace, it was a simple black square stone, and when I turned it over, it had a similar white one on the back.

"So, your ability to use blue to inflict pain comes from the stones?" I asked.

"Yes, it's used to control the magic, and with practice, you can use your magic for the opposite. Black with blue inflicts pain, green with black kills, and red with black creates a vacuum. The larger the black stone the more effective it is."

"Yellow with black does what?" I asked.

"Mind control. How can you not know that when you are using it right now?"

"Why the white stones?" I continued drilling her with questions.

"The theory is that it stabilizes or blocks magic. Though I haven't been able to use it, so something is needed to activate it that I don't have. If I could, your magic wouldn't be holding me."

"Why black and white together?" I asked.

"I don't have the ability to use black without the necklace. Even with the necklace, I shouldn't be able to inflict pain, but Annette has somehow put five percent of her magical DNA in between the stones. I guess it's like having a miniature copy of her powers. I paid her enough to ransom a king and queen."

I unlatched the chain of her necklace and put it in my pocket. Dr. Gobel whimpered a plea, "Please, don't take it."

"Tell me more about Annette."

"She is an independent magic auditor that works for the Nokuland Council. She uses dark magic to ensure I keep working long devoted hours. For her valuable services, I pay her from the embezzlement account. She has been a close personal friend since childhood."

"When will she visit you next," I asked.

"Kent's contract is over in a couple months. I'll need her help with that." It didn't surprise me that her security guard was still with her. I also had her give me Annette's elevator code.

At my demand, she had her assistant print out all the personal information on the indentured staff, current locations, full names, contract expirations, hometowns, social security numbers, bank details, and birth dates. I also took a printout of how the embezzlement scheme worked, including banker's names, account numbers, and access details.

"I'm going to need access to your apartment for this afternoon. Does your apartment have the same protection as the office?" I asked.

"Of course."

"How do I turn it off?"

"Good luck with that," she cackled. When I took a step closer and got right in her face, she went on to explain that if I had permission, or if someone had allowed me in, the alarm wouldn't have triggered.

"You won't go home until this evening; you will have no memory of my visit here today and you will give me permission to access your protected spaces."

I first stopped at the administrative assistant and gave her instructions that Annette was to be avoided at all measures. I warned her not to sign another contract without a trusted lawyer. Once outside the office, I took the stone designs off the wall. Then I released both the doctor and assistant from my magic. I went straight up to the doctor's apartment using Annette's code to get on the elevator.

Identical to her office, stone designs hung in the hallway on each side of her apartment door. With an upward push, they easily came down from the wall. Kent opened the door shortly after I pressed the buzzer. Being as the door was opened by staff, the protective net wasn't triggered.

"Dispose of these please." It was a command. He simply put them down a garbage shoot in the hall. Each staff member got the same instructions as Dr. Gobel's assistant received. It was heart-wrenching not to release them all at once, but that would draw too much attention. None of them would have any memory of my visit.

Upon returning to my room, I took time to regain my equilibrium and further strategize. By afternoon, the next step was carefully worked out. Back in the basement of the hospital, I entered the information technology department using my magic. After meeting the director and copying all the technology information he had available, I assigned myself the highest level of system administration privileges. The cyber security expert was extremely helpful in showing me how to evade detection and warned me not to use any devices that could be traced back to me. Next, he set up an administrator's account but not in my name. The new account was for Katie Holmes, and the approving authorities were Dr. Gobel and Dean Harrison.

At the bank, I tried to open an account under the new pseudonym. Caly had thought I looked like Katie. Whether it was true or not, I needed a name. Apparently, more than a name was needed because no amount of magic would enable the bank employee to give me an account. It made sense that the banks had extra protection. The security ward was sophisticated, subtle, and powerful. I needed a social security number and picture identification. Dang.

With several business hours left in the day, I caught the train to the nearest town. At the Social Security Office, it took several bursts of magic to get a number assigned, but in addition, they gave me a birth certificate. Not far away was the Department of Personal Registration, and with some more magic, I had a picture ID in my new name.

With just fifteen minutes to spare, I made it back to the bank and finally got my account set up. Dr. Gobel's illegal account was closed with the help of the bank manager. Not by coincidence, he happened to be the guy that assisted in making the embezzlement accounts. He had friends in high places in the banking and intelligence communities. We had the funds jump through several offshore accounts and a few government intelligence agencies before landing in mine.

He would have no memory of me or any the transactions he helped with today. The first transaction I made was to Mandy's account. One quarter of a million dollars was wired to her, of course, through the managers offshore accounts. I sent a message with the funds, so that when she asked her bank about where the money came from, the explanation was, "Reparations: promise kept." No amount of money would adequately atone for what she'd been put through. Hopefully, this would give her a sense that someone was doing something about the injustice.

For now, I left Dean Harrison's account open. Leaving only one tenth the amount the doctor had squirreled away, and I had plans for her.

Wednesday morning, I visited the institute's security office. One of Gideon's martial arts students was the officer in charge of the day shift. He had highly focused magic, he could send a pulse of red that mimicked a bullet being shot from a pistol. I copied that. With his help, I gained access to all surveillance cameras. His expert video guy taught me how to erase my visits to Dr. Gobel's office, apartment, and the bank. When I stumbled upon the dormitories' surveillance cameras, my interest was piqued. In the future, I would be watching the other students to help me determine what normal behavior looked like. With me having so much power and the pressing need to keep it hidden, I was quickly losing track of how to pretend to be an average teenager.

That afternoon, I visited the psychiatric ward. It was harder to get access, but with some extra effort and a story of how I really wanted to work in this field of study, I was allowed escorted access. My attendance required staying within the doctor's eyesight at all times. Each patient was so different. Some had physical abnormalities in their brains, others had electrical or chemical imbalances, and still, others had been through extremely traumatic events. I didn't get to heal anyone, but I did accidentally, on purpose, bump into the doctor. For the rest of the afternoon, I transferred as much of her knowledge as I could, overlapping it with Dr. Corona's information to make sure to eliminate duplicates. She had much more knowledge on human behavior. Her vast knowledge of drugs that affected the brain was new to me.

Thursday was dedicated to the financial offices. There were many more desks and employees then I expected. My goal was to find out who audited the books.

It was disappointing to find out no one inside the hospital verified the flow of funds. A brochure on a bulletin board explained anyone could be a whistle blower. I went in search of a disgruntled employee with purview over numerous buckets of funding. Sifting through one person at a time was taking up too much time. Knowing I was going to have a headache later, I opened the channels to hear everybody's thoughts at once, and then I simply strolled through the different sections. No one in this section had auras, which made it easier on my eyes.

One lady, way in the back that tracked donations, was threatening to quit but only in her mind. I closed the party mode of thoughts and simply walked up to her and touched her arm, sending a wave of calm through her. Externally, we carried on, chatting about her three adorable cats, while internally, I was getting to the source of her frustrations. She had been overlooked for promotions and was disciplined for pointing out missing funds to her neurotic supervisor.

Bingo. I sifted through her findings to make sure this related to Harrison and Gobel. Yes! Now, I drew her mouse to a "report fraud" announcement right on her computer screen. She absentmindedly clicked the link and began typing out her findings. When she had finished and clicked send, our interaction wasn't even a figment of her imagination.

Back in the dorms, I stopped at an empty desk, logged into my Katie system account, and deleted video of me visiting finance.

Friday, I set up deposits for the other contracted staff. The funds would land in their accounts a few weeks before their contracts expired. Giving them extra incentive not to sign another agreement.

Later, I found the library. It wasn't like any other I had seen. It mostly had medical books and journals for research. My magic drew me to a closed door. It was locked, and the librarian at the desk informed me I needed special permission to enter. Using my mind tricks, I convinced her to open the door. When she unlocked the door, she warned me not to remove anything.

"There is a tracer for each item, and an alarm will be triggered if any pass through the doorway," her voice irritated me enough to consider taking a book.

It was a small room lined with books. A small table with a computer and two chairs sat at the center. My magic vibrated and hummed as though it was singing. This was my new happy place. These books were about magic. I flipped through them looking for any references to yellow or mind magic. I didn't find a single mention. These books were about blue magic, which made sense, as this was a place for healing.

Pressing the power switch on the computer brought it to life. At the login screen, I used my admin account credentials, and it worked. I was in. The computer desktop only had one icon called search, a double click opened it.

My first search was for yellow magic. Clicking on an encyclopedia-type link provided some basics. Yellow is the rarest of all magic. It's used on the psyche of the mind. At its lowest level, it appeared to be similar to intuition. In its highest forms, it could control permanent thought and behavior manipulation. Levels could be checked at birth. If you have more than five percentile, you must be registered with the Nokuland Council and required to be on birth control. Reproduction is strictly regulated with stringent enforcement, in situations where a person holds more than twenty percent, sterilization is required. DANG. The book sitting at home in my dresser, *Legati Magicum Flavus,* was included in the further reading list. There was a paragraph about being able to take and give magic by use of spirit gifts and gemstones, but it had a highlighted notation that a reference was needed.

Clicking on spirit gifts opened a new tab. These gifts weren't connected to DNA, and many were quite powerful. Some ways to acquire these gifts of the immortals were by transference after the person was dead or by another spirit gift that could give and take these powers. There was a list of known spirit gifts. Overall, there wasn't much information.

Ability to self-heal

Ability to make yourself and objects that touched you invisible

Ability to bind magic

Ability to copy

Ability to use gemstones (most likely extinct)

That prompted me to search for gemstones. The first link was a page with lots of pictures of stones. It stated that though magic was no longer widely believed to have ties to rocks and gemstones, some historical documents linked them with dark magic. It pointed out that history should not be forgotten. It went on to explain that the ability to call on the minerals was lost through the Nokuland Council's restrictive reproduction laws. I was sure this wasn't true. The rocks in my pendant lit up without dark magic. Didn't they?

Continuing, the page theorized that if a person were to have enough magic, perhaps one hundred percent, the minerals could be used without dark magic. Well then, my magic levels must be one hundred percent because I could call on the pendant for extra support. My magic was powerful, but one hundred percent? WOW. Which explained why I was able to use so many colors. That must be why my scans showed double zero, the devices didn't have the ability to display higher than two digits. When anything near eighty was considered extremely high, no one even considered that the scanners would need to display a third digit. Reading further, it made sense that something about the elder's gift allowed me to blend one type of magic into another.

Controlling my ego and my magic without guidance or a mentor at the age of fourteen made me feel like I was barreling downhill without brakes. Like my parents, assassination might be considered if the council discovered my abilities. One pulse toward the librarian on the way out ensured she wouldn't remember me. Back at the dormitory, I deleted video surveillance of me being in the library.

Saturday, I spent in the Emergency Room. The institutes were built on or near the continental divide. This enabled them to hire support staff, mostly from Senaland. Only about ten percent of the entire staff had magic. It might explain some the strict rules students had to follow. It soon was apparent that the ability to self-heal was indeed quite rare. The ability to heal others was much more common. Most of the life and death emergency patients were flown in by drone helicopters. We had hikers that had fallen, traffic accident victims, and even allergic reactions, which in one case, were caused by green magic misuse. I was able to use my powers much more here than in the wards because the extent of the injuries wasn't always visible. I healed mostly internal damage. It was nice to let my energy do its work. At the end of the day, I imagined this feeling compared to a runner completing a marathon, drained but satisfied.

Sunday, when everyone was returning from break, a disturbance in the hall had me poking my head out. Sharlyn and Caly had collided into each other. A ceramic pot lay shattered on the floor. Caly was near tears, and Sharlyn was shaming her for being so clumsy. I rushed over to help pick up the pieces.

"This was my present for your birthday," Caly said, her voice weighted with disappointment.

As Sharlyn walked past, she shoved me right into Caly using her hand on my bared arm... We landed with a thump, just missing the broken shards.

"You should watch where you're going," Sharlyn said over her shoulder, in a sing song way that made my blood boil and magic pressure rise. Without a chance for me to stop it, a wall of force sprang from me and knocked Sharlyn to the ground. "You bitch," she hissed as she stood up and spun around, sending tornado-strength winds right at us. I covered Caly with my body and was able to put up a small bubble shield, so the air only whistled passed us. When we finally looked up, a guard was escorting Sharlyn to her room. Everything had been stripped from the hallway walls, including the trim, leaving a pile of garbage at the other end of the corridor.

I helped Caly get to her feet. We checked each other for any cuts, finding none, she grabbed her suitcase from the rubble, and we went to our room. We were both shaking.

"I never knew you could use force magic," Caly said accusingly.

"Neither did I," I lied.

"My mom made that ceramic pot just for you, that creep broke it on purpose. I can't believe you pushed her. She is not going to let you get away with that."

"What, sending a tornado at us wasn't retribution enough?" I asked.

"Nope. You've just made us her primary targets. She is so vindictive, be ready for anything."

"Oh great, just what I need," I groaned.

Just then, Caly saw the Bur$t bear on her bed. She gave me a huge hug. "This is so awesome! You're the best. Your new poster is a nice touch, too," she said, as an afterthought.

Looking over Caly from head to toe, I said, "Your hair looks great, just like the first day."

"Thanks, my mom did it." She held out her nails for me to see they matched her pastel highlighted hair and had sparkles.

"Very nice, your mom should be a beautician."

"She is a very good one, just a private one for the Hortons. Sharlyn had Mom do her hair and nails, too. Every year she says she won't sign another contract and every year she does. I don't understand why she does it." Caly's voice became much sadder talking about the contract.

"Do the Hortons know anyone by the name of Annette," I asked.

"Yes, that is the lady who handles the staff contracts. She comes in once a year, and she is incredibly good at retention agreements. Mrs. Horton brags about how not one of her employees has quit. Why do you ask?"

I noticed my blunder and had to smudge Caly's brain a little to make her believe she had mentioned Annette, not me. There was no chance of fixing the Hortons' staff problem from this distance, at least not without drawing too much attention. Stopping Annette was more urgent. Even if she could be located, how could she be convinced to quit binding people when it was making her rich. She was living proof that power and money brought corruption and feelings of entitlement. How was I ever going to save myself from the greed when my magic was so hungry for more?

REVALIDATION

DURING THE FIRST class of the new semester, Ms. Fine read from a report that the guard wrote. Sharlyn was cited as the instigator in the hall event. She was caught on camera bumping into Caly, pushing me, and then stumbling over her own feet. The attack on us was inappropriate and unprovoked, according to the write-up. No mention of my magic use. She lost all privileges for one month. No dayroom time watching television, no shopping, no personal technology use, and she had to pay for repairs. Though nothing was mentioned about her replacing Caly's ceramic pot. When I took a quick peek, her aura was glowing a very angry red.

After the reading, we had to get magic scans from a spectrometer for our official school record. The device was on a tripod, set up at the back of the room. Ms. Fine was taking the snapshots. Up until today, most of the students knew what each other's scores were from word of mouth.

No proof was offered, but everyone knew Sharlyn had the highest, and second was Caly.

While waiting for my turn, I decided to experiment. Pulling at Sharlyn's blue magic reserves, I nearly yanked all of it from her. I stopped and started much more gently, ensuring to shave off only a small slice. It took a few tries, but I finally pulled off a tiny piece that formed into a small blue bubble that floated over to Caly and added it to her reservoir. It did exactly what I intended. When the results were displayed on Ms. Fine's large screen, we got our first look at our scores side by side. Caly had the highest score in the class, and Sharlyn was second. When Sharlyn saw Caly's score, her aura nearly shown black.

No shocking surprise, my image was completely white, and the caption was still at double zero. Thankfully, it wasn't registering on the display. Ms. Fine pulled me into the hallway, "Sera these are disturbing results. I've never seen zero magic before. Ms. Mason will need to revalidate your scholarship. I'm sorry."

Ms. Fine kept to our pre-holiday agreement and escorted the entire class to the scholarship office so that the others could be assigned their spending accounts, and I could be evaluated again. No real surprise, Sharlyn and the other uber-elite kids had already been receiving their spending money.

When everyone had their access, all returned to the classroom except me.

"Please, don't cut yourself again," I pleaded with Ms. Mason.

"How would you suggest I validate your healing abilities?" she asked.

"Let's visit the Emergency Room."

After she explained what was needed to the head nurse, we were taken into one of the treatment rooms. It was agreed that I would get to heal the next visibly bleeding patient. Later, a mechanic with a torn and mangled hand was wheeled in on a gurney. Immediately, using the same combination I used on Dr. Gobel, I pulsed orange at the patient. It froze him both in mind and body. Placing my palm on his arm just above the injury, allowed blue to spring from me and pump into him. The energy waves were steady like a heartbeat. The healing wasn't instant like Ms. Mason's cut at Nana's house. Time was needed to repair nerves and bone. When I removed my hand, he wasn't perfect, but he had full range of motion, nerves, bones, and all vessels were repaired, and of course, no bleeding. In time, he would be back as good as before. He was from Senaland, so we weren't allowed to give him a speedy and complete recovery in minutes. We never knew if it would shock them to see magic. No need to scare them. Looking up, I saw Ms. Mason had recorded the entire process.

"That was amazing. Interesting how your blue magic calms the patient," she commented. There was nothing to gain by correcting her. It wasn't the blue but the orange that did the calming.

As classroom activities became more routine, I realized just how boring this was going to be for me. This section of teaching was on anatomy. UGH. I'd learned more in one afternoon by working with Dr. Corona than they would be teaching this whole term. I'd definitely be keeping my other activities going. Since the bratty princess had touched my arm when she pushed me, I now had access to her brain. Her brain wasn't the tar like goo I'd seen in Annette's brain all those years ago, but it was murky. The other students I had access to were like a crystal-clear spring in comparison.

Sharlyn was the most self-absorbed person I'd ever come across. Everything was about her and her family. From the time of her birth, she was groomed to treat others as subservient. The only people that ranked higher than herself were her parents, but that was because they controlled the money in her life. She hated how much time and attention her mother spent on her brother, Tifton—mainly on his arranged marriage, which wasn't actually contracted yet, and probably never would.

The family wanted a match with a Kendler girl. Of course, everyone knew the match was most likely too powerful for council approval, but that didn't stop the Hortons from trying. Thankfully, the adopted family was holding out to ensure the best match. I also learned she was now Audrey Milton.

Of course, Sharlyn despised me and Caly, we were the peons, as low as manure in her opinion. Hidden underneath, she was jealous of our physical appearance, believing we were much prettier than her. She wasn't unattractive, but her snobby expressions soured her features.

Randomly, during class, I would zap her with yellow to stop her brain in mid-sentence, especially when she was criticizing those she considered beneath her status. It was satisfying to see she was starting to worry about it. Once, right after she had mocked Jamyla about mixing up distal and proximal. I made Sharlyn's bladder muscles relax, and she peed her pants. She was losing credibility with her crowd and Ms. Fine. I did worry a bit about my moral compass, but if anyone deserved to have their pedestal lowered a peg or two, it was Sharlyn.

It was incredible how much our class worried about what people thought of them. Each one was insecure in their own way. They wanted to be popular and pretty. They wanted the other girls to be envious of their clothes. Caly wanted to be rich. Jamyla wanted people to think she was smart. She was, but Sharlyn mocking her, and getting some of the other girls to join in, was crushing her self-confidence.

Later in that first week of the new semester, we heard rumors about a high-level school official who was being investigated for stealing money.

Just when the world was feeling set to right, Ms. Fine took me aside and informed me that I needed to be in the Dean's office at ten o'clock on Monday to discuss my double zero score.

"But Ms. Mason approved my waiver," I protested.

"Yes, she did, but the dean has requested the council's lead auditor be at the meeting to investigate the curiousness of you using magic with a double zero score. I imagine they will want to poke around in your brain a bit."

That's all it took to ruin my weekend. I spent the entire two days trying to figure out what to do. I practiced blocking other people's magic. Since Sharlyn was grounded, it wasn't surprising to find her out back near the hiking trails. Taking a quick peek to see what path she was going to take, I selected the same one for my walk. Following behind me, she tried to push me down with her red force every chance she could. In her mind, it was my fault she trashed the hallway. She would've pushed me right off one of the cliffs if my magic hadn't stopped her. Her aggression was giving my responses a workout. When her force was sent my way, I would bend down to retie my shoe or casually step behind a tree. Each angry blast from her gave me practice in defending myself. By the end of the hike, I could form a protective field around me that her magic couldn't penetrate. All that work only to realize that what my magic did automatically in the hallway tornado was what I needed to do on command.

HELPING ANNETTE

I ARRIVED IN front of Matt's desk at ten-fifteen without an escort.

"Go in and have a seat, the dean will be back in time for your appointment." I was relieved to see the council representative wasn't in the office yet. The office looked different from the last time. Dean Harrison's nameplate, photos, and her medical certificates were gone. It almost looked vacant.

"Ma'am the dean won't need to see you today," I heard Matt say. I stood up and peeked into the front office, looking through the crack on the hinge side of the door. It was ANNETTE. It had to be; my protection shield reinforced automatically. Along with fear and hatred, strange feelings of loneliness bubbled up inside me at seeing her. Images of Mom flashed through my thoughts.

"I'm here to examine a student at the dean's request." I could see her use yellow on him, and she walked towards the dean's office. Before she could enter, Dr. Corona arrived. *What was he doing here?* I wondered.

"Annette, I won't be needing your services today," he said, confirming it was her.

"Where is Dean Harrison?" Annette demanded.

"She has been put on administrative leave, and I'm filling in until further notice."

Whew, that was nice to hear.

"I still intend to examine the student," and she sent yellow at him and walked into his office ahead of him. When she saw me, she sent yellow at me, and I was thankful it didn't make it past the shield. "What the heck?" My mind heard her exclaim. It was clear she wasn't used to being blocked.

Before she finished her thought, she sent yellow and black at me. It cracked the protection, so I dropped the shield and shot orange at her. When she stopped abruptly, Dr. Corona bumped into her.

"Pardon me," he said, and walked around her to sit behind the desk. "Both of you, please have a seat." I sat down, and with my internal voice, instructed Annette to do the same. "I certainly am no expert on the spectrometer readings, but I'm quite satisfied with Ms. Mason's validation, and I have reviewed the video. I see no reason for Sera not to continue in her studies here."

"Thank you, Dr. Corona, I do appreciate your decision," Annette said, much to my surprise. "I still will need some private time with Sera, the board would like me to inform them of my findings."

I put my protection back up as soon as she spoke, and just a second later, felt it crack again.

"Is there an empty office we can use; this shouldn't take long?" she asked politely.

"Ms. Mason's is just down the hall, and she is out until this afternoon, Matt can let you in."

The second Annette shut the door to Ms. Mason's office, she blasted the yellow black at me hard, and I let out a cry of pain. Collapsing into one of the chairs, hands on my head, with my elbows on my thighs, a groan escaped. She continued to scan my thoughts and it felt like an army of ants marching through my brain. Tiny zaps of energy buzzed through my mind, draining my physical energy. She was thrilled at the pain it was causing. I didn't understand the idea of someone finding actual pleasure in someone else's agony. Her grin was like a parent hearing their child say mama or dada for the first time.

The anger, pain, and creepy crawling feeling were too much, and my red blasted out and threw her against the wall and pinned her there. My head felt better, and she stared at me open-mouthed.

"You have blue, yellow, and I see red as well, how can you possibly be showing as double zero?" she questioned out loud. Not waiting for any response, "You're the kid we found with the Kendler couple, aren't you? You must have had a ward protecting you; otherwise, I would have known," she muttered in bewilderment. "Oh wow, *you* are their firstborn, this is why the child isn't showing as much promise as we'd hoped. Your double zero is really one hundred," she was shaking her head as if to clear it of the thought. I could see her mind putting everything together. "Your mom must have had a protective ward on you, so that people wouldn't see the truth."

"What are you going to report back to the council?" I asked.

"Oh, they don't know anything about you, I just told that to Dr. Corona to get you alone. I think you should come and study under me and be my apprentice, there is so much I can teach you." What she really wanted was to have control of my magic for her own twisted purposes. "You're the one who took Dr. Gobel's necklace and money," she accused.

"Well, it wasn't really her money, and she was using the necklace to hurt people," I said, defensively. "Do you realize that your magic feels and looks like sticky tar?" I asked. Pressing her against the wall was giving me time to recover from her assault.

"You see magic?" She raised her eyebrows and continued. "Well, one can't use dark magic without getting some sludge. I used to have a healer clean it but not anymore, she died from the last attempt. It leaves me sluggish, and my magic is harder to use because of the clogging."

"I can clear some of it for you, but you'll be sick afterwards." I was thinking this nasty stuff looked a lot like Navy's cancer. I was willing to try to clean it out as a ploy to get a closer look at her skills, but that sludge was going into her stomach.

"And just what would that cost me," she asked skeptically.

"Just some memory loss, mainly ever seeing my magic."

"Sure," she agreed too easily, and I could see she felt confident I couldn't remove the memory.

Allowing Annette to sit in Ms. Mason's chair, I then put my hands on either side of her head. Pulsing blue electric power at the dark goo, nothing happened. Even focusing on my mom's pendant didn't work. Instead, Dr. Gobel's necklace lit up from my pocket. Pulsing my blue through the necklace compelled the tarry stuff to start breaking into very tiny particles. Mixing the red with the black, I herded the loose pieces through the blood system and into

Annette's stomach. For a split second, I thought of letting it all pool in her heart chambers.

"There will always be temptation with your powers," Annette purred. "You really would make a good intern for me." She meant intern as an apprentice, but it resonated with me as imprisonment.

Suddenly, Annette grabbed the trash can and threw up several times until finally she was just dry heaving. The smell was awful. Both of us were gagging at this point.

Her brain was free of sludge and much easier to scan. Her magic channels were narrowed from years of abuse. No point of restoring them, that wasn't part of the agreement. Her and Dr. Gobel had argued recently, apparently the doctor had not paid Annette for the last two contracts.

Resetting her memories, all she would remember was my blue magic. "If you ever engage in using contracts to force people into servitude, I will remove all your magic." Possibly an empty threat, but neither of us knew for certain. Her protective shields were strong, and it took some time to make sure she didn't retain my secret. It would be nice to copy her skills, but she was recovering quickly. Her memory was adjusted so that she believed from this evaluation that I was a very normal blue healer but that some chemical or spell was blocking the spectrometer. That was her original theory before today. She would remember having a bout of flu to explain why her stomach was upset and would be afraid to force people to sign contracts.

Breathing through my mouth, I grabbed the plastic trash liner and tied it shut. I left the still nauseous Annette in Ms. Mason's chair. With all that sludge passing through her stomach, she might not be feeling well for the next couple of days.

On my way back to the classroom, I dumped the sack into the nearest hallway garbage shoot. No need to have Ms. Mason's office smelling if it could be avoided.

Strangely, I felt like my hands were covered in the black goo and bugs were crawling on my skin. Even after stopping to scrub with soap and water several times, the feelings remained. Physically, nothing was on my hands, but the feeling was annoying. Over the next couple of days, I tried everything to remove the sensation. I used hand sanitizers, soaps, and every combination of magic I could think of, but still, it remained. More than once I wondered if this was caused by my brief thought of killing Annette.

The next time I went out to the patio to water my plants, the basil plant was sending me vibrations. I pinched a leaf, but nothing happened. Once again, my magic wanted me to taste the plant. It made we wonder if my magic was an infant wanting to taste everything that sent me vibrations. I pulled the leaf and put it to my tongue. I could feel the white stone pulling. Some of the gooey feeling left, and when I chewed on it, the feeling completely vanished. White did help neutralize. It felt so good to not have the feeling of goo or bugs crawling on me. When I finally swallowed, even my head seemed clearer. It was exciting solving the problem. I was struggling with not having anyone to talk to about my magic. If I could've trusted Annette, it would've been so great being tutored by her and being open. I considered telling Caly and then wiping her memory, but without truly understanding any long-term effects, that wouldn't be a wise choice. I needed to use it to cover up my powers, not to feed my vanity. It wasn't worth risking her health.

Holding secrets was a burden; luckily, my first five years of life with my mom had groomed me to understand the importance of not telling even the ones you loved. Being on your guard all the time for fear of exposure was a lonely path. Even when people liked you, they couldn't be trusted with a secret this big. They didn't see the real you. If they knew, they might feel deceived, afraid, jealous, angry, or greedy.

At my next hair appointment, Dr. Gobel was at one of the beauty stations, so I listened in. She was obsessing on not getting her every whim fulfilled. Apparently, Annette had broken all of her contracts due to not getting paid. Dr. Gobel had no one to cook or clean and no security guards. Without being able to torture her staff for pleasure, she wasn't getting her normal tension releases. She still had an office assistant because the institute paid the salary, but several had quit within a few days of being hired.

She had been pestering the banker about her account being closed. She was sure he was lying and stole the money for himself. He had stopped taking her calls or visits. He even called her crazy.

Dean Harrison's attorneys were blaming the entire embezzlement scheme on her. It was Dr. Gobel's fault, but she was still angry they were blaming her. Due to the accusations, the Nokuland Council was discussing putting her on unpaid leave. She would've been distressed to know there was an arrest warrant being signed by a judge first thing Monday morning. I found that out by snooping through security documents and emails.

Having Chaz's gentle fingers tease my hair and finding out that Dr. Gobel was getting some of what she deserved put me in a good mood. I stopped at the pizza shop to pick up a pie for the suite. I used little bribes to keep them from resenting my ability to travel freely through the hospital and a little magic when needed.

When I got to our hallway, Caly was sitting against the wall, opposite our door. "What are you doing out here?" I asked.

"Don't touch it," she said, pointing to our door handle. A small crudely made doll hung from a thin loop of twine. It had several needles stuck into its torso.

"Is that a voodoo doll?" I asked.

"No, it's a talisman with a hex."

"What do we do with it if we can't touch it?" I asked. I knocked on Jamyla and Kya's door, then I sat down beside Caly and handed her a slice on a napkin. She took it and started eating right away. Jamyla and Kya opened their door.

"Are we having our party out here?" Kya asked. I handed them both a slice, and they sat down with us. In between bites, we talked about our options. The floor guards were too occupied with the pizza I bribed them with to pay us attention.

"You can come into our room and go through the bathroom, oh, except it locks automatically when you lock the entrance door," Jamyla said.

"When we're done with the pizza, we can use the box to knock it off the handle and carry it out to the garbage bin," Caly offered.

"Who did this, and what does it do if we touch it?" I asked.

"Most likely Sharlyn, but she wouldn't have put it there herself, one of her minions would've done it," Caly answered.

"And why can't we touch it?" I asked again.

"It'll have some hex on it. Your hand will swell, or you could pee your pants. In truly evil ones, you could die if it's strong enough. Fortunately, very few people can make hexes that strong and even fewer people can afford to buy them," Caly said.

"I think the pins in the stomach would probably make you puke," Kya offered. When we all looked at her, she said defensively, "My grandma makes mild curses, hexes, and potions."

"Wow, I'm your roommate, and you never bothered to warn me," Jamyla accused.

"Well, that would take away half of the usefulness if I went around telling people."

When she mentioned puking, I started to worry about Annette regaining some of her memory. We each had a second slice, and all visited the water fountain before we tried to remove the doll. After a few attempts, the figure was closed inside the box, and I offered to take it out to the bin. Before I went, I noticed Caly had used the bottom of her tunic to touch the handle after she had entered our code

I laid the box on the ground out behind a larg ster, making sure I was shielded from prying e⋎ it open with the toe of my shoe. I grabbed r dant and concentrated. I didn't get any r point to anyone I knew. I figured s⌐ made it and that whoever placed it ⊢

concentrated on red, and pulling on the doctor's necklace, I lit it on fire. It took several attempts, and I wasn't even sure it was possible, but lately, it seems like I can get my magic to do almost anything if I try hard enough. Now both of the stone pendants were on one chain and always under my shirt.

I let the fire consume the box and then just let it die out. There was a broom and dustpan attached to a pole near the bin. I swept up the remains and threw them away. I didn't want the needles left on the ground.

Before returning to my room, I made a quick visit to main security. They filled out an incident report. They were upset I removed the doll and burned it. "You destroyed our best chance at learning something about it," chided the officer taking my statement. I had them pull up the video of our hallway. It wasn't particularly useful. The culprit wore dark clothes with a hoodie hiding her eyes. She had an average build, shape, and kept her head down. It could've been Annette, but nothing confirmed it. The whole thing was less than a minute, with no one else in the corridor except the guard on duty. Even the guard didn't look up. It was someone with a code. So, I had them look at whose code was used.

It was the guards code who was standing at the desk on 'y. I was sure the guard didn't give it out, but they said would question the guard and let me know if they out anything.

NOT SO FUN SPRING BREAK

NORMALLY, THE SCHOOL schedule had just one break for the school year, between semesters at holiday time. This year we would have a spring break to honor the passing of the elder. He was a big enough deal for everyone to have three days of mourning. Once again, going to the ranch was denied. This really was ridiculous and frustrating. Someone was manipulating the situation.

Everyone left on Wednesday afternoon, and I was the only first-year left on my floor. Dean Corona asked that I be in his office at nine o'clock on Thursday morning. I was allowed to wear my regular clothes since it wasn't a school day.

When I arrived at Dr. Corona's office, Matt motioned me to go right in. The dean was sitting at his desk, and Annette was in one of the visitor seats across from him. My shields reinforced just at the sight of her. The dean motioned for me to take the other seat.

"Ms. Teufel has been telling me that the board would like further analysis on your magic. You're truly a unique individual, and they would like your cooperation on these evaluations." He paused and smiled at me like I should be so honored to have their attention. Sitting next to Annette was like being close to a hissing cobra, and he had asked me to follow her into a snake pit. Despite my fear, I kept my expression blank.

"What exactly would these evaluations entail?" I asked. The dean looked puzzled as if it never even occurred for him to ask.

"It won't require anything for your part, except being in the lab. I will simply be scanning your brain and testing your magic's reactions to different circumstances," Annette replied smoothly. She wanted me as her lab rat.

"Is this something I can refuse?" I asked. Dean Corona looked shocked that I would even consider turning down the opportunity to be of service to the board.

"It would only be for the rest of today and tomorrow, surely you can spare the time. Sitting alone in your dormitory room can't be that interesting," the Dean responded without answering my question. "Besides, this will look good on your record when it comes to future assignments."

This time, I addressed Annette, because the dean wasn't going to be of use. "Where will the evaluation take place?" I asked.

"The hospital administration office has been kind enough to offer up a patient room."

I was beginning to feel churlish. Knowing more about my magic would be helpful, and Annette would be a good source. Hoping that my magic would protect me from whatever Annette had planned, I agreed. "Sure."

"Excellent." Annette's grin looked like she'd won the lottery. "Let's get started right away, my time is precious."

I was sure Annette had manipulated both Dean Corona and me, but it wasn't obvious enough for me to pinpoint when she had done it. No bugs crawling through my brain, this time. She must have used a lighter touch. Dread drug behind me like an anchor as Annette escorted me to the psych ward, and that was another huge red flag. This part of the hospital had the most security, and I didn't like the implication that there was something wrong with my brain. After going through several doors and checkpoints, we arrived at a room with a sophisticated lock.

Inside the room was a hospital bed, a dentist-type chair, a big projection screen, a computer, extra lighting, and what looked like laser equipment. Annette had me sit in the chair.

"Is the council actually interested in me?" I asked. Annette just gave a look that seemed to say, *you're smarter than to believe that.*

"First we're going to do a series of simple requests, they will enable me to set a baseline of your responses," Annette informed me, as she pulled up a stool and sat beside me. "I'm going to ask you to do simple tasks. I want you to not do them and say 'no,' aloud." She fastened a helmet on my head and tightened it down in several places. It was connected to the computer by several wires of different sizes and colors.

A large screen lit up as if someone was projecting a kaleidoscope of colors onto it. Annette sucked in her breath when she saw the display.

"What's that on the screen?" I asked.

"That is a visual of your aura, quite pretty, isn't it?" She really was liking what she saw. "It not only shows your aura, but it also indicates enhancements you've received from touching magical people that have passed away. You're spirit energy." She walked over to the screen and pointed at some of the moving images. "See these light blue things that look like Zs? They tell me you've received a healing spirit. Probably from your father. These green dots indicate the ability to copy, most likely from your mother. These multicolored globes, I've never seen before; from your thoughts, I can guess they were received by touching the elder." The objects she pointed to were small and scattered throughout the design. You would have to know what you were looking for to see them.

She was looking at me for confirmation about the elder, but I wasn't going to admit anything.

"Anyway, let's get started," she said moving to the computer. "I will tell you to lift your left hand, you won't comply, and you will say 'no' aloud." She typed on the keyboard for a few seconds.

"Okay, lift your left arm," she instructed.

"No," I replied, doing nothing. She typed a bit more and it adjusted the four lasers that were now pointing at my head.

"Lift your right arm."

"No." My right arm didn't move, and she made more adjustments

"Lift your left arm."

I said, "No," but my arm lifted. She made more adjustments. I was getting extremely concerned and tried to reach up to take the helmet off, but I couldn't move. I tried to tell her to stop, but no sound came out.

"Lift your right arm," she continued. This time I didn't say no, and my arm obeyed. Absolutely frightening. She was controlling me through these lasers. My thoughts were racing, I needed to escape. "How had I not foreseen this?

Who could I tell? How arrogant, ignorant, and naïve of me to think she only trapped Senaland residents. Annette had subdued me without a struggle. She had total control. Her white whale was caught.

"Very good," she said standing next to me with a big creepy smile. She started inserting a small plate into each laser. She looked at me after the first one was in place. Her eyes glowing with anticipation. "The adjustment will be permanent. These little discs will help me melt your free will just enough so that when I tell you to do something, you will do it without thought, question, or hesitation." When the horror showed on my face, she wiggled in delight. Seeing me scared, excited her. "Oh, you will be so much fun to torture, but I don't have time today." Her lips formed a fake pout. No wonder she gave Dr. Gobel a sliver of her magic, they were kindred sadists. "If you have any ideas about resisting or breaking these adjustments, just know that the next step will be killing you and taking your spirits. The powers you've taken such care to keep hidden are ideal for doing my dirty work. No suspicion of me means much less effort covering up my work. You, on the other hand, will become very busy. If you even think of resisting, I will just take what I need from you by extreme force. Do you understand?" she asked.

I nodded without thinking. She continued adding the plates to the lasers. When she put the last one in and started toward the computer, her digital device buzzed in her pocket. She looked at it and then stepped outside of the room.

With her out of the room, there was a window of opportunity. Releasing energy in all directions was an attempt to find something useful. Dr. Gobel's necklace started to vibrate, letting me understand it could be used as a conduit. Using the focus technique I'd learned from security, I aimed a concentrated stream of red at the closest plate. Tiny cracks spiderwebbed across the surface. The damage wasn't very noticeable, hopefully it was enough to hinder the process. She'd warned me not to resist, but death was preferrable to being at a sadist's beck and call.

When Annette returned, everything must have looked the same. She walked straight to the computer and pressed enter. Each undamaged laser started to hum as they powered up. Three beams of light entered my brain right between my eyes. Self-healing blue energy rushed to my head. The damaged disc started smoking. She shrieked and leaned over to examine it.

"You did this," she accused and slapped me hard across the face. "Well, you've left me no choice." After shutting down the lasers, she threw a restraint on me as easily as throwing a blanket that was part magic and part spell. Gone was any ability to move. Shallow breathing worked, but just enough to keep me alive. She yanked the helmet off my head. Anger was billowing out of her. It even had a pungent smell, similar to rotten eggs or sulfur. She was worried about finding someone to pay for the millions of dollars' worth of the hospital's equipment just ruined. Nothing was ever her fault. So, someone else was going to pay for it. She knew I wouldn't have that kind of money, being a foster child.

Even though she had hinted that the next step was to kill me, she didn't want to do it here under the hospital's security. It would take a lot of cover-up, and her two main allies in the building had enough trouble. She needed space to think and burn off her emotions. She slammed the door as she left to find out if there was a replacement piece.

Alone in the room, I knew the damage to my brain needed to be assessed. If the three lasers had done any unrepairable damage, it wasn't apparent. Trying to get free from the restraint, my magic didn't work this time. Flashbacks of being stuck under my parents thundered through my thoughts. It was intentional. This was giving Annette a thrill knowing it would terrify me. It took some time and effort to wiggle my wrists, ankles, and head. Trying to shout for help, no sound came out. Closing my eyes to think, I curled my tongue and chewed on my lower lip. These were unconscious habits I'd used over the years to focus my energy. My hands were clenched in fists and every muscle was taut, straining to assist the magic in breaking the restraint.

With no idea when she was coming back, and not knowing how to break free, my fear escalated. After about an hour, my muscles and energy were completely spent from trying to break free. With nothing else to do but panic, I decided to pulse my brain, using what magic I could muster up on relaxation. Using too many jolts accidently put me to sleep. *Would I wake?* was the last thought to pass through my mind.

I did wake when a nurse opened the door. She was looking for a quiet place to take her break.

"I didn't know anyone was still using this room," she apologized and started to leave.

"Don't go," I pulsed at her. She stopped.

"Did you say something?" she asked, sounding confused.

"Please get the doctor in charge." I pleaded, not sure if my message was getting through.

She left, but no one came for several minutes. The head nurse came in next. She had some magic and not just the blue healing.

"What are you still doing in here?" she asked. She continued without waiting for an answer. "Annette said she only needed the room for a few hours." Then she shrieked when she examined the lasers. "She ruined one! Wait until the hospital administrator hears about this." Then she left me alone in the room, again. *UGH! Stop leaving me alone with restraints,* my thoughts screamed.

Several different people came in and chaos ruled the room for the next half hour. The hospital administrator wasn't Dr. Gobel. She had been replaced without a formal announcement, or at least I didn't see one, so it must have happened today. But everyone seemed more concerned about the equipment. They only paid attention to me when they wanted me to leave. It took them a while to figure out I was under restraint, and they finally brought in security. Security could not remove it, and they figured the restraint had a spell or hex attached.

The new hospital administrator's name was Dr. Jansen, he was short and slim with a very somber demeanor. "Make sure that Annette Teufel is out of this building and barred from entering until we're reimbursed for the damaged equipment," he instructed security. "Get someone in here to take care of this situation," he pointed at me.

Then the room emptied again, no one bothered to tell me what they would do next. Fear was replaced by hunger, thirst, and a need to use the bathroom. It was a while before the first nurse came back, she held up a cup with a straw. It was water. I just took a few sips, not wanting to add more pressure to my bladder.

"They have called for a spell-breaker, but the nearest one is an hour or so by helicopter," she told me.

I nodded my thanks. I put myself under again to relieve my mental and physical misery.

The spell-breaker shook me awake. He was normal looking in an I-just-stepped-off-the-golf course kind of way. He had a crew cut tinged with gray, making me think he was in his fifties. He wore a maroon polo shirt and khaki pants. Strange, I imagined some sixteenth-century gypsy type was going to show up. After digging through his leather satchel, which looked like a doctor's on-call bag, he placed a few items on the bed. He tried a spoken spell, then a gray powder. Next, he spritzed a smelly liquid, but nothing worked. As he dug deeper into his bag, he spoke to the security guard who had escorted him.

"This isn't going to be cheap," he said as he lifted a small bottle with an eye dropper. "About two thousand dollars a drop. Do you have the authority to approve the cost?" he asked the guard.

"It's going to be charged to Annette Teufel, so go ahead," the guard encouraged him.

The spell-breaker shuddered a little at Annette's name. The liquid was a deep purple, and he drew up a few drops into the stopper. He dropped one right toward my stomach. It sizzled and disappeared when it hit the restraint. There was a crackle, and my binding was loosened a little, I might have been able to break it at this point, but I didn't want to show my power. After each drip, the guard attempted to remove the restraint. It took a total of five drops to completely remove the spell. At the first moment of freedom, I ran straight to the adjoining bathroom without even speaking.

Returning to the room after relieving my bladder pressure, I asked the spell-breaker, "What's in the bottle?"

"Trade secrets," he replied without even looking at me. Standing next to him, I feigned weakness and wobbled just enough for him to reach out and grab me. No thoughts of what was in the bottle were readily available, so I asked, "No really. What's the amazing purple liquid?"

"It's made from a rare purple truffle found deep in the Evonwald Forest. Only those strong in green magic can find them." What he didn't tell me was that it took a special process to create the liquid, and his aunt was the only person he knew who could make it. She owned a tea shop in the capital of Redding. That was where Sharlyn and Caly lived. The tea shop was a cover for rare items sold in the back. His aunt only sold the liquid to a select few.

The security guard escorted the spell-breaker out, and the nurse escorted me off the floor. I hid my badge since I wasn't in my school uniform. No one paid me any attention, but my senses and magic were on high alert just in case Annette was still in the area. I stopped at the food court to have a late lunch. I considered telling Dr. Corona what happened, but it would bring up questions. More than I was willing to answer.

The rest of the semester went by fast. On one of the last days of the school year, I walked into my room to see all three of my suitemates talking excitedly.

"What did I miss?" I asked. Caly was grinning ear to ear.

"Today, Mom sent me word that none of the Hortons' household signed renewal contracts. They all decided to revolt. Apparently, the contract negotiator didn't show up this year. Mom already has a job lined up at the most exclusive salon in Redding. I'm so excited for her. She can finally move out of the Hortons' servants' quarters. This will be so great for her. And she will be making money!"

"I'm so happy for both of you," I said, giving her a hug and big kiss on her cheek.

"I know you planned to spend the summer break with Nana, but I would really like you to come up and meet my mom. It would just be for a few days. We're still in that dinky room, but she will be moving out right after we get there. We will definitely be celebrating. I think you should see the Horton house—it's insanely huge and so wrong for them to give us so little space."

"Let me check with Nana, I would love to meet your mom and see Redding, I've never been to any of the big cities."

"There's so much to do, shopping, movies, dance clubs, skating, and we can even go to the beach."

"I've never been to the ocean either. It sounds fun."

When I finally got a chance to talk with Nana, she said, we could take a beach vacation at Redding. She had some business in the city that the sooner it was dealt with the better. She knew of a beach house we could stay at that would be big enough for Caly and her mom to stay with us, if they wanted.

LIFE'S A BEACH

ON THE LAST day of our first year, Caly and I packed up everything, and we turned in our bedding and uniforms. Our rooms always had to be clean and tidy, but today, they had to be spotless. I was going to throw my poster out, but since Caly was keeping her rock and roll ones, she used mine on the outside of hers to give them a layer of protection. The gardener was allowing me to leave my patio plants with her until next school session. She pointed to the shelves where we first found the aloe, "They'll be all right over there." I took some leaves from all the plants and collected seeds from them as well. If she was surprised that we didn't only have aloe plants, her expression didn't show it.

When Ms. Fine inspected our room, she gave us each an envelope. Inside were our approvals for next year's scholarships. We hugged Jamyla and Kya; they both would be returning next year as well. We grabbed our suitcases and headed to the cable car.

Traveling by train off the mountains into flat lands, we arrived in Redding a little after noon. This city is the largest in all of Amaku, blocks and blocks of tall buildings. Sharlyn was on the same train, but she rode first class, and we rode in the cheap open seating car. There was an expensive sedan waiting for Sharlyn, and even though she had to walk right by us, she didn't offer us a ride. Not really surprising, but it would've made me not dislike her so much. Her driver stacked the suitcases and put them in the trunk of the car.

Our walk was about thirty minutes in very warm weather to get to the Horton house. In order to enter through a side gate, we had to walk past a big trash dumpster. We could see Sharlyn was already sunbathing by the pool. Further past her lounge chair, we could see a group of about six boys practicing Krav Maga in martial arts pants but no tops, making it easy to see their carved bodies. I wasn't paying attention to Caly, so when she stopped to point out Tifton, I stumbled into her almost knocking her over.

Sharlyn raised her designer sunglasses to look over and laugh. "Like you two plebeians have a chance at any of those guys." Then she lowered her glasses and lay back down, still with a big smirk on her lips. I could hear Caly's thoughts, she wanted to pounce on Sharlyn and pull her hair out. Heck, I wanted to make her pee herself again, but that would give her the chance to figure out who was messing with her. She looked good in a swimsuit now that a year's worth of healthy eating had trimmed her down, her breasts were impressive for a fourteen-year-old, and some of the boys were noticing.

"Let's go," Caly said, continuing to walk to the mansion. It was so big. We continued past the boys and most of them did stop to watch us. One even ran over to ask if he could help with our bags. He was smiling at Caly. "Brent, this is Sera, Sera, this is Brent, he is a good friend of Tifton."

"Nice to meet you," I said shyly.

"Likewise." He hardly looked at me as he grabbed Caly's suitcase handle.

"Hey, I get to help, too." I looked over my shoulder to see a smiling Tifton trotting toward us. "Who is this?" he asked as he grabbed my suitcase handle. Caly did the introductions.

"Nice. Do you attend the institute with Caly and Sharlyn?" he asked.

"I do," I answered, and for some reason it made me blush. He just grinned bigger. Man, oh man, huge vibrations from his magic washed over me. My energy wanted to reach out and mix with his. Holding mine back took some effort and it was persistent in its eagerness. He was gorgeous. Looking back at Sharlyn as we entered the house; she was standing with her hands on her hips and flashing electric dark red sparks. I bit my lower lip to keep from grinning. What a mess! Caly liked Tifton, Brent liked Caly, and Sharlyn liked Brent. Tifton and I were clicking together but

Caly being jealous seemed crazy. She was so much better looking and better at flirting. More important, his family would never approve of a serious relationship without knowing my real powers.

"Come out and join us when you get settled," Tifton invited us as they headed back outside.

Caly opened the door where they had left the suitcases. This hallway was nothing special, it even looked similar to our dormitory, but this flooring was marble. The room was tiny, only a full-sized bed and a dresser with a mirror. There was a small empty closet. The bed was completely covered in packing boxes. The view from the one tiny window was a little of the garden but mostly the brick wall fence.

"We do have a couple hours before Mom will be back, let's get into our bathing suits." My swimming suit was a plain one-color one-piece hand-me-down from Lysa. Caly's was a more stylish and form-fitting bikini. Once outside, we saw that someone joined Sharlyn on the lounge chairs. This whole scenario was making me self-conscious. They all were tanned to a bronze on the first day of vacation. My farmer tan made me extra self-conscious. Four of the boys were in the pool playing volleyball. We could see the boy's workout clothes thrown on chairs near the outdoor shower. Tifton and Brent were playing around, pushing each other, but they stopped when we approached the water.

"That is Brooklyn, Sharlyn's best friend," Caly whispered, indicating to the newcomer. "She is from a rich family but didn't get accepted into an institute, I don't understand how I'm still considered low life when clearly my magic is stronger." It did seem peculiar, Caly getting the scholarship should have bolstered her esteem in the Horton family's minds.

My eyes were drawn to Tifton as he stepped out of his pants, revealing swimming trunks. Caly bumped me with her elbow and whispered, "Don't make it so obvious." My cheeks turned red, and I looked away, Caly was laughing at me. But the next moment I was bumping her as she ogled Brent showering in his swimsuit. If it was possible, he was even more cut than Tifton. She was getting over her jealousy of Tifton paying me attention and that made me smile.

"You'd think neither of you ever saw a male body before," Brooklyn called out in a snarky voice.

I'm sure my cheeks got even redder as the guys started making bodybuilder poses for us. Brent even kissed each of his flexed biceps. Tifton did an impressive pushup while doing a very straight handstand. The other guys in the pool started making cat calls whistling at them, which made me laugh a little, relieving some of my embarrassment.

"Yeah, I guess seeing male bodies is nothing new to you, Brooklyn," Caly mocked her back. Her meaning was clear, she was calling the girl a slut. Which was unexpected because the girl was quite heavy. "She'll give anyone a blow job that even talks to her," Caly whispered not too quietly. The guys in the pool heard, and they started checking Brooklyn out with more interest.

Brent and Tifton jumped in the pool, each taking a different side of the net. Brent called out to Caly, "Come join us."

We went over to the shower, and I held up a towel I took off of a cart while Caly showered. She gave me a questioning look, but she held the towel when I showered. It was daunting for me to shower in front of this crowd, even with a swimsuit on. Back home, being in a swimsuit around the Bensons was natural, but this was the first time for being around the elite. The cool shower water was making both of our nipples stand out in protest, adding to my discomfort.

Caly jumped in on Tifton's side which made me pause for a second, but then I jumped in next to Brent. I grabbed his arm, pretending that I slipped, so I could copy his talent. I'd never played volleyball in water before. It was nice that this pool was all the same depth, and we could all stand. It was for laps, based on the lane lines on the bottom. It turned out that Brent was a lousy player and not a good choice to copy. Our side lost without scoring one point.

"It's too bad you all suck." A guy named Aaron mocked us from the other side of the net.

"Apparently, not as good as Brooklyn," Jacob from our team called back. The rest of us shushed and scolded him. Brooklyn jumped up without grabbing any of her things and ran into the house. Sharlyn followed her.

"Jacob, you're an idiot," Sharlyn called over her shoulder. From either Sharlyn or Caly's thoughts, or maybe both, I learned Brooklyn had a crush on Jacob.

Tifton had surfaced right next to me, nearly knocking me over. I had to grab onto him to stay standing. Oh boy, my magic jumped, spreading warmth through me, and Tifton felt it too. His face went from shocked to a bit gooey before he got it under control. He sucked in a sharp breath. "I'd ask you to pardon my behavior, but I'm enjoying being close to you way too much to apologize for it," Tifton said in my ear. My body shot out more warm gooey waves. I let go of him abruptly and pulled myself out of the pool and took a quick shower. My magic and feelings were starting to overwhelm me, and I needed to get away from that hot body. Caly followed right behind me. She wasn't completely over her jealousy.

"Thanks for the game," Caly called out to the guys as we headed back to the mansion.

"What are you guys doing tomorrow?" Brent asked.

"We'll be at Powder Beach," I said.

Caly cranked her head to look at me and asked, "We will?"

"If you want to, Nana is staying at a beach house there."

"We're on Powder Beach right now," Caly informed me, pointing toward a gate.

"What?" I asked looking around. There was a hedge that surrounded the yard as well as a tall brick wall. A path leading to a gate in the wall drew me over to look out the gate. There was a small building near the gate with a sign at the top that read "Surf Shack."

Sure enough, there was a gorgeous beach on the other side. The sand was multicolored with some specks reflecting the sunlight. Leaving the yard, I scooped up some sand letting it run through my fingers. It flowed like powder. Caly stood so that the gate wouldn't close and lock us out. Right in front of the Horton house, a long dock stretched out to accommodate four huge yachts. There was also two large, covered pavilions, a fire pit, and a volleyball net. The Hortons' house was the center house on the beach. Looking back at the house, I could see a huge balcony. When Caly saw where I looked, she said, "They have breakfast on that balcony most every day, weather permitting. I wonder where Nana and you are staying, there are only nine houses on this beach."

We eyed the homes trying to guess which one would be ours. Most every house had wall to wall windows making the most of the views. They were huge white sentinels with red clay shingles towering over the beach. Only the shutters had different colors. It was as if the same person designed the entire beach. It was so beautiful that magic had to be involved.

"She didn't really explain. I don't know if it's just a friend's place or if she is renting."

Caly looked both ways down the beach. "There is one place at the end that is mostly vacant. Just a gardener to see to the upkeep. I definitely want to see where you're staying, I'm sure Mom will let me, and she'll probably come as well." We went back to the room and changed back into our traveling clothes. I didn't want things to be weird between us, so I asked, "Are you upset at Tifton whispering in my ear?"

"Nope," she said with forced cheerfulness. But a thought flashed of her throwing hot oil in my face. Yikes! To her credit, she did chase it away quickly. I hated when people's words didn't match their thinking. It happened much more than most people believed.

Just as we packed away our wet suits in plastic bags, Caly's mom arrived with three other adults. Caly knew them all and introduced me to her mom. "Mom, this is Sera Webster, my roommate and best friend. Sera, this is my mom, Raine Pollin."

"You can call me Raine, hon." It was amazing at how young her mother looked. They could've been sisters.

The others were formerly the Hortons' chef, chauffeur, and Mrs. Horton's personal fashion designer. Every one of them had very striking looks. Seemed like you had to be good-looking to work for this household. After introductions, everyone grabbed a box, and we loaded them into a truck.

Nana was a minimalist by choice, but it was sad to know people were forced to live minimally as these ex-servants were. I was disheartened seeing it, and there needed to be payback for the injustice. Those illegal contracts stole years of their lives.

"Change of plans, sweetie," Raine said to Caly. "We all have been invited by Nana to stay the summer here at the beach. She told me I could invite who I liked!"

We drove down the street to a similar sized house. We carried the boxes into the guest bedrooms, *not* the servants' quarters.

Helping to unload the truck, Freya, who had been Mrs. Horton's personal designer, and I reached for the same box when our hands touched. As we each walked a box into the house, I asked her, "Why does Mrs. Horton dislike Caly so much?"

"Oh, I couldn't say for sure." I could see from her thoughts that she had a good idea, but after years of not being allowed to share an opinion, she chose the diplomatic response. Freya was there on the day Mrs. Horton shamed

Sharlyn. The girls were playing nearby while Caly's mom was giving Mrs. Horton and her best friend pedicures. The friend said in a very condescending voice, "Oh look, Caly is wearing Sharlyn's old dress. My, she sure is a much prettier girl. She makes that dress look much classier." As soon as the friend left, Mrs. Horton scolded Sharlyn about hanging around peons. Freya felt terrible because she had tailored the handed-down dress to fit Caly better. That dress ruined Caly's only childhood friendship.

By dinner time, the truck was empty. Caly and I had rooms that shared a bathroom. I didn't know when Nana had been in contact with Raine and arranged for this group of Hortons' servants to stay with us. This was the beach house Nana told me about, but she forgot to tell me it was a mansion on a private beach.

We found Nana in the kitchen. I ran and gave her a huge hug. Nana explained that Freya offered to be my chaperone if I stayed for the summer. This entire group was going to live here for the summer, each had assigned roles. Dion, the chauffeur, was to be the driver for the beach house and Alex was to be our chef. Raine would buy groceries since she was the only one with a paying job.

Mrs. Horton had spread terrible rumors about all of them, making it harder for them to find work, even though they were really good workers. Everyone pitched in for dinner. Nana said that was the way it was going to be, everyone helps each other.

"Where did you get these amazing vegetables?" Alex asked.

"They're from the ranch," Nana replied.

"I would love to try them right from your garden," Alex said.

"You all are welcome anytime you like, just know that if you visit, I'll put you to work," Nana warned with a smile.

Dion looked at his partner, Alex, and said, "Well, you'll have to do my share of the work; I won't want to ruin my nails."

Alex laughed and said, "That's the truth." With an arm around his shoulder, he gave Dion a reassuring squeeze that he wasn't laughing at him but with him. Alex, Deon, and Nana talked nonstop throughout the meal about Nana's favorite charities and her passion for giving people a hand up and not a handout. They were getting into some good friendly debates about the best way to do that.

The sedan Dion drove us in belonged to Nana and she offered it to Dion and Alex if they stayed and helped us out for the summer. Come fall, it was completely theirs, but even during the summer Dion could use it for making money.

After dinner, the adults enjoyed cocktails on the patio while Caly and I went down to the beach. There was a breathtaking sunset that lit up the infinity pool, and it did look like it was part of the ocean.

"Dion and Alex really seem to like Nana," I said.

"After all the cruelty of dealing with Mrs. Horton, they are enjoying someone with heart, even if she comes off a little rough."

We took a quick stroll not wanting to be out when the sun completely set. "Do you remember me telling you about the lady that got my mom to sign the contracts?" Caly asked.

I nodded.

"That's her place over there," Caly pointed at the house down at the opposite end of the beach. "I can't tell you how many times I wanted to burn it down with her inside; I hate her so much."

My heart did a few flips, it was exciting to know where Annette lived, but it was also scary being so close.

"Well, if you ever do, count me in. It's so wrong forcing people into servitude."

We took off our sandals and walked on the wet sand. The ocean lapped at our feet. "This is so amazing," I said, pointing at the water and sunset.

"Life doesn't get any better than this," Caly said with a contented sigh. "Especially, now that Mom is free. That yellow bitch, Annette, wrongfully contracted nearly every servant on this beach, turning what should have been a fantasy life into a nightmare," she said with venom. "I'm not certain, but I think this house is the only place on this beach that hasn't employed Annette's services. Doesn't it make you wonder why Annette didn't do it this year? It doesn't really matter why; I'm just so happy for it," she continued, without waiting for a response. "Maybe we can all teach you to surf tomorrow. Are you a good swimmer?" she asked.

"I can swim in a pool or lake; I've never been in the ocean."

"It's so much fun once you catch a wave and ride it; you have to try it. These aren't world-class waves, but they're fun." Caly kept looking towards the Hortons' house, where people were laughing and partying.

Looking at the ocean, my mind got stuck on how venomously Caly said, "yellow bitch." It kept echoing over and over in my brain. Did everyone hate yellow magic so much? I understood she had reason to hate Annette, I did too, but would she hate me if she knew how strong my yellow was? I wondered. It reminded me again of Mom warning me to keep it a secret.

I could've just asked her or searched her brain, but I was getting tired of people saying one thing while thinking another. It was truly dizzying to think about the differences. It happened all the time, simple things like when she said she liked my necklace, to more confusing exchanges, like when she said she didn't mind Tifton flirting with me, but she had a thought of throwing hot oil in my face.

Being here was so exciting until Caly pointed out Annette's place; now fear shadowed everything.

A RING, AN AUNT, AND A FIRST KISS

"WHO SETS AN alarm during summer vacation?" Caly had asked the night before.

"I don't want to miss my first ocean sunrise," I said, setting my alarm to take a sunrise walk on the beach. Caly decided she would rather sleep longer.

Nana said it was the best time to enjoy the beach. The peacefulness was amazing. The ocean's waves lazily lapping the shore, the wind tinkling the palm tree leaves, and an occasional bird calling all played a quiet symphony of calm. From this beach, both the sunrise and sunset would be spectacular. Twinkling sand ran a couple miles long, with the large dock stretching out into the deeper waters. Bypassing the smaller dock, I went straight to the larger one. Two yachts were parked on either side with their sterns backed up to the farthest end. Each had several decks above water level, and helicopter propellors were visible on two. They were so beautifully maintained that they looked new. Leaning on the rail at the end of the dock, I stretched out my energy to see all the creatures. Even though there were sharks, it was comforting to notice that none were nearby.

It was interesting to observe calm waters on our side of the dock and rolling waves on Annette's side. The anomaly could be the lay of the land, magic, mechanical means, or maybe a combination of each. Near our house, the beach stretched out into the ocean, making a hook shape at the end of the cliffs. There was a walking path that went to the top of the hill. I looked at the smaller dock and noticed a few nice fishing boats and Jet Skis in the calmer waters. Annette's side of the beach also had land that stretched into the ocean, but not as far.

Returning to the sand, I paused to study the pavilions. One had picnic-style tables underneath, and the other had four large cabana beds with side tables. Each pavilion had speakers in all four corners. Both had fans that hung down from the ceiling, and a misting system lined the edges of the roof.

A low rumbling noise drew my attention down the beach where something was cleaning the sand with a huge rake. It looked like a lawn tractor with an attachment being pulled behind. It was nice to see it wasn't running on fossil fuels. The house servants had done an excellent job of cleaning up from last night's parties, but this machine was sifting the sand and collecting even small objects that were missed. As it passed, it was clear that no human was driving it. On the side of the tractor was lettering stating property of the City of Redding. That couldn't be right. This beach was private. Only beach residents and guests were allowed. It reeked of Annette's meddling. Her moral compass wouldn't see anything wrong with manipulating the city into providing beach maintenance.

I walked behind the tractor in the fresh lines of cleaned sand. The beach was so soft, it felt like stepping on memory foam. Watching the machine, I noticed a collecting receptacle where small pieces of glass, gum wrappers, and something shiny bounced up and down. It was a ring. Focusing tiny pulses of my red magic at the shiny ring to make it bounce out, turned into a morning experiment. It took four attempts, but finally, it landed in the sand in front of me. Picking it up, I walked to the water to rinse it. It was a single large rectangular-cut yellow diamond mounted on a platinum ring; it was very simple in design but beautiful. Strong vibrations emanated through me just from holding it. After trying it on several fingers, I left it on my right thumb where it fit. Waving my hand around, it caught some sunlight. When the rays hit it just right, a burst of yellow radiated out from the gem. It hummed in a soothing way. It felt so connected to my energy, surely someone with yellow magic owned it.

Strolling in the direction of Annette's, the neighbor's house was as close as I dared, not wanting any security alarms to be triggered. Sitting on the freshly-raked sand, I called on my yellow. My thumb vibrated, and my magic was able to stretch and search as far as it wanted. I focused my attention directly on finding Annette. She was sleeping. I pulsed yellow with some black to keep her in dreamland.

Poking around for information, she had recovered her memory of me, but not on her own. She had someone else do the recovery in exchange for sex. *Oh eew, come on, Annette, have more respect for your body,* I thought. It seemed like sex was her number one bartering tool when magic couldn't be used. She didn't want to kill me; her main goal was to figure out a way to control me. She loved that my magic was still a secret. It would be much easier to manipulate me if no one knew.

The talisman on our dorm door was from her, and she delivered it. She figured I deserved the stomach pain, and she was still upset about me interfering with her most lucrative sources of income and for the damaged lasers. She didn't have any shortage of wealth. She could easily live out the rest of her days in luxury without taking in any more income, but that wasn't enough to stop her greed. Being rich and powerful didn't satisfy her hunger. Apparently, there was no such thing as too much wealth by her way of thinking.

She was still using yellow to manipulate people in exchange for money and valuables. She just wasn't using contracts anymore. She felt it was acceptable to exploit the loophole in my threat. The Hortons already had a new set of household help, some had even stayed. Caly's mom and friends got away because they had somewhere to go.

Annette's continued use of dark magic brought back the tarry goo, and it was giving me the feeling of bugs crawling on my skin again just by tapping into her memories and thoughts.

"Annette, what are your worse sins?" I asked her sleeping brain.

"Murder. Greed. I used my magic to get my sister legally assassinated so that I could steal her magic and raise her kid. I use dark magic as much as possible."

"You're raising a kid?" I asked, feeling extremely sorry for the child.

"No, the council barred me from raising her. The joke is on them because it ended up that the child wasn't showing any extraordinary powers. It was a huge disappointment that I wasn't able to get my sister's magic. Her body didn't share with me." Her thoughts were on the cabin where she found me when I was five.

"Was your sister Crystal Kendler?" It was disgusting just thinking it was a possibility.

"Yes."

NO-NO-NO-NO! It can't be. She cannot be my aunt! My thoughts were making it hard to stay inside Annette's head. Sweat and nausea were building from the knowledge of being related to such evil, and thoughts of panic raced through my mind. My whole body started shaking.

"What did you do to get your sister assassinated?" I asked her, after pulsing some calm to my mind.

"I wanted her magic. Being firstborn, she was always more powerful than me. I manipulated the council into believing it was really the only way to make things right. Then I volunteered to get the job done. They were conditioned to think it was appropriate for me to handle it being as she was my biological sister."

"How did you kill them?" I asked. My jaw was clenched so hard it hurt.

"I took their magical codes to the top hex maker. He made the death bomb to only kill them and no one else. It was quick and painless. Because my code was too close to hers; I didn't want to risk my life. We were twins. I was out of the area when the spell was activated."

Twins? That was hard to wrap my thoughts around.

She disgusted and infuriated me. Bundling her yellow magic, I pulled it toward me. If this didn't help her mend her ways, I was going to remove her magic completely. I decided to leave enough yellow magic for her to understand what I did. Using the doctor's necklace, her magic came bubbling toward me. Thankfully, not all her goo came with it.

Using this amount of magic from this distance exhausted me, and I needed to organize my magic to fit hers into my body. The two yellows needed to separate. Some day she might find a way to get hers back. Fortunately, the two wanted to stay apart.

The sun was completely above the horizon, so I just laid back on the cool dry sand and let the sun warm my skin. Dozing off, I woke to the sun being blocked by a muscled figure. Before opening my eyes, I knew it was Tifton. My magic jumped and stretched out to him.

"Hey, sleepy head."

I barely opened my eyes to look at him. "What are you doing up so early," I asked.

He laughed. "I don't think nearly ten is early." He squatted down so his haunches were resting on his heels and pulled a small tube out of his pack. He squeezed a white strip that looked a bit like toothpaste onto his finger and then rubbed it on my nose. "You're going to burn if you don't get some sunscreen on, this zinc oxide will keep your nose from peeling." It was silly how thrilling it was to have him touch my nose. His finger moved slow and hovered above my mouth for just a moment.

"I can't believe I slept so long," I said, as I jumped up. "I just came out for the sunrise." He had a three-quarter length surf suit, and his board was nearby.

"Sunrise, wow, when the days get hotter, we'll be out at sunrise to surf." Then I noticed he had three of his friends with him.

"I better get back to the house and see what Caly is up to."

"She is out on the water already," Tifton said, pointing out to her reclining on a floating chair not too far from the shore.

"Well then, I better get back to the house to get into my swim gear," I said, waving in Caly's direction. She waved back, and I motioned toward the house. She nodded her understanding.

Heading back, the crawling bug feeling was so strong that I started to run to have something else to think about. Running on sand was awkward compared to running on solid ground. By the time I got to the patio, my breath was coming out in gulps. Nana was sitting outside at the table, watching me with curious eyes.

"I thought you'd be back after sunrise," she commented.

"I fell asleep. Guess I'll get something to eat and get changed into a swimsuit unless you need me for anything."

"Not today I don't, but I need you to come with me on Monday."

"Oh, that works great because Raine will have the day off, and I'm sure Caly will want to be with her."

"Where'd you get the ring?" she asked, grabbing my hand.

"I found it on the beach."

"It looks expensive. Maybe you should ask around to see if anyone is missing it."

"How about a sign to tape to the pavilion, letting people know a ring has been found, and if they can describe it, they can claim it?"

"Sure, that will work."

Breakfast was a quick bowl of cereal in the kitchen. In my bedroom, I put the ring in the bag with the plant leaves and seeds. Chewing on a seed stopped the wiggly feeling, but I also threw up. It was covered with the gross, smelly goo. Once that goo was out of me, the crawling bug feeling stopped, and I felt hungry, again. After rinsing my mouth several times, I put on my swimsuit, went back to the kitchen, and ate again. When I passed Nana on the patio on the way to the beach, she handed me a flyer about the ring, it already had tape on it. I just needed to put it up at one of the pavilions. She also handed me a towel, suntan lotion, a large jug of water, and pointed to an outbuilding.

"You'll find some ocean toys in there."

"Seems like every house on this beach has a shack," I muttered. Grabbing a floating chair that looked like the one Caly was on added to my burden. It was even harder walking on the sand, loaded down with everything.

I dumped my items down next to Caly's stuff, it had to be hers, the towel and water jug matched. I took a big drink from my water before attaching the flyer on the closest corner of the first pavilion, applied some suntan lotion, and then grabbed the chair to join Caly.

"The view is great," she said, tilting her head toward the boys. They were all waiting for the next wave. I climbed on the float and started bobbing up and down beside her. The mild wave motion was tickling my stomach in a good way. This morning she was more interested in watching Brent than Tifton.

"Oh great, here comes the circus," Caly said, looking down the beach. She wasn't wrong, Sharlyn and an entourage of friends had on so many bright, shiny colors, you'd have to be blind to miss them. Some of the new Horton household help were setting up food and drink on the picnic tables. The entourage spread out their bags on the cabana beds. We could hear beach music coming from the speakers.

"Looks like a circus that brought the party," I said wistfully.

After the next wave, the guys all headed their way and my jealousy popped up. Using our arms to paddle, we turned our backs to them. Closing my eyes didn't stop me from thinking about them. Self-consciousness creeped in about wearing a very plain, powder blue one-piece. The same one from pool volleyball. Even though their new-looking bikinis didn't have much material, they looked expensive. I relaxed and scanned the ocean for the second time today. There were many little creatures at the bottom in the sand. Observing the swimming fish was the most relaxing.

My chair felt like it was moving faster than normal. My energy jumped to greet Tifton. "What are you smiling about," he asked, his breath touching my face, and just as I was going to open my eyes, soft, light moisture touch my lips. Warmth spread from my lips all the way down to my toes, and when it ended, my eyes popped open to see light whisps of magic swirling between us. He was still close enough to kiss.

"Should I have asked for permission?" he whispered. As he talked, his lips lightly grazed mine. A slow moan escaped from somewhere deep inside and his smile widened.

"Stop making a scene, everyone is watching," Caly hissed with jealousy. I really should have resisted by pushing Tifton away. It took a moment to muster the strength. I pulsed some magic, and it moved him a few feet away. It looked like a wave had moved him, not me. The few feet removed the influence he had used on me.

Caly feeling bad made me feel sad. I'd thought she was over Tifton. Maybe she was because when I looked to see if people were watching, Brent was leaning in close to one of the girls. She was pretty but not nearly as good-looking as Caly. Caly's negative feelings were not for us. Curling my tongue to concentrate a pulse of blue to Sharlyn's gut, she passed some loud, smelly gas. It was like someone had thrown a firecracker in the cabana. Everyone jumped and scooted back. The guys laughed, and the girls screeched. That did the trick in separating Brent from the girl. They were not sure who passed the gas. With practice, one day it would be more obvious.

Once Brent was up, he looked around for Tifton. As soon as he spied us, he jogged out toward us and then dove into a wave when he was deep enough, popping up right next to Caly.

"Dude, you're so lucky you weren't over there, someone let out a big smelly one," he said, laughing.

"Who did?" Tifton asked in amazement.

"I don't know, don't care, just needed to get away," Brent was now rocking Caly's chair teasingly, and she was giving off pleasant vibes.

While they all talked and joked, I copied Tifton's swimming and surfing skills. He really enjoyed catching the big waves. He was into me or at least determined to get in my pants. At dinner last night, Sharlyn was trying to convince the family that Caly and I were completely terrible human beings. Tifton didn't believe a word of it. He knew his sister was jealous of Caly. I popped out of his head when Brent said, "Bet I can get Caly to the dock before you get Sera there." And the race was on, we were being pushed toward the dock. Both Caly and I laughed. They won because Tifton couldn't reach the bottom and was having to do a lifeguard rescue pull instead of pushing.

We stayed under the dock's shade for a while. They talked about the waves they surfed this morning. Tifton had one hand on my float, and the other was absentmindedly stroking my shin, sending tingles up my spine.

"Tifton, Mom wants to talk to you," Sharlyn called out. I could see that he thought his mom was going to admonish him for hanging out with Caly and me. Both he and Brent went inside.

We stayed all day at the beach, only going to the house to eat and use the bathroom. The volleyball net was the main activity for the afternoon and into the evening. Every household seemed to come out to watch the competition, many joining in and inviting friends. When Caly and I needed to cool off, we watched from the floating chairs. When Brent and Tifton were not on one of the teams, they rocked the chairs for us. It was such a silky feeling, and it was stirring up longings I never knew before this summer. Once, while sliding off the chair to walk to shore, my foot touched and glided down Tifton's thigh and calf. He stopped and gave me another kiss. This one was longer and deeper, I felt his tongue and pulled back.

"Too fast?" he asked in a low deep voice that made me want to pull him back. I resisted. From his thoughts, he had reassured his mom that he knew my place in society was too low for anything serious. *Wow! That hurt.* He stayed out in the water when I went to shore.

That evening at sunset, the Hortons' help was busy at work building a fire and bringing out more food. I went over to offer to help and to touch one of them. When I got inside one head, I realized what Annette had done. This new batch of servants didn't sign a contract, but they believed they had. It was so frustrating, I wanted to release them all but knew it would draw too much attention. I made sure that the one I touched realized they didn't need to be here unless they wanted to stay. They stopped working at once and walked away. My heart ached for the others. Somehow, there had to be a way to release everyone she had exploited. The depravity of her actions cemented my decision. I was going to completely end her magic.

SURFING UNDER SIEGE

SUNDAY MORNING, SEVERAL of us met on the beach again. The guys were determined to teach me to surf.

"You're looking excited," Nana commented on my why out.

"Surf lessons, Nana," I exclaimed.

"You take a beginner longboard and dress in a wet suit. Both are in the shack." She pointed for extra emphasis.

Caly grabbed a shorter board, confident in her ability. She picked up a couple of items from one of the shelves. They looked like handles with a hook. "Here, let me show you how to use this claw. It'll make carrying the board so much easier."

When we met up with the guys, Aaron helped me attach the surfboard leash just above my right ankle.

They showed me how to stand on the board while we were still on the beach. They told me about surf etiquette and who has the right of way. They showed me how to get to my sweet spot on the board for paddling out. The trick was to not let the nose get too high or too low. Within an hour, I was catching waves. Thanks to no small help from Tifton's skills that I copied, but it did need adjustments for my body's center of gravity.

"Wow! You're a fast learner," both Jacob and Aaron commented from the beach.

Later, we were all just relaxing on our boards, away from shore, waiting for more waves. The water was much calmer, and the slight movement was lulling me to sleep. One moment, the gentle rolling was relaxing, and the next, I was violently overturned into the ocean.

Saltwater rushed up my nose, sending a gush of pain to my brain. Panic rushed in. Getting to the surface became my only goal. Tugging on my surf leash enabled me to grab the board and pull my head above water. A violent cough spewed the water from my airways. One good breath was all I got before I was yanked down again. With air in my lungs, I opened my eyes and mind to see what was happening.

Right below me was Annette in SCUBA gear. She had my unleashed ankle in her hand. She was angry and determined. From her mind, I could see she planned to drown me and take all my spirit gifts. My death would look like an accidental drowning. Not sure if it was a spell or just me panicking, but I couldn't use red to blast her away. The self-healing blue was at work having my lungs use as little oxygen as possible, but the air wouldn't last for long. At one point, I was able to kick enough to knock the regulator out of her mouth, but she quickly recovered it. My yellow wasn't working either, at least I couldn't get her to let me go, but she was wondering why I wasn't unconscious yet.

Apparently, she didn't know about my self-healing, even though she pointed out that I got my dad's spirit. Perhaps it wasn't widely known what powers a blue spirit could give.

The struggling and lack of air were weakening me. In desperation, I used all my green energy to call in any large fish in the area, and it worked. She must not have thought it was necessary to block the green. Just my luck, the first to respond was a shark. Thankfully, it swam right in front of Annette. She was distracted by its tail swishing in front of her face, just long enough to loosen her grip on me. I kicked as hard as I could and pulled at the leash at the same time. When I surfaced, Tifton was nearby.

"Help me!" I gasped, and he grabbed my hand and pulled me up on my board.

"What happened to you? I was so worried when I saw your board bobbing."

It took a bit to get my breathing back to normal. Now that Annette wasn't touching me, my magic returned. I pulled as much red as I could and blasted it at Annette. It should have been enough to harm her, but I didn't see any effect. Maybe she had a protective charm, or maybe my magic was weak, or the water cushioned the strike. She was swimming underwater toward her house. Even though she was retreating, my mind was on high alert.

"I'm not sure," I lied. "I fell asleep and maybe hit my head on the board trying to get to the surface, and then water rushed in; it's all a blur." I coughed a few times for effect.

"I can relate, hitting your head and sucking in water can be terrifying. I saw a shark fin, which is odd because we have some magical deterrents set up. Let's head back to shore."

"Yes, please."

That wrestling match with Annette kept me out of the deep water for the rest of the day, putting me closer to Sharlyn and her crowd. Tifton had left his board with one of the Hortons' older servants to wax it.

"Just leave yours, Jesse will wax it,"

Knowing how the Hortons treated their staff, no way that was going to happen. Kneeling beside Jesse, I tried to imitate his actions, but it was obvious he had years of experience. Caly just sat by watching. When Jesse was done with

Tifton's board, he took it to the surf shack and came back out to help us.

At one point, I bumped against Jesse's shoulder and was then able to copy his surfboard cleaning and waxing skills. He had been a world-class surfer. His surfing skills replaced the ones that I copied from Tifton. Jesse had so much more finesse. He had been hired to teach Tifton how to surf and ended up never leaving the Hortons'. My heart ached for him because he hadn't seen his family in years. Even though he had not signed a new contract, he was part of the group that Annette was able to convince that they had signed.

She was such a yellow bitch, I wanted to scream. I smudged out the belief that he had signed a contract but put a delay on it. I didn't want someone to noticed that every time I touched one of the help, they walked away.

Caly was playing touch Frisbee. She had taken off her surf suit and was only wearing a swimsuit. I was hungry, tired, and scared.

Still intimidated by the entourage's beach outfits yesterday, today was going to be extra hard. I wore the same powder blue one-piece every day because I didn't have another one. Tomorrow there might be time for shopping for more. Everyone else had a different suit each day. Caly only had two of her own, and she was able to use her mom's suits as well.

"Hey, I'm going back inside. Swallowing so much saltwater has given me a stomachache." Caly stayed, which gave me the much needed time to recuperate.

After a long shower, I was still trying to wrap my head around the fact that Annette had tried to drown me. Once dressed, I went to find Nana. Of course, she was in the gardens. I could see Alex and an older man discussing a roped-off area while Nana was digging in a flower bed."

"Can I have a few planters and potting soil," I asked her.

"Sure, help yourself" she said, as she pointed to the garden shed.

I went back in to get my seeds and leaves from my dresser drawer. I chewed on the basil-like one. It seemed to help me align the control Annette had disrupted in the ocean. I took the ring out of the bag and left it in the drawer. So far, no one had claimed the lost ring.

I planted a few seeds of each plant and watered them.

"Are those seeds from your plants," Nana asked over my shoulder.

"Yes, I left the plants at school but brought some seeds and leaves." I held my small bag up for her inspection.

"I did a little research on them. They are quite hard to grow. You should go ahead and plant all of them. I could get you a good price for each plant at the next farmer's market. The seeds are not as sought after because people can't seem to get them to grow. The parsley-like plant is much more popular." Taking her advice, I planted most of the seeds in biodegradable pots. I retained a few seeds for personal use.

Later, inside, I asked, "Nana is that meeting tomorrow going to take all day?"

"It should only take the morning."

"I'd like to do some clothes shopping in the afternoon if that's all right. I still have most of the spending money you gave me. There isn't much to buy at school."

"I'll see if Freya is available to go with you. Did you know she has a fashion degree?" Nana asked. "She isn't working yet, so I'm sure she could use the extra money if you want her to sew some clothes."

"Sure, that'd be great, I need so much. I've outgrown everything from last fall," I waved my hand over my growing breasts and snug shirt.

"Oh shoot, I forgot, Mrs. Benson sent a box of things that Lysa has outgrown." She disappeared down the hall toward her bedroom. "I meant to put this in your room," she said putting a box down on the couch.

I rummaged through the contents, separating summer items from the other seasons. Yay! There was a cute two-piece swimsuit. On the ranch, I would've been thrilled with these clothes, but here at the beach among the children of the elite, it all felt sadly lacking.

"Tuesday morning, I'm going back to the ranch. This city life is too fast-paced for me. You're welcome to stay here. Raine, Alex, Dion, and Freya are going to spend the summer here in this house, and they all assured me you'd be well looked after. I think you'll have more fun here, but I do want you to come to the ranch for the last couple of weeks of summer break." I gave her a quick hug.

"I'm enjoying it here, but let me think about it. I might want to go back with you." I was thinking I might want as much distance as possible between Annette and myself. Though being around Tifton would most likely keep me here. "Nana, do you own this beach house or are you renting it?"

"It has been in the family for years. I spent my childhood summers here. It's mine now, I just enjoy the country life so much more. I have held on to it just for this reason. I thought one day you might enjoy the beach. I wasn't sure it would ever happen, but when I contacted Raine and they all needed a place to stay, I thought this would be a fantastic opportunity for you. Plus, it gave me an excuse to check on the house."

"Who has been taking care of it for you?" I asked.

"Mr. Levitt, I don't know if you saw him, but he was in the garden earlier. He stays in the gardener's rooms. He is very meticulous about checking the condition of everything. He is a widower in his seventies now. He seems pleased to see the house getting some use. He is helping Alex set up a vegetable garden."

Gathering up the clothes to carry them back to my room, "I was wondering who that was," I said over my shoulder. With everything put away, the box was used to pack up all the outgrown clothes. Freya could find some use for the material and buttons.

The new-to-me swimsuit I changed into fit loosely. The green halter top was a bit plain but could be adjusted to give me some nice cleavage. Before heading out to the beach, I carried the box to Freya's room. She motioned for me to put the clothes on her bed. From her closet, she pulled out a small suitcase bursting with all sorts of ribbons, buttons, and jewelry.

"This will brighten your suit up a bit," she said, as she pinned a yellow plastic flower with a smiley face right below my cleavage. I checked it out in the mirror and was amazed how one thing could wake up the look. She took off my necklace, "This shouldn't be worn with the flower. I'll make a bracelet with the smaller one. They really don't go on the same chain."

"Please be super careful with those, the rock flower is the only thing I have of my mother."

"I will," she assured me.

"This yellow pin is so cute, thank you. If you're free tomorrow afternoon, I'd love for you to come clothes shopping with me."

"I'm going shopping with Raine and Caly, but I'm sure they would love to have you join us, that is if you don't mind us checking out second-hand stores first."

"Cool," I said, giving her a hug.

Passing through the kitchen, Alex stopped me and handed me a basket. Inside were two sandwiches, a bag of cheese puffs, a couple of apples, and two large fruit drinks. "For you and Caly. You need to eat, or the wind will blow you away."

"You're the best," I said, giving him a hip bump. After picking up the basket and a towel from the surf shack, I went to find Caly.

Nearing the group, I saw Sharlyn sitting on her blanket and using some red magic to push Caly down as she was about to set the volleyball for a spike. She and her friends laughed as Caly pushed herself up. Sand was plastered all over her front. I rushed over and started brushing the sand off with my towel when Sharlyn called out in her snarky voice, "Oh, it's nice to see you do actually own a second swimsuit." That brought on another round of laughter. Holding myself in check took fortitude. The urge to send a tornado at those cackling hens was begging to be released.

It would be justice to send them head over heels across the sand.

Pulling Caly from the team, I laid the towel down next to hers and put the basket on top. Someone from the sidelines jumped right in to take her place in the game as I knew they would.

Caly was embarrassed and angry. "She's been doing that every chance she gets," Caly hissed still wiping sand from her legs.

Her frustration of having so little red was evident in her thoughts. That frustration was no different than having it but not being able to use it freely. I opened the puffs and handed her a sandwich and a drink. She dug right in. Being near the social elite was more important to her ego then making time for eating. We watched the game while we munched.

Brent went up for a spike with a big grin on his face, and with great force, he smashed the volleyball right into Sharlyn's face, well, with a little help from me. He ran over to apologize and tripped on the edge of a beach towel. As he fell, he plowed into one of the staff carrying a large bowl of cut fruit and it spewed all over everyone in the area. That accident didn't have any help from me.

"Get out of here, you oaf," Sharlyn shouted as she pulled watermelon from her hair. She stood up and marched back to the house, one hand to her face and shaking juice from her other arm. Her gaggle of friends followed right behind her in hot pursuit. Brent was running to catch up, I assumed, to apologize. The Hortons' help rushed in to clean up.

"Oh, that was priceless," Caly said. Both of us hiding our grins by taking bites from our sandwiches. "That's a cute swimsuit, where did you get it?" she asked.

"It's from a box of Lysa Benson's handed down clothes. The pin is from Freya," I said, using my pinky finger to point at the sunflower because I still had a sandwich in one hand and a drink in the other.

It seemed like the commotion ended the volleyball game. Tifton plopped down beside me, leaving his friends to mill about nearby. He snatched up the bag of cheese puffs. Before he even took a puff, he used his finger to trace around the yellow flower. It was an excuse for stroking my cleavage. A bolt of energy shot down my spine, and my nipples decided to stand up and pay attention. My cheeks turned red, and he removed his hand to grab into the bag. He had a smirk of satisfaction on his face as he popped a puff into his mouth.

Tifton's friends were ribbing each other and snickering, so I use my scanning to hear what was going on. Tifton bet one of them he could have sex with me by midnight tonight, and his smug thought was that getting there was going to be as easy as eating a piece of cake. As soon as that registered, I switched off the thoughts. My disappointment was exhaled through pursed lips. This was to keep me from building up too much anger. Controlling my breathing didn't calm me enough, so I pulsed some yellow. My appetite was ruined. It was a game to him, and my body was the toy.

"Are you all right?" Caly asked, concerned. My demeanor had changed enough for her to see. I gave her a nod of reassurance.

About that time, Annette strolled by with a dog on a leash. We watched as they passed. When she reached the end of the beach, she turned around to come right by us again. Our eyes met as she got close. "Enjoy your meeting tomorrow," she said, sugary sweet.

After she had walked by and was nearly back at her home, Caly grabbed at my arm, "Do you know that mentalist?" she asked horrified. The derision in her voice was dripping with disgust.

I rolled my eyes and leaned back in the sand, "Remember the spectrometer scores at the beginning of second term, when afterwards I had to see the dean, she was up there to interview me. She was really creepy." Caly using the word mentalist with such disdain reverberated how much I needed to keep my yellow secret.

"You should have told me. We should get you checked out to make sure she didn't mess with your head. How does she know you're going with Nana tomorrow?" Caly wondered aloud.

"She's a yellow witch, she probably knows everything. I didn't know what she was capable of at the time, I certainly didn't connect her to your mom's contract," I lied.

"What's that about Raine's contract," Tifton asked, looking genuinely clueless.

"As if you don't know your mom makes people her puppets using that mentalist's magic," Caly spat out as sour as I ever heard her. She stood up, gathered her towel and her water jug, and headed back to the house. I gathered the rest up and followed her.

Over my shoulder, I heard Aaron comment, "Seriously, dude, are you that stupid? Even I know the whole beach pays Annette to bind the help, except their house."

I stayed at the house for the rest of the day, helping Alex with dinner by peeling and cutting vegetables. Then I watched the sunset from the pool. I could hear the gang down the beach having fun and roasting marshmallows at the fire pit. Caly joined them, she definitely liked being around these people much more than me.

I picked up enough bits and pieces of their thoughts to realize some of the older crowd's friends brought booze, weed, and pills. Most of the Security Institute students left for the day, they didn't want anything to do with the drugs and alcohol, but Tifton and Brent stayed. Tifton had an excuse, he lived there, though he could've gone inside. Brent talked Caly into sharing a joint with him, and they walked away from the crowd.

Several of them were betting on when Tifton was going to take my virginity. I decided that I wasn't going to give Tifton a chance to win his bet anytime soon.

I expected Caly to come into my bedroom to tell me about smoking weed with Brent and anything that happened afterwards, but she didn't. Her mind was reliving the sex she had with Brent tonight on the beach. She was super happy about it, even though it hurt a bit, thankfully, he didn't last long and used protection. I curled up in the fetal position feeling sorry for Caly and then myself. She didn't trust me enough to share such important life events with me. Even though we were best friends, we sure had secrets from each other.

BRACELET FROM GLENN

THE NEXT MORNING, after indulging in Alex's fabulous stuffed French toast, I took a shower. Raine fixed my hair with a fancy, tight braid in the back. She then had me curl my bangs and sides under her instruction. I wore a yellow sundress with small white polka dots from Lysa and white dress sandals. Freya gave me back my necklace, and now I had a very pretty bracelet, too. Caly had not even gotten out of bed by the time Dion drove Nana and me to our appointment. He dropped us off in front of a huge government brick building with the word Nokuland across the top. I started to feel strange and began to reach inside Nana's brain, but as we walked through the doors, my magic stopped working. Nana told the receptionist our names, and she directed us to the top floor. Once there, another receptionist asked us to take a seat.

Reaching for my magic again, I could feel it was still there but not responding. I turned to Nana and asked, "Is there something strange about this building?"

She looked up at me and blinked a couple times. "Not that I'm aware of." She seemed almost in a trance.

"What's this meeting about?" I asked suspiciously.

"I wasn't told, just that I needed to bring you here."

"And you didn't ask?" I questioned. That wasn't like Nana at all.

"No, I didn't think to, it all seemed normal." Her voice was bland and her eyes vacant. I was sure someone had used magic to get us here. So, magic could not be used here, but if it had been in place when we arrived, it seemed to remain active.

Why hadn't I asked Nana more questions before we got here? I was too busy with stupid girl stuff, I scolded myself. I wasn't a nail-biter, but I sure wanted something to chew on right now and decided to gnaw on my cheek and lower lip. I grabbed my mom's pendant and tried to call my magic, still no response. This place had some heavy-duty wards and spells in place.

Right at nine o'clock, the receptionist stood and asked just me to follow her. I looked at Nana, who was just staring at the wall. Oh great. The young lady brought me into a room that looked like a court room. Everything was wood, including the ceiling and walls. The front of the room had a judge's bench with seating for nine people; the middle seat and desk were slightly higher than the rest. *More like a supreme court,* I thought. There were desks for the defense and plaintiff, along with room for the respective attorneys. Just like a court room.

I was walked to the closest desk and introduced to my counselor, Ms. Sharp. My brow was getting a little sweaty. After the receptionist left, Ms. Sharp told me that we had thirty minutes to discuss my case before court started.

"What case?" I asked completely confused.

"Annette Teufel has made a formal complaint. First, she accused you of having a large amount of unregistered yellow magic, and then, recently, she amended the complaint to also accuse you of stealing magic from her. She wants it back."

I pulled out a chair and sat down. *So much for secrecy,* I thought.

Ms. Sharp continued, "I'm here as your legal advisor. First, if you don't already know, magic can't be performed in this building. Second, you will be compelled to tell the truth when answering the judges' questions. Due to your young age, only three judges will preside today. Third, this is the Nokuland Council Court, there is no higher court to make any appeals, their decisions are final."

After a pause, she asked, "Do you have any questions?"

"What kind of punishment can they give out?" I asked.

"All the way up to complete removal of your magic, but that is extremely rare. Usually just restrictions on the use of your magic. They can impose monetary fines, work hours, and imprisonment. Though given your age, I doubt they would put you in lockup."

"Why is my case already at the highest court?" I asked.

Ms. Sharp genuinely looked confused, "That is strange." I knew it was Annette's doing. My advisor rifled through some paperwork she had. "The reason given for you being brought straight to the Nokuland Council is that you have several unique circumstances. First, your magic scores of double zero. Second, is your ability to take someone's magic. Third, she accuses that you have several spirit gifts, which implies that she thinks you might be a killer." When Ms. Sharp looked up from reading, her eyes were large. She must not have read the circumstances until now.

Even before our thirty minutes were up, Annette and her counselor walked in and sat at the other desk. Her expression was so smug, I couldn't look at her for more than a moment. She had years more of experience working with the council, and I'm certain she had used her magic to manipulate them. I looked around the room slowly, taking in the name plates for each judge. The high seat in the middle read, Justice Horton.

At nine-thirty, a court recorder walked in and announced that we all needed to stand. We did. When Justice Horton sat down, everyone else did the same. Only three of the high seats were filled. Judge Horton sure looked like he could be Sharlyn's and Tifton's father. The other two judges were female, Mrs. Kim, and a Ms. Parks.

First, the recorder read the charges against me. Then Annette had to swear the accusations were true. Finally, they had me give a condensed version of my life story, including my knowledge and usage of magic to include my actions against Annette.

When they announced that they were going into recess to discuss my future and my punishment, I asked, "Don't you want to know why I took Ms. Teufel's magic?" Everyone stopped what they were doing and waited.

Justice Horton said, "Yes, we would like to know, please continue," but his face was concerned.

"She is using dark magic to bind people into servitude in exchange for money." The entire court room gasped, except Annette and me. Annette glared at me with murderous eyes. What? Didn't she expect me to reveal her secrets? This can't have been a surprise. Unless her ego believed she could control every situation.

Next, they had Annette tell the court of her use of dark magic. Horror and disbelief were on every face as she went on and on. "How could this happen? Isn't she audited every year like all the council members?" the judges were asking each other.

Ms. Kim asked, "Annette, when was the last time you were audited?"

"More than seventeen years ago," she answered truthfully.

If possible, the court members gasped even louder.

"Ask her how much she has manipulated the council," I urged.

"Yes, please tell us," Justice Kim commanded.

More information poured out about how she had convinced the council to assassinate my parents, the Kendlers. How she had been sleeping with Justice Horton in exchange for getting his cooperation. As chief justice, he could override the audit requirement. It was strange to see even Horton gasp. Seriously, he didn't know? Now I knew where Tifton got his cluelessness. They went into recess, knowing these new facts.

Annette's tone was so livid while she was explaining her misuse of magic, I didn't dare to look at her. During the break, I went to check on Nana, but the receptionist told me she had left and would be waiting in the parking lot later. So, I went to the first floor to get a drink from the cafeteria and bought a coffee for Ms. Sharp.

Shortly after I got back to the court room, the two female justices returned without Horton. Which made sense if his position as chief justice was under review. Annette was to have her magic completely removed, forever. It was amazing that she didn't receive a fine or have any prison time, which was disappointing. I was allowed to continue at the Healing Institute but would have to wear a bracelet blocking my yellow magic until further notice.

"At eighteen, your sentence can be revisited, and we will evaluate you for sterilization at that time," Ms. Parks explained. My mind went numb. It all felt so wrong. Maybe they should consider having a therapist handy for statements like that.

Ms. Sharp escorted me to the basement. I was able to watch as a technician attached a bracelet that blocked Annette's use of magic, and then she was free to go. Unbelievable! That wasn't removing her magic. That was just a barrier, and knowing Annette, she would find a way to get around it before the end of the day. As she left the room, she gave me a stare that chilled my blood, not magically but no less terrifying.

I was so nervous when Annette was in the room with me that I hadn't noticed much about the technician. A name plate on his shirt said Glenn Levitt. I studied him while he used a tablet to program my bracelet. My mind was extra imaginative today, this guy looked like he could easily be related to the Hortons. His muscles were not as chiseled as

Tifton's, but he was still good-looking. He had longer, darker hair and was slightly older, so maybe eighteen. Here on Amaku, Nokuland, we were educated at a much faster pace than the rest of the world. When the mainland United States was graduating high school, we were done with what would be a four-year college degree for them.

"Are you related to the Hortons?" I asked.

Without stopping what he was doing, he commented, "Funny you should ask. I just recently analyzed my magic code as well as my DNA, and it said Justice Horton was my biological father. I've been in foster care my whole life since the day I was born. And his wife is my biological mother. So how I am a foster child would be a mystery if I didn't know the court rules. Digging through council records, I found the contract that allowed those two to get married if they gave away their first child. Firstborns receive the highest amount of magic, and this was their process for dissuading powerful families from building dynasties. Can you believe two people would make a decision like that?" he looked up as he asked me that.

"That's really sad, I'm sorry you had to find that out on your own."

"Nothing like living as a ward of the government, knowing you're poor and unwanted, only to find out your parents are alive and are the most powerful family in all of

Nokuland. It does mess with your head," he said and then continued typing.

"Does anyone know that you figured it out?" I asked.

"Nope, and I'm not really sure what to do with the information. Some days I want to knock on their door and say, 'Surprise, I'm your firstborn you gave away.' But then on the plus side, I have a lot more magic than I ever imagined. I guess that explains why I've had control training since before I can remember."

"So what career are they training you for?"

"Mostly, law. At this point, I could probably represent you better than your counselor did. I think they groomed me that way, expecting that my magic levels would one day put me on one of the councils, either as an auditor or maybe even a judge. Ever since I found out, I have just wanted to get out of this city and away from all this falseness."

He stopped typing and attached my bracelet. "This will be a blessing and a burden. It will be nice not to know when people are lying to you or when they dislike you, but you're also going to miss it." I looked down to see a similar bracelet on his wrist.

He lifted his wrist, "This worked for a while, now it's just for show, people feel more comfortable around me if they think I'm limited on my magical use."

"Are you serious about getting away? I could probably find a nice ranch for you to work on over the summer."

"I would jump at the chance, but I can't imagine any ranch wanting a city slicker like me. I've never been out in the country."

"I know someone who is waiting for me right outside that might take you in for the summer. Would you like to meet her?"

He thought about it and said, "Sure, I could use a break. It can't hurt to meet someone. How do you know this lady?"

"She is my foster mother," I said with a grin.

"So, you would be on this ranch, too?" he asked.

"Not until the last two weeks of summer, I'm getting to spend time here. Before last week, I had never been to a big city. Would you be able to leave this job to go to the ranch?"

"Yep, I'm just volunteering, it's a strategic place to find out what's going on in Nokuland. Though, they will miss me because they have me doing several jobs. Another reason I want to get away, they're taking advantage of my helpful spirit. They give me enough assignments to keep me busy fourteen hours a day, which doesn't leave me much personal time. It would be nice to get some space to figure out what's next for me."

As we left, I noticed he brought his device with him. "Why are you bringing that?" I asked, pointing to his bag.

"It's mine, I take it everywhere."

"They let you do Nokuland business on your personal device?" I asked, incredulously.

"Well, I didn't ask permission, I have lots of administrative rights, so I approved its use for myself. I'm not planning on doing anything illegal, I just don't want them monitoring what information I'm researching."

I knew my yellow magic was blocked, but the moment we stepped outside, I reached for it and found that Annette's yellow magic in me wasn't locked. Nice. All my magic was excited and began reaching for all the power in Glenn. He stopped, grabbed my forearm, and held it.

"What are you doing?" I asked.

"I'm teaching you some tricks to control your magic, right now it is being super enticing to me, and I really don't want to be attracted to a fourteen-year-old girl."

"Oh." I pulled my magic in and paid attention to what information he was sending. It was great to finally have someone that could help train my magic. While he was doing that, I split my attention and poked around in his head for information on getting into the Nokuland council databases and information storage. I left an order for him to create access and an administrative account for Katie Holmes the next time he logged on. And I could see he was attracted to me, even before we stepped outside, but once my magic reached for him, it overwhelmed him to the point of almost losing focus. He did want that to stop. He didn't seem to be aware of me using Annette's magic, or he was ignoring it.

Glenn went back inside to take care of something he forgot. Ms. Sharp walked out of the courthouse with the recorder. I froze both. I walked over and touched both, having them forget my name and face. Erasing the whole court proceedings seemed like overkill.

Neither the car nor Nana was anywhere in sight, so when Glenn rejoined me, I offered to buy him lunch at the courthouse diner across the street. Inside, Mrs. Kim and Ms. Parks were eating with several others. Glenn and I both ordered the lunch special.

He pulled out his device to make an admin account for Katie. While he did that, I used the orange to freeze the entire room. I went and touched everyone at the judges' table. I was able to use the freeze magic and have everyone forget anything that happened during the freeze in just one step, so I was back to my seat in less than a minute to release the freeze.

One long table was just judges and auditors. Justice Horton was not among them. Most of the diner's customers worked at the courthouse. Glenn continued on the computer while I checked to see how Annette had manipulated each of their minds. Because it was Annette's yellow magic, it went straight to corrupted thoughts. She convinced one justice he was a pedophile and used that to blackmail him.

First, I verified that he wasn't one, then removing the conviction. Another she had convinced they had murdered someone, most likely someone Annette had murdered. One thought they were a blackmailer, another an embezzler, and the last believed they had incestuous relationships. Every one of Annette's planted beliefs were false, and with her magic, I easily removed them. Adjusting their memory of court today, they understood the accused was related to the Teufels, but I removed my name and face from their memories, too. They were all more relaxed than before the freeze.

It was nice to see that they had figured out the current fulltime auditors were not high enough in magic levels to fulfill the job, and they were going to replace them immediately. Most likely due to Annette's meddling in court business. One justice was currently on their device searching the database for prospects. Since they were already logged on, I had them approve my new administrative account. Before the judges left, I compared their auras against Glenn's, and he was packing more magic than any of them. I could feel all theirs, his lack of projection must be part of the control training he mentioned.

While we waited for the bill, Glenn put both of his hands around my bracelet. When he lifted his hands, I asked, "What did you do?" The bracelet looked exactly the same.

"Well, it's invisible now. Isn't that enough? It's one of my many talents," he gave me a playful smile. "People won't be freaked out seeing a court bracelet on someone so young."

This statement made me question his sanity, but then I remembered I could see things that others couldn't, ever since the elder passed me his spirit.

"Thank you, maybe one day you can teach me how to do that."

"It's not something you can learn; what little I've found says it's a hereditary spirit gift."

Dion and Nana pulled up just as we were leaving the diner. After introducing everyone, both Glenn and I climbed into the car. Nana was interested in Glenn working on the ranch. Dion dropped me off at the thrift store and they went back to the beach house. Inside, Raine and Freya were trying to decide between two different pairs of jeans.

"Which one do you think I should get?" Raine asked me.

"Why not both?" I asked, seeing the price tags were less than five dollars each, and then realized they didn't have much money to spend.

"We're trying to make my last few days of tips from the salon stretch as far as we can," she answered, not embarrassed at all. Clearly, she was happy to have any spending money.

"Have you tried them on to see how each one fits you?" I asked.

"Oh, good idea," she said, as she headed toward the changing rooms.

I walked over to an idle cashier and asked if they sold gifts cards, and they did. So, I purchased one each for Freya and Raine and put two hundred dollars of credit on each. They both tried to refuse the cards.

"This is not charity; I fully expect you two to earn it. Freya is going to make me some clothes, and Raine, you will be doing my hair and nails all summer." They both thanked me and gave me hugs. When Caly saw what I did, she placed two tops and a skirt in her mom's shopping cart.

Instead of going to the mall next, Freya convinced me that we should go to a fabric store in the same building just a few doors down.

At the fabric store, Freya obviously knew her way around. "Fasteners are in isle three, and threads along that wall. What do you want me to make first?"

"Swimsuits!" Caly and I said at the same time.

Freya first picked out buttons, zippers, ribbons, and anything she thought would improve the thrift store clothes.

Then we went to find fabrics. The sales assistant guided us to the newest material, perfect for swimwear.

"How much do you want to spend?" Freya asked.

"Both Caly and I probably need at least two new suits."

"She needs like four new super cute ones," Caly inserted.

When we decided on some colors, Freya had the sales assistant cut some lengths from six different bolts of cloth. She said we won't need much material. She talked me into even shorter lengths of shiny stretchy material for some highlights. Everything totaled together was less than one hundred dollars.

"Do you have good scissors?" the sales assistant asked.

"Freya?" I looked at her questioningly.

"Well, it never hurts to have extra." She added three different sizes to the basket. They ended up being the most expensive part of the shopping.

Back at the beach house, Freya was so excited by our purchases. We piled the fabric store bags in the crafting room, and we laundered the thrift store clothes. Freya measured both Caly and me. Using our current swimsuits for patterns, she started cutting and assured us we would each have our first new suit by morning.

"Here, take this," Freya handed me a sample packet for self-tanning, "It'll even out your skin tone so that you won't have tan lines. Use it after a shower tonight; by morning, it will have full effect." Its label showed it was from a magical supply outlet.

"Where'd you get this?" I asked.

"Raine got some from the sales representative at the salon. She'll need to give them feedback on how well they worked."

"You should use it. Raine gave it to you."

"Pssh, I'll never impress those beach snobs, but you have a good shot at it."

Even with all of today's spending, I still had most of Nana's generous allowance from the past school year. She put money in my account every month. Thankfully, no one asked me about my court appearance. I didn't want to talk about it.

Alex, and Nana were in the kitchen preparing dinner. Glenn had not gone back to the courthouse, but he had contacted them to transfer his work assignments. Dion would take Glenn back to his foster home later tonight, and then in the morning, Nana would meet him at the train station. They both agreed to a trial period with the understanding of no hard feelings if the arrangement didn't work out. I knew Nana made that agreement because no way would she fire anyone from the ranch, short of them being a criminal. She had a huge weakness for strays like Glenn and me.

After dinner, Caly, Glenn, and I walked along the beach. Glenn was amazed, "I have never seen a beach so well maintained and clean."

"That's Justice Horton's house." I pointed out before we got close. Being as it was Monday night, not as many people were on the beach. No bonfire or volleyball, but Brent, Tifton, Aaron, and Jacob were practicing Krav Maga with Sharlyn and Brooklyn nearby, pretending not to watch. The guys started to show off as we approached, and I could see they were eyeing Glenn when they thought we weren't looking.

"Caly, do you want to throw the Frisbee with me," Jacob called out. He was so ignorant to Brooklyn's feelings.

"Sure," she replied and broke away from Glenn and me.

We continued down the beach, and I pointed out Annette's house. Now that Glenn had shown me how he calmed magic, the next trick he started teaching me was how to have my red always maintain a protective shield without draining the magic. Red maintaining the shield gave me a strong physical barrier with just magic. I didn't want to walk by Annette's house, but Glenn kept strolling, so I matched his pace.

When we turned around to walk back to Nana's house, I felt a sharp poke at my side, rib level. It had so much force that it knocked me into Glenn, and we both fell.

"What the heck was that?" he asked.

"I don't know, but something sharp poked at me." I turned my torso so he could look at my side. "Am I bleeding?" I asked. He lifted my shirt to look, and I blushed.

"No bleeding, but you might get a bruise here." He lightly touched my skin, I gasped.

"Ouch, what did that?"

"I think that was a blast of red intended to hurt you," he said, as he quickly added extra shielding around us.

We both looked at Annette's house, the direction the blast would've come from and saw someone was lying on their back, feet facing us, right in her gateway. The gate was trying to close, but it was blocked by the person on the ground. We hurried over to look. It was Annette, and she was bleeding from her chest. My best guess was that whatever she blasted at me ricocheted off my shield and came right back to her.

"Can you try to heal her?" Glenn asked. "I know you're just a first-year student, but still, you can probably stop the bleeding. I'm going for help," he called as he ran toward the Horton house.

Slowing the bleeding, I wasn't ready to completely heal her yet. First up was removing every bit of magic she held. Making drastic decisions when pissed and in pain wasn't a good idea, but sometimes emotions block logical thinking.

Anyway, this should've been done at the courthouse. Pushing the gate back to kneel beside her, I started gathering her magic. Not wanting to look suspicious, I put my hand on her as though healing her. Caly and Sharlyn were on their way. They could heal her and be the heroes.

By the time they arrived, I had removed every bit of magic and did an extra sweep just to make sure. Her pulled magic flowed into my body. I certainly didn't need any more, but where else could it go? Sifting through her memories, her bank account information was easily copied. She shared one jointly with Mr. Horton. It had an obscene amount of funds.

I stepped back so that Caly and Sharlyn could each grab an arm. They didn't heal her much, even though they completed first-year at the institute. Not one minute of the schooling had taught healing. Still, it was surprising that they weren't able to use it via instinct. My magic could have healed her completely, but no way that was going to happen.

An ambulance arrived as well as a security guard. While the rescuers put Annette into the ambulance, I went to tell the guard what happened. Glenn was already giving a statement. I just nodded along to everything he said. He didn't accuse Annette of shooting something at me, he wanted the guard to come to that conclusion on his own. When the guard had finished collecting statements, we all strolled together back toward our houses.

"She would have died if I hadn't been here to stop the bleeding," Sharlyn bragged.

"She is lucky you were here," Aaron said.

"Do you know her very well?" I asked.

"Well, her and Dad are good friends, she consults for the high council and, of course, my dad is Chief Justice," she added the last part just to brag a bit more. Her bragging didn't make me jealous. Soon enough, she'd realize that her dad probably wasn't going to be on the high court any longer.

Slowing my steps, Glenn matched my pace. My nerves were frazzled, and I touched his arm seeking out comfort. His energy jumped at my touch, and for a few seconds, I felt warm and gooey, but he pulled it back.

"Here, let me show you how to calm your feelings," he said, as he touched my elbow.

I wanted to tell him I already knew, but glad I didn't because his way was much more effective.

"Wow, thank you so much. I've learned so much in just a brief time with you."

Tifton was listening and he let out a derisive snort.

"Hey guys, this is Glenn. Tomorrow he is leaving with Nana to help on her ranch," I said. "Glenn, this is the beach gang. This is Tifton Horton and his sister, Sharlyn. That is Brooklyn, Aaron, Jacob, and Brent." They all nodded to each other, but the guys lost interest, knowing Glenn was leaving tomorrow. Sharlyn and Brooklyn tried to flirt, but he didn't respond. To his credit, he didn't gag having his sister hit on him.

"You know, you could be Tifton's brother, you'd look like twins if you had your hair as short as his," Brooklyn said to Glenn. He gave a small cough to clear his throat.

"I'm way more handsome than him," Tifton said pushing out his chest. He was in better shape from all his training, but they looked so much alike.

"What's your family name," Jacob asked.

"Levitt," Glenn replied, pointing at the name tag on his shirt.

"Oh, like your gardener," Sharlyn mocked in my direction.

"No relation," I said, glaring at her.

Everyone stopped walking in front of the Hortons' house, except Glenn and me.

"Caly, do you want to walk the beach with me?" I heard Brent ask. He slyly wiggled a joint at her.

"Sure," she said eagerly, and they headed back in the direction we had just come from.

When we were back at the patio, Glenn asked, "Why didn't you heal Ms. Teufel?"

"You think that saving her life wasn't enough, that I should've rushed to heal the person who had just tried to kill me?"

"How can you be certain she was trying to kill you? It could've been an accident, and healing her would've been taking the high road." He leaned in as he tucked his chin a little and raised his eyebrows.

"So, what if I healed her, and she zapped me again as soon as she was conscious?" I challenged.

"Since you took her magic, I'm quite sure that would've been impossible," he was eyeing me with such intensity, my magic wobbled enough to feel it in my bones.

Damn! How did he know I did that? His eyes were so light blue, and my lungs could only pull in tiny amounts of air. My heartbeat was so loud, it seemed to be partly catching in my throat, moving in a circle between my ears and heart. I was warm and tingly all over, and I began to wonder if his magic was trying to seduce me.

"I have pretty much the same magic as you, but I've had a lifetime of training on how to use it, there isn't much you can hide from me," he informed me. "I expect better from you, especially if you expect me to continue to train you."

"Well, you're leaving tomorrow, so that point is kind of moot, isn't it?" I was able to say in a husky sass.

He leaned in further and put his face really close to mine, and my breathing stopped completely. He lifted my chin with his finger and said softly, "When you grow up, we will be spending a lot of time together. I'd like the person I'm sharing my future with to be someone I trust and admire." He dropped his hand, walked into the house, and told Dion he was ready to go.

It took me a few minutes to recover. My whole body tingled with electric fuzz. I pondered what he meant about spending a lot of time together. For the first time in my life, the future couldn't get here fast enough.

For the rest of the evening and the following morning, I stayed close to Nana. We decided she should take most of my plants with her to the ranch. Each had at least broken the surface of the soil. "If they stay alive, you can do whatever you like with them." During our goodbye hug, I transferred as much of Annette's green magic to her that her body would accept. Carrying around extra magic just forced me to use it more often, and I was still trying to keep my own levels a secret.

THE YACHT

THE SWIMSUITS FREYA made were fabulous. They certainly were on par with, if not more stylish than, any of the top fashion designers. We decided to wait until later to wear them when more people would be on the beach. Caly went surfing this morning. Raine was cutting and highlighting my hair. While the highlights were setting, she gave me a mani-pedi.

"Freya told me that she gave you the tanning potion. It looks great," Raine commented as she worked.

Later, a stranger was looking back at me from the mirror, between spending time in the sun and Raine's highlights, I was now a blonde. My tan and swimsuit complimented each other. It was a bright white one-piece, with nautical blue piping around the edges, the shoulder straps, even lining the deep cleavage. Lightly padded cups pushed up my chest. As with most swimwear, the best part was the tailored custom fit. A grown-up elite was staring back at me from the mirror. Sharlyn just might choke on her comments about me not having another swimsuit.

The regret that Glenn wouldn't be here today to see me was stronger than my excitement for Tifton seeing me. Thinking of Glenn made me wonder why Nana had left me here and why I didn't insist on returning to the ranch. It was out of character for both of us.

When Caly saw me in my new swimsuit, she stopped and gasped. "You look so awesome and grown-up." It made me sad to see the jealousy in her thoughts, she was putting up a good show supporting me, but inside, it was eating at her confidence. Her swimsuit was a twin to mine, tailored to her shape, but it had red piping. She made me wait while her mom styled her hair so we both would be sporting cute ponytails.

When we were finally leaving the house, Freya stopped us to add belts that matched the piping and cinched up my swimsuit straps. I now had some more cleavage, but it was tight. "If it gets too uncomfortable, just have Caly loosen the straps in the back, but not until everyone has had a good look," Freya said, and she gave me a wink.

There were several people on the beach, more than just the usual gang. Near the volleyball net, Sharlyn had set up a contest for the servants. All the beach house servants were invited. If they could throw a Frisbee through a small slot in a board, they could win a bolt of cloth from her mother's storage. Sharlyn said the cloth was out of style so they didn't need it anymore, but I could read the real reason. They had lost Freya, no one could make clothing from scratch like she could. It was sad how excited everyone was to have a chance because I could see Sharlyn was using her red magic to block the slot. No one's Frisbee was getting through, but they kept trying. I'm sure if any of them had won a bolt of cloth, they would've brought it to Freya to have her make something. Our house had not been informed about the contest, so Freya wasn't even here to see the competition.

We were standing at the back of the crowd and had put on our long T-shirts, so that our surprise wasn't competing with the contest for attention. Working my way to the front, I asked, "Can I have a go at your little contest?" My mock innocence sent a flash of irritation across Sharlyn's composure.

"Well, if you consider yourself *a servant*, sure, have a go," Sharlyn purred. She was so sure that I would miss the slot that she didn't even block it. This was my first attempt at throwing a Frisbee, but I had copied the skills from several people. Standing on the towel she had laid down as the throw line, I curled my tongue and bit on my lower lip to help focus my red. I spun the Frisbee on my fingers, helping me to get the feel for its weight, and then it sailed straight through the slot. It bounced off Sharlyn's stomach, causing her to bend from the pain. The crowd cheered so loud that the rest of the beach stopped to see what had happened, and even more people joined to watch.

Sharlyn picked up the Frisbee, walked over to me and shoved it into my stomach. "Do you want to go for double-or-nothing?" she asked, with a challenging smile.

"It is a ridiculously small slot. If I can do that again, you should let me have three bolts of cloth." Upping the ante didn't even faze her.

"Done," she said and went back to stand on the other side of the board, but not directly behind it.

Sharlyn had strong red and blue and didn't need to be on any registry. Just yellow and baby-making were closely watched. Sharlyn and Caly had seen me use a little red, but I didn't want to tip my cards to the rest of the onlookers. Tifton had joined the crowd, and I reached out to his thoughts to convince him to help me. When Sharlyn had put up the red block, Tifton knew to remove it, even though he couldn't see the color. Maybe siblings had connections. When the Frisbee was airborne, he pulled it through the slot. It landed right at his feet. Sharlyn threw a tantrum and ran off to tell her mom.

"I will have to escort you to the storage room to pick out the three bolts you just won," Tifton said close to my ear, and my toes curled.

"I would really like Freya to help pick them out if that is acceptable?"

His smile dampened a little, but he said, "Sure thing."

When Caly, Freya, and I came to pick out the cloth, there was a line of servants by the storage door. We picked out our three, and then Tifton let all the other participants pick out a bolt. He was allowing each participant to select material even though they hadn't gotten the Frisbee through the board. He was doing it to impress me and make it up to the staff for his sister's cruelty.

We each carried a bolt of cloth back to the house. Freya was so happy. "We got three of the best ones there," she said proudly. "This one will be great for making dress jackets," she said, lifting the one she was carrying.

As soon as we dropped the cloth off in the crafting room, Caly and I went back to the beach. The large crowd had dispersed, but some people were playing volleyball, some in the water, and others just sunbathing. We took off the over-sized T-shirts and began to lengthen our strides.

People started to notice us. The sun was reflecting off shiny pieces of our suits. We were barefoot because our sandals would've weakened the look. It felt so good to have the new swimming suits, but now, I was self-conscious of our cheap sunglasses and using a T-shirt for a cover. Trying to keep up with fashion was a carnival house of mirrors. It could make you dizzy, wondering which way to go next. Even if we got the fashion glasses, sandals, and cover-ups, we would then need the right beach bag and the expensive towels. There was always something lacking: jewelry, party invitations, the right friends, and even cars. The more you acquired, the more you still wanted. The solution was to settle the unworthy thoughts and just enjoy the moment instead of worrying about what we didn't have.

By the time we spread out our towels and sat down, both Brent and Tifton had joined us.

"Do either of you need help rubbing on sunscreen? I would be happy to help," Brent said, squeezing some lotion in his hand. Without waiting for a response, he warmed up the lotion by rubbing his hands together and started on Caly's shoulders. She lay down on her stomach and he knelt over her, his knees on either side of her hips and continued applying the lotion.

Tifton raised his eyebrows at me questioningly. I rolled over on my stomach, and he began giving me a wonderful relaxing massage using the sunblock. He untied my suit at the back of my neck, leaving me feeling a little exposed. His moistened fingers tended to roam under the fabric of the bottom of my swimsuit every so often, and my body was loving the tingling. He made sure every inch of flesh he could reach was protected from the sun, from the sides of my breasts to my inner thighs and including between my toes.

My body felt so good, I started to believe he was using some form of magic on me. Every time he touched me, my magic responded by reaching out to his. Floating in a seductive haze of his magic fingers, I still could pick up on his current thoughts. He was reveling in the thought that everyone was jealous of him getting to be so intimate with my body right out in the open.

"Would you like a tour of our yacht?" Tifton asked softly near my ear.

Perking up, I said, "I would love to. I've never been on a yacht."

Tying the top of my suit at the back of my neck was priority before standing up. Gathering my towel and beach gear caused Caly and Brent to look up.

"Do you want to see the Horton yacht?" I asked Caly. She probably wouldn't make a good chaperone, but it was better than going alone.

"Oh, definitely," she said, jumping up.

From the dock, we walked onto the yacht via a railed plank.

"This is the swim deck. Please remove your shoes," Tifton instructed.

He took us up the first flight of stairs. It was jaw-dropping beautiful. It had highly polished teak wood flooring and cabinets, leather, and gorgeous fabrics professionally designed. We stopped at the main deck bar. Caly went in search of a bathroom. Tifton poured us all alcohol drinks.

Even a small sip of the whiskey left a trail of heat on my tongue and throat. Seeing my pinched face, Tifton then added cola to the whiskey and encouraged me to try again. This time it was enjoyable until he bragged that the whiskey was twenty-five years old and over a thousand dollars a bottle. I almost choked, swallowing the next sip.

"That's crazy! Won't you get in trouble for drinking it?" I asked, eyeing the large portions he poured for Brent and himself.

"Nah, but even if Dad did get upset, I would just blame it on the help." His grin told me he had done that before and was happy with the results. His comment appalled me so much that the seductive mood broke. He further bragged that the yacht cost several hundred million, but he wasn't sure the exact amount. After taking me to see all the main spaces a guest would visit, even a gymnasium, he ended the tour in his bedroom. We separated from Brent and Caly at the bar.

Tifton had me take another sip and then took my drink and put it down with his on a dresser, after a seductive spike from his magic, we started kissing, and he tried to pull me down on his bed. Pulling back, I noticed that the covers were disheveled, and the room had an odd musky smell. Sliding into his thoughts, he was so certain I was going to be his second round of sex in less than a day, and he was pumped about being my first.

His thoughts were bouncing between me and the other girl. It was one of the girls that hung out with the druggies. Eew, he had someone in here last night. Stepping away from him and his bed, I clutched at my stomach to keep from throwing up on him. There was a trash can in the corner by the dresser, so I tilted my head over it. Inside were several used condoms. This was where most of the smell was coming from. Yanking my head away from the nasty mess, I edged toward the hallway.

"That whiskey didn't settle too well. I'm not used to alcohol." I lied about why my stomach was churning. Being disgusted with him and at myself for not seeing him for what he was is what was making my stomach turn. Bending over and groaning was all a ploy to get me out of this situation.

"I need to get back to the house, really quick." I turned and ran out of the room, calling for Caly.

"Busy," she shouted back; it sounded like she was between kisses.

"I'm headed back. I don't think my stomach is handling the whiskey," came out as a groan.

"All right, I hope you feel better soon."

I grabbed my stuff from the bar and ran all the way back to the house without looking back. Passing Freya at the patio door, she reached out an snatched my arm. "Hold up. You smell like alcohol," she said sniffing at my lips.

"I had three tiny sips."

"You're not allowed any sips, you're fourteen. Do you want to get sent to the ranch?" She asked in a disciplinary tone.

"Right now, that doesn't sound bad." The words tumbled out with a sob. Freya then pulled me into a full frontal hug.

"What happened?" she asked.

I told her everything, except about Caly being on the yacht and being inside Tifton's thoughts. I just beefed up the used condom smell and how cocky he was being.

"Honey, you need to stay away from the Hortons, they're bad news."

"I wasn't thinking, I was excited about being on a fabulous ship."

"Put your stuff away and come out here and give me your opinion. I've been sketching your next swimsuits."

Mostly, I just watched as Freya sketched and held different pieces of fabric together. We were listening to a music station when we heard an announcement about a contest for concert passes for Bur$t.

"Oh, that's Caly's favorite band," I said. According to the band's portal, the concert was for this coming Friday evening. Winners of the contest would receive concert tickets and be able to meet with the band. "Caly would be over the moon if I got those passes," I said. Freya didn't even look up but nodded her agreement.

"Those tickets have been sold out for months," she said, "you'd have to win."

"We should probably keep off this station, so she doesn't hear about the concert and get depressed." Even though she probably already knew all the tour dates and locations. What good is magic if you couldn't use it to make a friend happy?

After an hour online, I found the address for the office handling concert tickets. Each of us now had a separate contest form submitted. I shouldn't have used their names without asking, but I wanted as many chances to win as possible, just as a backup. All my magic and wiles would be put to the test to get us tickets without winning the contest.

I'd recruit Dion to drive me. In addition to getting tickets, we needed to stop by the bank that held the account shared by Annette and Mr. Horton.

I decided to browse through the court database. Once logged in, right on the courthouse web portal was a large announcement about Mr. Horton having a court date with the Nokuland Council. Abuse of power was the main charge. Adultery was listed as a supporting factor for his unfitness to retain his position. He was already relieved of his duties. Annette would be there to testify.

Annette's name had a link to click on, so I did. Up popped her personal information. Full name, date of birth, social security number, address, parents, and much more. I clicked on Mother, Jennifer (Sander) Teufel, my grandmother. Jennifer's personal information filled the screen.

There was no date next to deceased, so she was still alive. She had three births listed, but the eldest, my mother, was put in foster care. Seems to be quite the trend with the rich and powerful. Based on how Annette turned out that was probably for the best. My grandfather, Matthew Teufel, had a different address than Jennifer. Further searching led me to my dad's, Justin Kendler's, record, and both his parents were still alive. His mom was listed as Norma L. Kendler address unknown. Perhaps because she was passed the age of childbearing, they didn't need to keep close tabs on her. His dad, Dr. Erick Kendler, had an address in the next largest city in Nokuland, Blue Canyon.

Every one of my grandparents were on the registry for yellow magic. It would be impressive if just one grandparent had yellow, but all four, that would never ever have been sanctioned by the council.

Freya was inside sewing when Caly returned. Her eyes were glassy, and she had a goofy grin. She sat down on one of the lounges. "Being with Brent is so much fun," she said dreamily.

"You look high or drunk," I accused.

"What's it to you. You should try it. It'd help loosen up your prudishness," Caly slurred.

"OUCH! It didn't help your bitchiness."

"Oh, don't be so mean. I'm just repeating what Tifton said. They've been letting me have hits of weed for over a year now. It's no big deal."

"Some people would say it's a big deal."

"You're telling me that you've never tried smoking weed?"

"Until this summer, I'd never even seen it."

"Not possible."

"Nana keeps our ranch life as wholesome as possible."

"What about Lysa?"

"Well, she's older, but still she decided it wasn't something she wanted to get into."

"You country folk are ducks of a different color," She slurred the messed-up metaphor.

I peeked inside her to find out not only had she drank whiskey and smoked a bit of weed, but she had also popped a pill. She was definitely feeling no pain. Of course, they had sex on the yacht, twice. They left the yacht when Mr. Horton came aboard and found them in his bedroom. Mr. Horton was half blocking the doorway, and he deliberately touched Caly's breasts as she passed. Gross. When Caly got back to the beach, Brent headed straight to the older crowd. That crowd didn't have anything to do with us, which was fine by me, but Caly wanted to be a part of their group. After waiting around about a half an hour, Brent had not come back to sit with her, so she left. Since I was already in her head, I poked around to see if she had any addiction tendencies, and I was glad I did not see any.

"Have you ever noticed how Brent and Tifton act like we don't exist whenever anyone from the older, druggie crowd shows up?" I asked.

"Yeah, but that's how he gets his supply, so he has to hang out with them," she said, defending Brent.

"Tifton and Brent had sex with a couple of those girls on the yacht last night," I said.

"How would you know, and why would you say that?" She looked at me with accusing eyes.

"I overheard them bragging about bedding two different girls in less than twenty-four hours when you used the bathroom. They assumed they couldn't be overheard," I lied. Caly looked crushed, making me feel like a louse.

"So, you know I've been having sex with Brent?" she asked.

"Why didn't you tell me?" I asked.

"I figured you'd say I was too young."

"Oh, heck yeah! Though the temptation is understandable. You guys better be using condoms. Why are you doing drugs with Brent? That is worse than having sex."

"Who says I'm doing drugs?" she asked indignantly, obviously forgetting we just talked about it.

"Umm, you did, and I saw him wiggle the joint at you the other night, and your eyes right now are so unfocused."

"Oh," she said weakly. "If he's sleeping with other people, I'm definitely done with him, nobody deserves that. And yeah, he used condoms. There was a lot in Mr. Horton's drawer. Isn't that weird?"

I gave her a squeeze, hoping she would be all right after finding out about Brent. Using magic, I pulled the alcohol and drugs into her lower colon. She sobered up and excused herself and ran to the restroom.

Dion drove me to the bank the next day. On the way, he told me that he and Alex had lined up employment starting right after Caly, and I headed back to school. Both jobs were beneath their capabilities, but they were happy. Dion would be driving a truck for a delivery company, and Alex would be working at a restaurant in the business district. They were looking at houses to rent. They wanted at least three bedrooms so Raine and Freya could move in and help with the bills.

At the bank, using just enough magic to get into a private office with a manager, I froze him, locked the door, and lowered the window shades. He was already logged into the system. We closed the shared account between Annette and Mr. Horton, splitting the money and sending it into their individual accounts. Then, using the offshore accounts of the manager at Dr. Gobel's bank, we withdrew the funds from both accounts. We bounced them around the world, and they landed into my Katie account. From there, generous amounts of money were scheduled to land in Dion, Alex, Freya, and Raine's accounts in the fall, with the explanation of reparations. The rest of the funds would go to a charitable organization yet to be determined.

Giving money wasn't really an adequate way to make up for the abuse, but it was all there was for now. These transactions would also be bounced around the world and even be exchanged in and out of crypto currencies. Of course, the manager would have no memories for our time together. Next stop was the bank's security office to replace any video coverage of me in the bank. The whole visit took less than an hour.

Next, at the ticket office, every office personnel's mind was searched to find a name of someone who knew Bur$t's manager. They had to make outside inquiries to finally disclose the band managers private contact information. A message was sent that a rich fan would like to have the hotel information of the band when they performed in Redding, so that she could send them some very select whiskey. Specifically, the label that we had drank on the yacht. The manager apologized that he couldn't give out the information, but he gave us the tour manager's contact information for when the band would be in town. The tour manager would send me a message when the band checked in.

Caly had decided to stay off the beach for the day. After Freya had her try on some designs, Caly helped Alex in the garden and kitchen. We played board games in the evening. It was encouraging to find that she hadn't run back to Brent.

BUR$T

THE REST OF the week went by slowly. We did surf in the mornings but stayed away from the guys. Whenever Brent or Tifton tried to come near, we went indoors. At first, they were simply curious why we were avoiding them, but by Friday, they were just angry. Both of them kept getting in our way on the waves and producing waterspouts in our path. Finally, Tifton even knocked me off my board by ramming me with his. I tumbled and hit the water hard. A moment later, the surfboard hit me right on my temple, and my vision went a little blurry. Swallowing salt water, it took a while to get on my feet. My stomach hurled the salty water right in front of the Horton crowd.

"Not much of a surfer," Sharlyn mocked.

"She just caught the wave wrong," Brooklyn said, each word dripping like syrup.

Crawling out of the water on my hands and knees, dry heaving every few feet, Brooklyn and Sharlyn started talking about what they were going to wear for the concert tonight. My pain was no longer interesting. The conversation hit its intended target. Caly was getting upset. Everyone that hung out on the beach had purchased their tickets months ago, except us. Caly helped me stand and we went back to the house.

"I can't believe how jealous I am that they are all going to Bur$t," Caly confessed.

"If all goes right today, you'll have something better but don't ask. It's a surprise."

After a shower and a change of clothes, Dion let me know he was on standby to drive me this afternoon, and hopefully, we would need him to drive us tonight. The moment the alert came in, I contacted the tour manager to arrange a meeting, letting him know he should expect something nice for the band. I didn't have anything for them, but then nothing was needed.

Dion dropped me off out front, and even before we were introduced, I froze the manager.

"What tickets, pass, and merchandise do you have available?" I asked. Not surprisingly, he had a stash that he used to get girls. He transferred four tickets with passes to meet the band before the concert to my communication device. From his bag, he gave me two band hoodies and two

T-shirts. The four tickets were for me, Caly, Freya, and Raine. Later, he would surely be puzzled about who got the tickets and gear.

"Hey everyone, I snagged four Bur$t concert tickets for tonight." I announced, walking into the living room.

Caly ran up to me shrieking. "How did you get them? They've been sold out for months."

"We won the radio contest. Dion just took me down to collect the prize." I held up the bag with the hoodies and T-shirts. Caly grabbed it and dumped it on the sofa. "There are four tickets, plus we get to meet the band."

Caly squealed with excitement, "Who gets the tickets?" Caly's eyes were wide with anticipation.

"Well, you because you're their biggest fan." She jumped up and hugged me. "I was thinking Freya, Raine and me for the other three." I surveyed the room watching for reactions.

"I'm not going." Raine said quickly. "I have plans."

"I'll go." Alex offered, surprising the rest of us.

"Dion, you can have my ticket." I offered.

"It's not really my scene. I'm fine with just driving. I'll listen to my music while I wait."

The band meet-and-greet was in a huge wine cellar at the hotel, where I met with the tour manager. Wine bottles in wooden wine racks lined the walls with locked glass doors protecting the most expensive wines. The center of the room was cleared, and the band members sat behind narrow folding tables in front of the glass doors.

We went through a receiving line to get our shirts autographed. Each band member signed over their own image. Caly was excited and the happiest I'd ever seen her, except maybe when she found out her mom didn't have to work for the Hortons. Caly talked me into wearing the T-shirt for the autographs. When Andy, the lead guitarist, standing second to last, groped Caly while signing her shirt, I was appalled, but Caly played into what she thought was fun. The last member was the lead singer, Bjorn, and I'd been watching him hand out his photo to fans he liked. He gave one to Caly, and she shocked everyone around by throwing it in the air and saying, "I don't want *your* photograph, but if Andy has one, I'll take that!" I grabbed the photo as it fluttered to the ground, and I smiled at Bjorn apologetically.

While placing the photo on top of the stack, Bjorn clasped my wrist, pulling me close to him. He leaned over and kissed my cheek, saying, "You can keep that, sweetheart." In that second, I could see how pissed he was at Caly; he wanted to revoke her ticket and pass. He then signed my T-shirt.

Andy stepped out behind the tables to catch up with Caly. "Here, this will get you up close to my side of the stage," he said, putting a sticker on Caly's and then my pass that we had hanging down from lanyards.

When he went to kiss her, Alex pulled him back, "Hey buddy, she's fourteen years old." Andy shrugged and headed back to where the line was backed up waiting for him.

Freya and Alex held the hoodies, it was too hot to wear them. They were just getting them signed for us. When they got through the line, we went outside to find Dion and the car.

Caly talked nonstop on the way to the stadium. She was so impressed with Andy. I honestly couldn't see the appeal. None of them seemed physically handsome, but they weren't ugly. Their confidence made them attractive. Andy was now Caly's favorite member. His groping eliminated any chance of being in my good favor.

All the members had touched me enough that I was able to get into their minds. The wisps of thoughts I did pick up only reaffirmed they weren't concerned with the rest of us. Andy and Bjorn were forever clashing over who was the most popular with the fans. Most thoughts were somewhat normal, about money, sex, friends, and family, though most were larger than anyone else's life. But their egos were HUGE when they were together as a band and on tour. They felt so entitled to everything, and they argued about everything that took away from their own special status.

They had fought about who got to be in the center of the band photo enough to stop speaking to one another. The fight about who got credit for writing the latest song nearly broke up the band. They were all from Senaland and none of them had much magic. Though I couldn't help but think magic had a hand in their fame.

The stadium had fifty thousand seats and the concert had sold out in five minutes of being released for sale. At the concert, Alex and Freya had assigned seats, but Caly and I were in the mash right in front on the left side of the stage. We sang, cheered, and clapped from the beginning of the opening band to the last encore of Bur$t.

During one of Caly's favorite riffs, Andy winked in our direction, and Caly nearly fainted. It was easy to see why these band members were referred to as rock gods. The moment the emcee announced them, the stadium became an ocean of cheers. Girls on top of boyfriend's shoulders took their tops off to show their boobs. Several people shouted that they loved them. Panties were thrown on stage. The crowd went wild at everything. This was why their egos were so huge. At times it was hard to hear the band because all the fans were singing so loud. Even when the lead singer wiped sweat from his brow and flung it at the fans, they cheered. YUCK. At the end, they came out and did two encore songs. It took a while for people to start leaving. As the crowd thinned, I did see the beach gang, but they didn't see us.

"That crowd was so wild, I feel like I've been trampled by a herd of stampeding horses," I said on the ride home, and Caly agreed. My white canvas shoes were now gray from so many people stepping on my feet.

"Still, that was the best day of my life," Caly sighed.

"So far," I corrected. She laughed when I winked at her, trying to imitate Andy.

Without even washing the T-shirts, we wore them over our swimsuits the next day and walked the beach end to end a couple times. It was the weekend crowd, and several people stopped us to ask about the shirts. You could not buy these at the concert, and they did have autographs of the whole band. Several times we were offered obscene amounts of money for them. Not one member of the Horton crowd approached, but I could see they were curious and jealous.

During a volleyball match, Aaron strolled over and asked, "Why did you start avoiding Brent and Tifton?"

"Umm maybe because they were having sex with other people," Caly said, and she lifted her sunglasses to give him an eye roll.

"What makes you think they're having sex with other people?" he asked.

"Used condoms and then them bragging about it," Caly answered.

"Well, that isn't cool," Aaron said, staring at the ocean. "That doesn't mean you should freeze us all out," he said, looking at Caly with puppy-dog eyes.

"Aaron, get over here, you're up," Brent called, indicating he didn't like Aaron talking with us. It wasn't Aaron's turn. Brent had just decided to take a break.

With a sigh, Aaron trotted back over to the game. We watched as Brent asked Aaron what we were talking about. Brent looked over at Caly in sort of an apologetic way. I'm sure only because he was caught, but I could feel some of Caly's distaste melting. In her mind, seeing Brent pull Aaron away from us meant he had feelings for her. It was probably true, but it didn't make up for the lying and cheating.

Caly was using her Bur$t T-shirt for a swimsuit cover-up nearly every day. Freya had made us each a few more suits. These were even better than the first ones. She had more time to work on them. Coming in from the ocean, dragging our float chairs, we noticed our gear was rumpled. When we went to straighten the towels, we saw someone had shredded Caly's band shirt into pieces.

"Oh my God, who would be such a bitter bitch," I said, loud enough for Sharlyn and Brooklyn to hear.

Caly was so upset, she alternated between dry heaving and sobbing. Her eyes and nose were running from the flow of tears.

"You can have mine, I'm not that big of a fan," I said, trying to comfort her.

"It's not the same," she hissed between sobs.

Of course, Brooklyn and Sharlyn were smirking. Sharlyn mouthed, "Oopsie" and then covered her mouth with a hand.

Caly was going to rip into Sharlyn. With all of Sharlyn's red power, everyone knew who would win that match. Physically restraining her, I pulled her toward our towels, and finally convinced Caly to go inside with me. We gathered our stuff, but she clutched the torn shirt to her chest. She held onto it for the rest of the day, even taking it to bed with her. The following morning, she had thrown it in the trash can. Scooping up the pieces seemed hopeless, but Freya would know if anything could be done to fix this.

That day, Caly, Raine, Alex, and Dion went to check out some house rentals while Freya and I stayed home.

From the T-shirt pieces, Freya salvaged all the names, photos, and graphics by using some backing and ironing them together seamlessly. She then used fabric ink to fill in any missing parts. She said she got the idea from a canvas restoration class she had in college. She then made a lightweight, white robe and we tie-dyed it with bright yellow. After it was set and dried, she sewed what used to be the front of the T-shirt on the back of the robe. She sewed the guitar and Bur$t logos on the front pockets. It was so awesome. Freya created amazing things. My band T-shirt would be going to Caly. We wrapped the robe and T-shirt in gift wrapping paper and placed it on her bed. We then swam in the infinity pool and sunbathed.

Shortly after they got home, Caly came shrieking out of the house with a garment in each hand. She hugged both of us between her excited bounces. It felt good to see how happy the gifts made her. It was totally worth the effort. The next day, we walked past Brooklyn and Sharlyn, this time we were the ones smirking, and I even blew them a kiss and then smacked my butt.

Since we really were not wanting to hang out with the Hortons and their friends, we decided to befriend the younger crowd to have some social interaction on the beach. Our closest neighbors were the Kims, an elderly couple. Mrs. Kim was on the Nokuland Council, and I was beginning to see that most everyone that owned a house on the beach was connected to the high council, except maybe Nana.

"Where is your court-ordered bracelet?" Mrs. Kim asked me.

I walked over to her and let her feel my wrist, "It's here, just invisible."

She gave me a small curt nod and went back to her reading. It was strange that she remembered I was supposed to be wearing a bracelet, but she didn't connect me being the teenager that stole Annette's yellow magic. Without having had training, my magic was a bit sloppy at times.

Two of the Kims' grandkids stayed with them for the entire summer. The older was a thirteen-year-old boy named Jae, and the other was Gi, an eleven-year-old girl.

They could only play on the beach if an adult was watching nearby, and they helped watch their younger cousins when they visited. They were not allowed to surf yet, but they did have body boards. Nana's surf shed had a few, so I asked Jae to teach me. Caly decided to join in the fun. We leashed them to our wrists instead of our ankles and we used fins on our feet. When the water was calm, we put masks on and snorkeled under the surface.

"Do you girls want to join us for supper," Mr. Kim asked, he looked ready to go SCUBA diving.

When he saw my questioning look, he said, "I'm going out to grab lobster for supper and was wondering how many I should catch."

"Oh, we'd love to join you," I said with a smile.

"How many should I catch?" he asked.

"How many can I invite?"

"Everyone, if you want."

"If you can wait one moment, I'll go find out," I called over my shoulder as I ran to get Alex.

Alex came out and met Mr. Kim. They agreed if Mr. Kim caught the lobster, Alex would cook the meal. Alex made an excellent lobster boil. He had added potatoes and corn on the cob with wonderful seasonings. We scrubbed down a picnic table and covered it with parchment paper form the kitchen. When the boil was ready, Alex drained the water and dumped all the food right onto the paper-lined table. Mrs. Kim added a bowl of fresh kimchi, which I had never seen before.

"Oh, we used to do this with crab and shrimp," Jae said, when he saw the food just scattered. I had never seen anything like it. "Oh, yum. Grandma made fresh kimchi. You have to try this," he said, using his chopsticks to put a small mound on my plate.

At first bite, I fanned my mouth and reached for my water. "Oh, that is hot."

"But good, right?"

I just nodded, afraid to open my mouth.

For the rest of the summer, Mr. Kim and Alex took turns hosting dinner on Sunday evenings. Mr. Levitt would join us as well.

One day, Caly and I followed Mr. Kim, Jae, and Gi up the trail to the top of the cliffs. It was only a twenty-minute walk. They were in water shoes and swimsuits, no towels or water bottles. At the top, they shocked us by just diving off the cliff. I ran over to look down. All three had surfaced and were laughing. Down there, under the water, is where Mr. Kim had caught the lobsters. He would poke a stick into holes in the cliff and out would come the lobster that he grabbed with gloved hands. If they were of legal size, they went into his netted bag. I didn't realize they used this same area to cliff dive. Caly and I took the path back down.

Later, when all of us were back, Mr. Kim asked us if we wanted to learn how to dive. Caly and I said, "No way."

Gi knew how to make realistic sand sculptures, and she gave us all lessons and every day we had competitions. Gi always won, and if the younger grandkids were visiting, they got to knock them down. We flew kites, played catch with Frisbees, and made huge soap bubbles. Sometimes we just played board games on the patio.

Mr. Kim took us out fishing several times, Caly never joined us. We had fresh fish regularly for the rest of the summer. Dion would even fish off the docks. When the Kims took us out on Jet Skis, Caly was always with us. She liked the speed and almost never let anyone else drive. Gi rode with her, and I rode with Jae. If the younger grandkids were visiting, we usually didn't get to go.

It was fun hanging out with the younger kids, but Caly started spending the evenings around the fire pit. She was sitting with Brent again. Jae was finally comfortable enough with me to ask about my parents. Not wanting to tell him they were murdered, I said, "I lost them when I was young."

"Dang! I thought divorce was tough." He was sad for me not having either parent alive.

Wanting to lighten the mood, I quoted Oscar Wilde, "To lose one parent may be regarded as a misfortune; to lose both looks like carelessness." Just as Jae laughed, Tifton strolled nearby to pick up a wayward Frisbee.

Tifton's face had such an ugly sneer, "I guess you're not up to handling more than a boy."

We just gave him a blank stare until he was headed back, then we looked at each other. "Can you believe I used to think he was hot?" I asked.

"I still do," Jae said wiggling his eyebrows.

"Pretty sure he's into females," I said, trying to cushion his blow of disappointment.

"Well, I'm pretty sure he let me release his sexual tension last summer," Jae said, his facial expression and voice clearly mocking me for thinking I was the expert on Tifton's sexual preferences.

"Seriously?" I asked with shock.

"Yep, then he raped me, called me a faggot and ever since, pretends I don't exist," Jae said, in a sad sing-song tone.

"Dang, he is such an asshole, and that's criminal."

"Yep, and I'd probably let him do it again."

My head rolled back like he'd slapped me. "Jae, you need to have more respect for yourself," I chided.

"The heart wants what the heart wants," he said, as he gave a sad one shoulder shrug.

I gave him a one-armed hug and sifted through his mind trying to find someone else for him to be crushing on. If there was any way to help him get past this with yellow magic, I wouldn't hesitate to use it. This elite beach life was in drastic contrast to the simplicity of the ranch. Some people here were so abusive and foul, it made me appreciate Nana even more for sheltering me from this side of life.

"Do you want to sleep out under the stars with me tonight," I asked.

"Sure."

"Cool, if you have a sleeping bag, bring it, otherwise, I'm sure we can find some blankets."

Sleeping under the stars started back on the ranch. Nana would check the weather forecasts, and any night when the temperature didn't fall below seventy degrees, we slept outside. On the ranch, we used netted tents to limit bugs and crawly things. With no city lights nearby, the sky was luminous. You could see thousands more stars there. Even though the sky wasn't as bright here, it was still an enjoyable tradition.

Sleeping in the pool cabana a couple nights a week with the canvas top open grounded me. It would easily accommodate the two of us. When I told Freya, she started to protest, but Alex assured her there was nothing to worry about.

It turned out that Mrs. Kim would only allow Jae to sleep outside if it was on her patio. They just had lounge chairs and no cabana. Apparently, she had protective wards on her house that extended to the patio. Gi joined us. When the sky was dark enough, we talked about the major stars and constellations. At first, the brightest light was a planet near the horizon. Gi was the most interested, but she fell asleep before we did. Sometime during the night, Jae had moved his chair right next to mine and I woke up with him spooned to my back. It felt right.

MIDSUMMER PROPOSITION

AS MIDSUMMER APPROACHED, the beach had small amounts of fireworks going off most every night. Here, by the ocean, the holiday was celebrated on the water, especially if you were rich. Everyone wanted to be on a yacht for the fireworks show out at some island. We could hear Sharlyn talking loudly, confirming which of her friends would be on their ship. Both Sharlyn and Tifton could each invite three friends.

"We should hang out near the dock tomorrow morning at sunrise," Caly told me.

"Why?" I asked.

"Just in case one of their friends can't make it, then maybe we would be asked to go."

"Don't hold your breath." I couldn't believe she thought that was a possibility.

"Even if we don't get asked, it is interesting to watch. All the passengers will be the elite crowd. They are always fun to watch. It's like having front row seats to the latest fashion show."

Our conversation was overheard by one of the Hortons' next-door neighbors, Maxwell. His long, lean body was stretched out, sunbathing on a lounge chair. He was about twenty-five. I'd never seen him in the water, yet he still looked the part of a beach bum surfer. He was attractive, but his age, superiority complex, and total lack of empathy only marked him as someone for me to avoid. He was one of the main drug suppliers for the beach. His crowd never paid us any attention, so I was surprised when he spoke.

"We have space on my parent's ship, but I would really want you to ride on my yacht," he offered. He lifted his expensive sunglasses to the top of his head and raised his eyebrows at me, checking to see if I understood.

Caly clearly wanted to accept, I wasn't sure if she caught his double meaning, so I said, "I'm pretty sure we wouldn't be allowed."

"Why's that?" he asked.

"Umm, because you're like ten years older than us," I sassed. "And besides, we don't know you or your family." *And you're a perverted druggie*, I added to myself.

He looked me over real slow from head to toe and back up. "You're the virgin Tifton wants to bang, aren't you." It was more of a statement than a question. His eyes suggested he was high. I turned my back to him. "A girl's first time should be special; with someone that knows what they're doing, you could definitely do worse than me."

He was using a mild form of orange magic on me, it didn't freeze me, but it was making me really want to touch him. We hadn't touched before, so this shouldn't be happening. I looked over my shoulder to see him smile as if he heard what I was thinking. His face looked predatory, like a cat playing with a mouse whose tail was already under his paw. I didn't put up a hard block, curious what he was doing. He wanted me to be curious and tempted by him. I was, even though I hadn't been until right now. He was using a trick of some sort for me to even be considering this. His magic continued pulling on mine to bring me closer to him. He laid back down and the pull became stronger. Taking advantage of the pull to crawl the short distance over to him seemed natural. My hand reached out to touch his arm. His eyes popped open when I blasted him with my orange.

Max had some yellow but not enough to get into my mind without touching me. I poked around and found a familiar vibe. It was similar to Annette's but not her magic. It felt like mine but also different. It had to be a relative. My guess was that she had gotten someone biologically close to both of us to put this lure out to catch me. It was scary to wonder how many other guys on the beach would have the magic planted in them. The spell probably laid dormant until an opportunity arrived. But why would she care if I slept with this guy. Max's brain answered. "She just wants me to get you alone, where she can trap you, but having a sweet morsel to myself first makes me a willing man."

One of Max's groupies grabbed my arm and pulled me away from him. She was beautiful. Her skin was caramel color, but she bleached her curly, short hair white. When she touched me, I turned to realize that she was the girl in Tifton's head. She was the one he slept with on the yacht, and it wasn't the only time. I asked her brain, "Why are you sleeping with Tifton?"

"I'm part of the deal when Brent buys drugs, they all get a turn at me," she answered with her thoughts. My eyes widened when I realized that Max was pimping her out. I reached into her brain to release her from this terrible situation but was shocked to find out that she wanted to do it. Her hunger for drugs was stronger than her self-respect. Being one of Max's girls meant she was around the upper class, and this was the only way she was allowed to be part of the group.

Sometimes, when you have power, you have a social obligation to help someone make the correct choice. Following her thoughts on drugs, the magic teased out the chains that kept her bound in addiction. Freezing and pulverizing the strands of her addictive cravings left tiny particles. They were channeled to her stomach. All the current drugs in her system were also sent to her stomach. Extra effort was spent on sealing off her cravings to forget reality. It wasn't my decision to make, but I justified it to myself by saying it was for her own good. When the process was finished, she started throwing up, right on Max's legs.

Backing away from Max, I said, "You could definitely be fined for that." Referring to his proposition to take my virginity. "Does the term statutory mean anything to you?"

"Ah, suck my Moby Dick and call me Ishmael, you little tease," he spat the insult at me. He was furious about being puked on. He thought me ignorant for turning down such a great offer, and he was mad at himself for stooping so low as to proposition a slaveborn nobody. Now, it was one hundred percent clear that he wouldn't have even talked to me without the implanted magic.

With a huff, I gathered my stuff and moved further down the beach, Caly followed reluctantly.

"We could have been on a yacht tomorrow, why did you turn him down?" she whined.

"You're fine with me losing my virginity to that guy so you can be on a yacht for midsummer?" I asked, upset.

"You could've just pretended you're going to give it up but then changed your mind."

"God Caly, that is wrong on so many levels, and then we'd be stuck on the ocean with that cretin." There was a wide chasm between what she'd do to get her way and what I was willing to do, even for a friend.

THE PARADE

JAE AND GI were spending the midsummer holiday with their dad. Caly dragged me out with her at sunrise to watch the parade of people getting on the yachts. She was still a bit peeved at me, but she wanted my companionship more.

First aboard were the ship crew members and then the catering staff, pulling coolers and crates of food. Next came the entertainment, a few DJs, singers, bands, and even comedians. Finally, the guests, all dressed in the latest ship fashions, started boarding. Lots of nautical blue, white, and splashes of red were in their wardrobe choices. I was worried we would look pathetic for standing out there, but we weren't the only ones. Camera crews from every national and local station were set up all along the dock. It seemed like everyone from the beach who wasn't going on a yacht was standing with us to watch. Caly pointed out a few local media celebrities; I had no idea who they were.

The Hortons didn't come as a family; each was with their own set of friends. Both, Sharlyn and Tifton's groups ignored us, except Brent did look at Caly. I didn't want to know what any of them were thinking. Their friends were all so animated and excited that it did feel like we were missing out.

Max walked by with several people, and he didn't look happy. Miss bleach blond curls wasn't with them. I did pop into his head to find out why his shadow wasn't here. When he woke this morning, he wanted her to give him a blow job, just like every other morning, and then he would give her a fix in exchange. A blow for blow was what he called their arrangement. She didn't want the fix; so, she didn't give him a blow. For punishment, he left her behind. He had not kicked her out of his house, but he was angry at her. Guilt threatened to raise its ugly head. She would be missing all the fun, though from the looks of Max, it might not be all that fun to be on the same yacht as him.

Mr. and Mrs. Kim joined Justice Parks on her ship. As the Parks' guests walked by, Caly listed the famous people, many from all over the world. An A-list movie star, an athlete who was in commercials, and a preacher who was on the networks several times a day all trailed Justice Parks. It was shocking how many of her guests were famous people from the outside world.

"How can outside people be on Anaku?" I asked Caly.

"They think they are on the big island of Hawaii. They were most likely all brought out on the same private plane from Los Angeles."

"Won't their GPS tell them where they are?"

"Nope, you must have Amaku mapping to see anything here, theirs will just show they are somewhere in the Pacific Ocean. They usually think their devices are glitching. If anyone asks about it, we usually say they must be near something magnetic."

"Won't they be shocked if someone uses magic around them?"

"Nope, not many people recognize magic, and when they do, it's more often considered coincidence, their brain playing tricks, or an act of nature. If something totally obvious happens, then they must bring in someone with mind powers, but there is rarely a need. Most people with enough money to own a yacht have enough prestige and power to fix any anomalies. Sometimes I forget how sheltered you were out on Nana's ranch." That little jab about the ranch hurt because she sounded condescending.

As Annette walked by with several people, I shrunk behind Caly, the fun of this morning was sucked right out of me. She gave me a quick withering stare that made me shiver. Some of the people with her could be my relatives, but if they were anything like her, I was better off not knowing them.

When a man, woman, and a child stepped on the dock, Caly grabbed my arm and shrieked in my ear, "There she is."

"Who?" I looked to where her finger was pointing to see a girl about Gi's age walking with her parents. She had a brown ponytail pulled through a pink visor. She had on a long T-shirt, shorts, and deck shoes. Over her shoulder was a pink beach bag.

"That's Audrey, the girl Mrs. Horton wants Tifton to marry, even though the council would never approve. She's bound to be the most powerful magic holder that ever lived. The whole island is excited and scared of when her magic is activated. It shouldn't be for a year or two, but with that much magic, you'd think some of it must be spilling out. All the reporters want to be the first to announce how and when it comes out. Her scans show high scores, but some jealous people claim they aren't spectacular. I figure she'll show them all in her own time."

The world seemed to stand still for a second. This had to be my little sister, Tatiana. A chill rippled over my skin. My eyes were glued to her every move. I wanted to find and reunite with my sister, but seeing her walking among the elites had my stomach turning. Her visor put her face in shadow, so I couldn't get a good look. Not remembering what my parents looked like anymore, I wasn't sure who she resembled. As they came closer to where we were standing, I was able to use yellow to get into her head. It had to be her, otherwise that wouldn't have worked on a stranger.

Caly's shout of, "Hey Audrey!" was mixed with several others vying for her attention.

"Tatiana," I whispered in her head. Her footstep faltered, but she didn't fall. "Do you remember your sister, Sera?" She was looking around now with wide eyes. Her mom asked if everything was all right. Our eyes met, but she didn't recognize me, she kept searching near me. Her dad grabbed her hand and pulled her back in step with them. She kept turning to look our way as they headed toward the yachts.

From her thoughts, I could see she didn't remember a sister, but her mind was curious. *Where had that thought come from?* she wondered.

"She was looking at me," Caly grabbed my arm excited. "Did you see? She was looking right at me," she repeated out of giddiness. Her touch pulled me out of the focused tunnel of shock. You'd think she was talking about Andy from Bur$t. Honestly, my emotions were heightened too, but for completely different reasons.

Audrey didn't just dazzle us; she stopped us in time for a second. Everyone on or near the dock seemed to stop what they were doing to watch her. It was a spell, not her magic.

For the first time ever, my blood seemed to boil with jealousy. My feelings were still raw from Max calling me slaveborn. Jealous that Caly was so thrilled at just the thought that Audrey was looking at her. Standing right beside her, being her best friend, she'd never gotten this excited over seeing me, and my firstborn power was maxed out.

It was a struggle holding back. My magic wanted to raise up and roar. Maybe even try to blast everyone off the deck.

Inside Audrey's head, this was all very normal for her, and she even expected it. She felt entitled to the attention. Being firstborn to powerful parents made her believe people should show her extra respect. It was so strange. Without any evidence, she believes it's the truth.

It also annoyed me that she was so arrogant. That was my birthright that made her so confident. My birthright that made people pay attention to her. A part of me wanted to shout out that she was second born. Tamping down the negative feelings took effort. Being a spectacle to be gawked at or controlled wasn't a reason to be jealous. Anyway, in a couple of years or so, she and everyone else was going to be disappointed when her magic turned out to be strong but nothing extraordinary.

Tifton was on the dock near their boarding ramp. As Audrey approached, he started to ooze with charm and put on a disarming smile. His magic started curling around her. It was mostly red but had a little yellow mixed in. She lit up like a Christmas tree. Her aura glittered with excitement.

Inside Tifton's head, it was surprising to find that he had no interest in Audrey. He was only going through the motions for his mother. He was confused why his magic wasn't attracted to her magic. In contrast, he had a super-strong reaction to mine. His intense response to me and then me rejecting him, fueled clashing feelings of desire and hatred for me.

Audrey and her parents were getting on the same boat Annette had boarded, but if her parents had not been there to stop her, she would've gotten onto the Hortons' ship. Annette was covering all angles with trying to control her sister's children.

Being around her made my emotions bounce around like a ping-pong ball. Now, I wanted to protect Audrey from being magically seduced by a creep. Pulling images from Tifton's mind that showed him having sex with several different people, I sent them to Audrey's thoughts. Before she got on the yacht, she looked back and gave him a disgusted look, but his back was turned, so he didn't see it. Hopefully, those images of him stay with her forever.

Watching, I hoped to get another look, but one by one all four yachts left the dock. They went in three different directions. It wasn't just my imagination that the Hortons' ship followed the one Audrey was on. We watched until they were out of sight. It was tempting to stay by the docks until the yachts came back to get another look at my sister, but there was no way of knowing when they would be back.

It ended up being a fun day. Many of the servants that didn't have to be on one of the yachts, got to spend time relaxing. They played volleyball and surfed. In the evening, they sat around the fire, singing and roasting marshmallows. We could see the fireworks display, and even from the beach, it was spectacular. The nicest thing about the day, other than seeing my sister, wasn't having to hear snarky remarks from spoiled numbskulls.

Caly and I slept in the cabana that night. "What would you do if you had all of Audrey's power?" I asked Caly while looking at the night sky.

She got up on one elbow and looked at me. "Anything I wanted. Duh." She laid back down with a sigh.

"No, really. Haven't you ever thought about it?"

"I think more about getting a powerful match."

"And what will you do when you get one?"

Her thoughts flooded with fashion designer clothing. Being on a yacht. Riding in luxurious cars and air travel. Servants waiting on her.

"I suppose just live as an elite."

"Don't you think with all that power you should do something good?"

"Like what?"

"Maybe try to fix corruption! That doesn't appeal to you?" With everything that happened to her and her mom in the Horton house, I really thought she'd be more determined to make a difference.

"We have courts for that. Why are you asking? What would *you* do with all that power?"

"I'd probably want to help people."

"Well good for you and good luck with that." She rolled over signaling our conversation was finished. Her thoughts turned to Audrey, and my interest piqued. It was strange to see hatred and jealousy toward Audrey just hours after paying homage. Caly was thinking she deserved the attention. She was prettier than Audrey. It was so whacky to be excited for someone to notice you and hold such negative feelings about that person too. Caly had a chip on her shoulder for Sharlyn and the other elite offspring. She would blow a fuse if she ever realized how I deceived her.

We slept through the elites' return to the beach. All four ships were back on the dock at sunrise.

The following night, while on the patio, listening in on the bonfire crowd, the subject of Mr. Horton's upcoming trial came up.

Sharlyn and Tifton were quite bitter about the young witch who had gotten their dad into trouble. They were not referring to Annette, but they knew the fiend was connected to her somehow. From their thoughts, Tifton and Sharlyn had overheard their dad order Annette to "kill the little bitch." Since Annette no longer had any magic, he told her to get a pistol. They hadn't pieced together that I was the one Mr. Horton wanted dead. Apparently, he had seen me run off the dock and that is why he went to check on the yacht. He wanted to find out what I was doing here at the beach. Brent was clueless and said he didn't know about a girl running on the dock. Mr. Horton thought he must have imagined the girl was me.

The crazy thing about the pistol was they were illegal in Nokuland. Very few permits were allowed, mostly just used for putting down dangerous animals. To get a pistol without magic would probably cost more than the hex that killed my parents. It terrified me that two people wanted me dead, and both lived on this beach. Bullets were hard to stop with just magic. Spending most of my time near Nana's and the Kims' house seemed like the best plan.

Inside, everyone was talking about the trial as well. Being former victims of the Hortons, they had each received summons. The prosecutor wasn't sure if their testimony was needed but wanted them there just in case.

They were discussing what outfits to wear. Freya was able to use her thrift card and the bolts of fabric from the

Frisbee contest to make Raine, Caly, herself, and me dress jackets. Dion had bought suits for Alex and himself at second-hand stores with some money made from driving. Freya had already updated their suits. Everyone would have business attire for court.

"Why do I need court clothes?" I asked Freya.

"You have been summonsed as well."

Dang, I really would've liked to sit this one out. It wouldn't take Sharlyn and Tifton long to figure out that I was the young witch that derailed their dad's prestigious career, and then four people living on this beach would want me dead.

ANOTHER TRIAL

WE WERE AT the courthouse by eight-thirty, and the line was already long for the nine o'clock trial. Because we had summons, we could enter through the side. Dion had dropped us off and went to park the car. When we got into the courtroom, most of the seating was already filled. We asked several people to move so we could all sit together on one bench.

We all placed our purses between us so we would have enough room to scoot together when Dion joined us. He was barely able to squeeze in to sit down. Raine had her arm around Caly, Freya's arm was around me, and Alex's arm was around Dion so we could sit more comfortably. Extra cameras were set up near the front for online viewing and for broadcasting the trial. Everyone wanted to watch what happened to the most powerful man in all of Nokuland. There was so much excitement in the air that the courtroom felt alive.

Annette, Mrs. Horton, Sharlyn, and Tifton were all in the front row behind Mr. Horton and his attorney. They were sitting quietly, looking straight ahead. At one point, Mrs. Horton stood up and walked out, probably to check her makeup in the bathroom. I watched as she walked to the side door. She was so pale, petite, and thin, she looked like a skeleton with a big bobble head, huge boobs, and a wig. It seemed odd to me what the elite considered fashionable.

Entering the courthouse sparked my nerves. Anything that limited magic was something to be feared. We'd be in a crowd of uncomfortable people. As with everything magical, I was forever testing and experimenting. Everyone was tense, so it was natural to want to send out magic to comfort them. Since sending any warmth or reassurance was blocked, I tested sending Annette's red magic to all five of my group, and it worked. Wow, that was interesting. This court hadn't covered everything in locking out magic usage.

Giving these five an extra boost of magic felt right. Carrying around the extra magic required me to use more magic, making it necessary to burn off the extra energy. Too much extra energy, and I would get jitters. If I didn't use the magic at the jittery point or eat a leaf to release magical tension, it started spilling out uncontrollably. Wanting to keep my abilities secret, less was better.

Giving away the extra would make my life less stressful. The ability to take and give magic let me suspect that spirit gifts weren't blocked. Annette only getting a bracelet instead of her magic removed made sense. They didn't know how and probably couldn't remove the magic. *Was I the only person who could?* I wondered.

Scanning the room with blue magic worked. No health issues stood out. Using group mode to listen to everyone's thoughts and see auras was available, but within only a few moments, a headache made it unbearable. Copying wasn't blocked. In the time we waited for the trial to start, I copied Alex's chef training, Raine's hairstyling, Freya's fashion education, and Dion's driving skills. The information transferred, but the creativity was elusive.

Born of an atypical lineage with copious amounts of extraordinary magic was daunting enough. In addition, the marvel of my spirit gifts, especially from touching that elder, channeled me into a vessel of power unknown to this time. So much power and most of it was used to keep me safe from detection.

Glenn was the closest thing to a magic trainer I'd come across. Not spending the summer with him on Nana's ranch was most likely a mistake.

My understanding as to why my mom had wanted to keep me a secret was growing. I must have received most of this from her family. Even Annette, being second born, had more powerful magic than any of the council members. Twins carried the same concentrations of magic, so the Teufel's lucked out getting to keep Annette. It seemed a strong mentalist raised by a strong witch was extremely powerful and fertile breeding grounds for corruption.

The trial started the same as mine had, we all stood for the justices to enter. I saw Mrs. Kim come in with the rest. All nine seats were filled, and now Ms. Parks was in the center chair. The auditors were not the same ones from my trial. From the side of the room, the court recorder read the charges of abuse of power, noting several subcategory infractions. Next, the prosecutor asked questions, and Mr. Horton was compelled to answer truthfully. He blamed everything on Annette's manipulations, he must have believed it to be true or he could not have spoken the accusations.

Annette testified to what magic manipulations she used on Mr. Horton. Her testimony blamed the greed of her victims. "Without their greed, none of this would've been possible."

My thoughts were on whether or not she'd gotten her hands on a gun. I couldn't even look straight at her without trembling.

"Does anyone here in the courtroom have anything to add to the record?" Ms. Parks asked the summoned spectators.

One brave young woman stood up and told her story. Currently, she was a household servant. Mr. Horton had sexually molested her numerous times. The courtroom made a collective gasp at the harsh and humiliating details.

The prosecutor waited for the room to quiet down and then he asked Mr. Horton to confess any molestation and torture he had perpetrated, and not just on the household staff.

Mr. Horton's testimony went on for over an hour. He had sexually assaulted and tortured nearly everyone he had encountered, men and women, and even his own children. It was horrifying to know that everyone I came here with was one of his victims. Freya, Caly, Raine, Alex, and Dion all had tears in their eyes. My eyes were leaking in empathy at the horror.

At the front of the room, Sharlyn and Tifton had their faces buried in their hands. My head couldn't stop its shaking from side to side in disbelief. Mr. Horton must have used magic to smudge their memories because I'd never seen any of the abuse in any of their minds.

When court adjourned for the justices to decide the sentence, I slipped out of the courtroom to visit the basement room where Glenn had attached the bracelet to block my yellow magic. The technician seemed surprised to see me. Due to the building's magical blocks, no ordinary magic would work on him, so I reached for both dark stones and blasted the orange freeze at him; and it didn't work, but he responded to a verbal spell. The bug-crawling sensations started immediately. Dang! I should have brought some leaves. I instructed him not to be alarmed when I entered the room again and to forget I was here before returning to join the others.

Mr. Horton's sentence, like Annette's, included having his magic completely blocked. He was to be hospitalized to undergo brain treatments for the sexual assaults. Hopefully it wasn't laser treatment from the hospital equipment that got damaged. Most of his assets were now frozen and were to be sold to create a fund to assist the victims. It was named the Organization to Help the Victims of Magical Abuse, and it would arrange counseling for all as well as relocation support. The remaining balance of Annette's and Mr. Horton's joint account funds would be anonymously donated to that organization.

As soon as they read that his magic was to be removed, I headed for the basement. My commotion of getting out of the packed row caused Sharlyn and several others to glare at me. Annette stood up as well. This was my only chance to get close to Mr. Horton, and I wanted to ensure his magic was truly removed, not just blocked. Even though using more dark magic would increase the sensation of creepy bugs crawling all over me.

Dodging camera detection was mostly keeping my face toward the ground and following larger people downstairs. There was a small dark hallway near the bracelet room that was empty. This would be a perfect place to wait. I had only been there a few seconds when I felt something poke me in the back.

"Walk backward slowly and move to the open door," Annette said calmly.

Not wanting to make it easy for her to kill me meant cooperating but avoiding going into the room at all costs. Looking over my shoulder, the door she was talking about was visible. I also wanted to see what hand she used to hold the gun.

Slowly stepping back, she moved with me. Before entering the room, using one of the Krav Maga moves copied from Gideon, I spun around with my arms spread out from my body and knocked the gun away from my back. Pain flashed through me when a bullet grazed my side. I felt more than heard the gun go off. It had a silencer attached. Continuing with the spin, I used one elbow to lock her gun arm against my side and my other elbow to strike her in the face. My knee thrust hard into her stomach. Reaching around, I grabbed the gun from her loosened grip.

Even while I was grappling with her, my magic was hungry and started copying from her. It was frantic and reached for anything close to the surface. It found and copied how to condense magic.

Still bent over, she pulled her arm from my grip. I didn't see a need to hold on to her since I had the gun. She turned and ran, shouting, "She has a gun." Oh great, now I was holding the illegal firearm, and guards would be on their way. Flipping the safety on and wiping down the weapon with my soft undershirt, I tossed it through the open door. After quickly closing the door, I hurriedly went to the bracelet room.

Thankfully, Mr. Horton was there. I used the dark stones and started pulling his magic. From his expression, he could tell what was going on, but since they had him restrained in a chair, he could not do anything about it. He was furious. Every electric molecule of his power was out. This time I didn't draw it into me. It was giving off heat just from being condensed and contained in my hands. My magic was searching and found his skill for making a protective shield. It was much more complex than the one Glenn taught me, so I copied it.

Thundering footsteps on the stairs told me the courthouse was emptying in a hurry. Several were rushing into the basement. These were the guards Annette called to catch me with the gun.

Leaving Mr. Horton with the knowledge of what I'd done wasn't an option. Using the stones again, I blasted mind freeze at him, enough to probably wipe out his entire day. Dang! Nothing happened. Shoving the now golf ball-sized wad of Mr. Horton's magic into my pocket, I hurried to the security office. Footage of me being downstairs needed to be replaced but with the guards near, I decided to do it remotely through my account.

Rushing outside was easier than it should've been due to all the chaos and confusion. On my way to the car, I finished condensing Mr. Horton's magic. It ended up being about the size of an aspirin, and I returned it to my suit pocket.

Everyone was already waiting in the car for me. Alex stepped out of the front passenger seat and let me into my place between him and Dion. Thankfully, this old sedan could hold the six of us.

Still jittery from the dark magic, my hands felt covered in goo.

"Where'd you go?" Raine asked, apparently irritated at having to wait.

"My stomach was so upset at what I heard in court today, I needed to throw up. You all are so strong to take this in stride."

They all started talking about their experiences. It seemed to be healing them to talk about it. It was nice to see that they would be strong enough to carry on. There was a lot of congestion with several vehicles trying to leave the parking lots at the same time. Sitting back, I stared out the window, trying to ignore the unpleasant sensations buzzing around in my body. I wondered how Annette was able to tolerate this when she had megatons more forbidden magic.

Almost as if thinking about her made her materialize. A guard was giving her a small bundle about the size of the gun. They were standing on the lawn near the courthouse. My magic should've demolished that gun when I was fighting with her, instead of copying her skill. *Note to self: fix your priorities.* When the guards found the weapon, they should've retained it. Just my luck that one of her mind-altered minions had to be the one to find it.

When we arrived back at the house, we could see a crowd of protesters gathering outside the Hortons' mansion. Scanning their house with yellow showed the family wasn't home, at least not Sharlyn, Tifton, or Mr. Horton. I hadn't met Mrs. Horton yet and definitely hadn't touched her.

We went in the house and changed out of our dress clothes. I kept Mr. Horton's magic with me and went back out to the garden to get some leaves off one of my plants. It took chewing three before they worked. There had to be ways to handle the sludge without puking. YUCK. Though it was so nice to have the goo and the feeling of crawling bugs gone.

Listening to the crowd, it seemed most everyone here had suffered from Mr. Horton's actions or was here to avenge the abuse of a family member. There was no crowd control on location. People were trampling their garden, pounding on the windows, and climbing fences.

Needing to expend a lot of pent-up energy, I blasted so much orange that it froze the entire mob. Wow, that was amazing and totally terrifying at the same time.

Taking out Mr. Horton's magic, I then crumbled it into dust particles and scattered the tiny pieces into the crowd. It wouldn't make much difference in their lives, being so spread out, but they deserved the boost.

When the dust had settled, I released the freeze. The frenzy continued, windows were broken, and soon the doors were opened, and everyone rushed in. People started looting everything. Furniture, clothing, jewelry, paintings, and even stuff from the kitchen was being carried away. They even broke into the surf shack and emptied that. No one ever came to protect the property. When there was nothing more to take, the people finally left.

GRANDMOTHER

FOR THE NEXT couple of days, the beach was quiet, but by the weekend, the beach families came back to surf, play volleyball, and sit around the fire. None of the Hortons returned. No one was at their house except a guard at the front door. No one could figure out what he was protecting. Caly and I crawled in through a broken window from the beach side, just to see. It was empty, just dust and the flooring. The view from their balcony wasn't damaged. I started to hang out there to see when Annette was at home, which was most of the time. It was important to track her whereabouts. She had the gun.

Her mother brought it with her when she came to stay for a few days. Listening in was difficult at times. I could only hear Annette's thoughts, not my grandmother's. Annette wanted to borrow her mom's ability to take someone's magic just long enough to steal mine. So, I wasn't the only person in the world that could pull magic from someone.

Then she promised that once she had her magic back, she would return the ability. My grandmother was interested in meeting me, and Annette was trying to use that as a bargaining chip. From what I could gather, hearing only Annette's side of the conversation, was that the ability to steal magic wasn't something my grandmother wanted to loan to her daughter. It was too powerful. She was sure the magic would be too seductive for Annette to return it. The visit ended without Annette getting it. Whew, I didn't need another reason to fear her.

It felt strange not to have any warm feelings for my biological grandmother. She'd done a terrible job of raising Annette. She was a cog in the powerful corrupted elite machine. The only things I felt about her existence were fear and dread. Another person to avoid. There was some curiosity, but not enough to risk my life.

The Hortons' mansion and the yacht were both put up for sale. Caly was hanging out with Brent whenever he was on the beach. He visited to get drugs but stayed as Caly's guest. I wasn't comfortable with that but didn't say anything. Brent told Caly that Mrs. Horton and Tifton had moved in with her sister, and that Sharlyn was living at Brooklyn's. Brent wanted Tifton to stay at his house, but his parents wanted the story to die down before letting Tifton live with them.

One night, I asked Caly, "Did Mr. Horton take your virginity?"

"I don't think so. Mom was smart about keeping me away from him. Truly, I can't be certain, so I'm choosing to believe he didn't. In the court-ordered counseling, Mom confessed that Mr. Horton was my dad."

"WHAT? No way! Tifton and Sharlyn are your half-siblings?"

"Yep! He charmed Mom when she was just sixteen. He paid for her to attend beauty school and provided for us during that time. Then he brought Mom into his household to be Mrs. Horton's beautician. She was in love and thought he would leave his wife for her. When she had finally figured out that he would never leave his wife, she was already bound into servitude. He lost interest in her except for occasional sex, just like all the other people under his roof. Mrs. Horton made sure all her female staff was on birth control, not wanting any more bastards running around. Even Sharlyn and me have been on birth control from the time we began menstruating, so she knew she was married to a pervert."

"Oh, Caly, that is disgusting! I'm so sorry you all were subjected to his depravity. It explains why you and Sharlyn have the same blue spectrometer scores."

"Our counselor said that Mr. Horton's mother was attacking the victims on the news, saying the stories were made up. Which was super weird because he confessed to it in court. She says denial was quite common inside incestuous families. No one wants to be related to that type of creepiness. No way would she accept her precious son was a monster, even when it was one hundred percent true. By accepting the fact, she'd feel responsible for the behavior or would have to face demons from her own past."

Ever since the trial, Mrs. Kim had been extra nice to me. Before Mr. Horton's confession, she wasn't sure what to think of me. She was glad the corruption was exposed, but she wanted to give Mr. Horton the benefit of the doubt, or at least wait until he confessed his guilt. She even invited me to join her on her sunset beach walks. Sometimes, Alex, her grandkids, or Mr. Kim would join us, but many times it was just the two of us. Her aura shimmered much more than everyone else's, and my magic wanted to mingle with hers, not in a sexual way, but it was drawn to her. I had touched her in the cafe, so entering her mind was possible, but because she had so much sensitive court information, it didn't seem wise to access her thoughts, in case she had protections.

I wondered about her motives for befriending me. She could've just been curious about my talents and ancestry, but she was being protective toward me. She knew what Annette had done to her and the council. And, of course, she might remember the charges Annette brought against me. If that was the case, she was intelligent enough to know Annette would want revenge.

On these walks, I was always on the lookout for Annette. Always staying away from her house if she were anywhere near the beach. One night, so focused on watching for Annette, we walked right passed her mother standing at the shoreline looking out over the water. We'd never met, but her countenance reflected an older Annette. My magic started swirling when we passed behind her.

"Hi, Jennifer." Mrs. Kim greeted the living statue.

"Hi, Bernadette, how's everything going?" she asked, with an air of distraction. Her gaze raked me from head to toe.

"Much better than expected with all the court changes lately, those of us still on the council are hoping that another scandal doesn't drop."

"Poor Annette is at her wits end. She is furious over losing her magic."

"It was the least we could impose, many wanted her to go into confinement," Mrs. Kim mildly apologized.

"She was quite lucky, but she doesn't see it that way."

As they chatted, catching up on each other's grandchildren, Jennifer Teufel studied me. It was all so unreal. This was Annette's mom, my grandmother. She was dressed casually but was very stylish. She could've easily stepped onto one of the yachts and fit right in with the elite. She probably was on Annette's for the midsummer cruise, but I was focused on Audrey. From the top of her hair to her toes, she was finely polished. She had an air of entitlement that comes with power.

Settling my power using Glenn's technique when she glanced at me questioningly took concentration.

Mrs. Kim introduced us, "Jennifer, this is Sera Webster, our neighbor. Sera, this is Jennifer Teufel, Annette's mother." We nodded politely. I was hoping my face was neutral because my magic was wanting to explode. Her strong energy was swirling, too. She had to be feeling it. Her eyes squinted ever so slightly while she studied my flower pendant.

"So, Sera, where is your family from? What do they do?" Mrs. Teufel inquired. "I'm not familiar with any Websters."

"Ranchers in the foothills," I replied, my chin lifted a little in pride and in challenge.

She wrinkled her nose, and the nostrils flared, but just barely. No outward event led to us quietly facing off like two angry dogs, but it sure felt aggressive just talking with her. It was frustrating that my eagerness to learn about family was soiled by Annette's evil. The necklace indicated to her that we were related. Her biological granddaughter being a rancher from the foothills was unacceptable. Or maybe, my being proud of it was too much for her sensibilities.

Since she was repelled by my upbringing, I decided to let her see the complete picture. "I was raised very simple. Some people even compare our country living to the Amish, but we aren't associated with them."

"Oh, and what is the reason for you living so plain?" she asked disdainfully.

"Mostly my family wants to leave the planet unharmed." She winced a little at the word family. No way was this snob going to make me feel any shame because I came from what was considered the boondocks.

A small black and white dog came running up to me to sniff at my feet. It had extraordinarily little hair on its hindquarters and was shaggy around the head and shoulders. She was extremely well groomed.

"Here, Dotty," Mrs. Teufel said as she picked up the dog. I wanted to remind her about leash laws because she had just let Dotty do her business without caring that it needed to be cleaned up.

"What type of dog is that?" Mrs. Kim asked.

"Löwchen, it's hard to find a good breeder for them," replied Mrs. Teufel. Which was her way of accentuating that they were rare or special.

Little Dotty startled me with her sudden barking, and the hair on the back of my neck stood up. Annette came to join us, and an involuntary shiver slithered up my spine. My glance swept over her to ascertain if she was carrying a pistol.

Reading my discomfort, Mrs. Kim shifted her stance a bit to shield me from Annette, which was unnecessary because she wasn't carrying a weapon. Mrs. Teufel would be the threat if anything went down.

Seeing the movement, Mrs. Teufel asked Annette, "Is this the child you brought charges against?" She must have just wanted Annette's confirmation because I was certain she already knew.

Annette gave a curt nod. Losing the leverage of being the only one of them who knew my identity.

Mrs. Kim broke the tension by saying, "Well it's getting dark, we should start back. It was nice catching up," she addressed the elder. It was time to get back, but I didn't want to turn my back on these two women.

Grandma, fully understanding the situation, gently nudged Annette toward the house. Walking a few steps backward before turning felt right. Taking deep breaths to calm my nerves helped some. Nothing like being terrified of your blood relatives.

Mrs. Teufel started walking the beach with Dotty at sunrise every day. It seemed she decided to stay longer. This morning, when we passed close, she tugged at my magic or maybe she was searching for Annette's. On its own, my readiness shot up to DEFCON one and my shields reinforced instantly. Her eyebrows betrayed her shock. She was testing me, and my automatic response had surprised her as well as pleased her. After the encounter, I decided to break the bracelet binding my yellow power. I wasn't planning to physically break it, just adjust the setting in the database.

Before reaching our patio, Mrs. Kim came out to greet me. "Sera, do you have a moment?" she asked, motioning me to come sit on her patio.

"Sure," I answered and took a seat. She sat down opposite of me.

"The council would like you to enter into a special training program." She paused to watch for any reaction from me. When none came, she continued, "We're not as useless as our past behavior might indicate. We're quite aware of your uniqueness. There are several incredibly talented tutors for your caliber of energy." I doubted that but was curious.

"Uniqueness?" I prompted with a raised eyebrow.

"We do believe you stole magic from Annette, she couldn't have lied in the courtroom. That capability is extremely rare. With the chemistry between you and Mrs. Teufel, I would wager that you are her biological grandchild. The missing puzzle piece in the Kendler situation. We would like to have our new auditors examine you."

Reaching for her thoughts using Annette's yellow magic didn't work because she had a shield blocking me, most likely a ward or spell. I could've broken past with some force, but I didn't want to be abusive. She frowned at my effort.

"Your yellow is supposed to be locked down. When did you touch me?" She looked at me confused.

"It is, but Annette's wasn't included in the block." I ignored her second question.

Her shocked expression told me they didn't really understand me as much as they thought. I was rubbing my forehead in an unconscious effort to get my brain to produce some solutions.

"I've asked Mrs. Teufel to assist in your compliance if you decline our offer."

Looking in the direction Mrs. Kim indicated with her head tilt, I see Mrs. Teufel and the dog standing about six feet away.

"Nana made me promise to spend time at the ranch before summer's end," was all I said, my mind was frantic with panic.

"We would like to start you right away in our program, but it only seems fair to give you time to visit. We have an ankle bracelet to trace you," my grandmother explained while putting the band on the table between us.

Oh, heck no! I didn't want to wear a tracking device. It would be a link Annette could use to keep tabs on me. My data base access might be able to adjust the settings before anything terrible happened but waiting would be dangerous.

"You will need to turn in the pistol Annette has before I'll wear a bracelet," I said, looking Grandma straight in the eye. I heard Mrs. Kim gasp.

"What a horrid accusation," Mrs. Teufel said, looking indignant and amused.

Just the thought of wearing a tracking device supercharged my fear and desperation. Taking a jolt to calm my mind, I started to evaluate the situation. Knowing that some of the elite were starting to understand my potential put me in incredible danger.

Sending the strongest blast of orange I could summon, thankfully froze both of them. Reaching across the table to touch Mrs. Kim allowed me to easily get past the blocking ward. First thing to check was whose idea it was for the special training, and it wasn't from the council. It was dear ole Grandma. She had supplied the ward and the bracelet.

Next, smudging Mrs. Kim's memories of anything to do with this conversation, training me, or being audited took a minute.

Grabbing the ankle bracelet, I attached it to Mrs. Teufel, touching her for the first time. The contact knocked me back on my heels. Her personal wards and protection were strong enough to stun me for a moment. She would most likely just discard the bracelet the moment she realized it was there, but it was to make a statement.

She was much harder to smudge, but with repeated efforts, most of her thoughts about me were jumbled. She started to stir, so I sent another shot of orange at her and ran to our house, where I could watch and listen from the secrecy of our patio. Once I was safe and caught my breath, I released the freeze.

"Can I help you with something, Jennifer?" Mrs. Kim asked, sounding confused that Mrs. Teufel was on her patio.

"Sorry for the intrusion, Dotty was being nosy." The dog yipped as she picked her up and she headed back toward Annette's house. She did glance back in my direction but only for a second. *The Wizard of Oz* quote, "I'll get you my pretty," faintly reverberated in my mind.

This whole incident put one more layer of mistrust between me and other people. I could be betrayed without the person even being aware of their actions. When Mrs. Teufel was out of site, I went into the house and logged onto the council's database. After turning off the bracelet block, I felt so whole and complete with my magic's return. Then, I searched for the ankle bracelet, only to find it wasn't listed, verifying that the council had nothing to do with the tracking device. It was obvious now that Annette had learned her manipulative habits from her mother. Mrs. Kim and the other council members needed protection from people like Mrs. Teufel and Annette.

It was sad that there wasn't a special training program I could participate in, but then it was nice to not have auditors digging in my brain.

With my own magic back, I discovered that Mr. Horton's protective shield design could help block intrusions. He must have let his guard down to let Annette get so much control. Strange that this wasn't available using Annette's magic. I created a knitted invisible shield of yellow, blue, and red to surround me automatically at all times. It was perfect for providing my magic something to do while lessening the need to come up with ways to burn off the excesses that built up.

That afternoon, hanging out at the Kims' pool was entertaining. Mr. Kim was giving Jae and Gi diving lessons. They already knew how; this was just getting them closer to competition level. Their pool was made for high dives. It was at least eleven feet deep under the diving boards. Mr. Kim offered to give me lessons, too. Watching was all I would do until there was a chance to touch him.

Mrs. Kim was on a lounge watching. I moved to the seat right beside her. We made small talk for a few minutes, and then she started reading from her digital pad. It looked like court summaries. While she was reading, I entered her mind, pausing to see if she would react. With no changes on her expression, I instructed her to be completely absorbed in her reading. Then I asked some of my typical questions. What are your sins? What's your best accomplishment? What do you do exceptionally well?

She was exceptionally good at potions, hexes, curses, spells, and wards. Her mother had been good at all of them and taught Mrs. Kim from the time she was young. They both were skilled in making and breaking occult magic. Eagerly, I copied it all, not interested in doing any of the magic, but I definitely liked having the knowledge. She had been on a team that worked on the court bracelets.

One last question: "Did you have Annette make your staff indentured?"

"Absolutely not."

DEFINITION OF INSANITY

ONE LAZY MORNING, I was sitting on the large dock with my back toward the yachts and the sand at my feet. Using a twig to draw stick figures and digging in the sand with my toes was a relaxing activity to relieve some boredom.

A few nights ago, I put the yellow ring back on my thumb because no one had made any claims. Something about it calmed me and made me feel more secure.

Mrs. Kim was watching Jae and Gi flying kites from a folding chair nearby while periodically reading from her digital pad.

Light footsteps padded on the dock behind me, and Mrs. Kim looked up, tilting her head in curiosity. Before I could turn to see who it was, Mrs. Kim stood up with alarm radiating from her entire demeanor. My physical shields added extra reinforcement faster than the hair could stand up on my neck.

"LOOK OUT!" she called, as a tremendous blow landed between my shoulder blades. The force struck me so hard that I ended up on my knees with my head bouncing off the sand. Everyone was shouting and running toward the dock.

Mrs. Kim ran to my side and started checking my back. She pulsed blue through me, but my own self-healing hadn't been activated, so nothing needed healing. She tried to have me lie down, but I insisted on standing. It hurt a little to take a deep breath, but otherwise, everything was fine.

"I don't understand how you're not hurt," she said dazed.

Turning to look at the dock, I could see someone flat on their back and completely knocked out of their deck shoes. I had to see who was on the dock. Up close, I recognized it was Annette with part of her face and head gone. "No one needs to see this." I warned Mrs. Kim, who had gone back to make sure her grandkids and others knew to stay off the platform.

The gore and mess had me unfocused. There was the pistol on the dock not far from her body, and suddenly, it all made sense. She shot me. The bullet ricocheted just like the magic before, but this time it killed her.

Further down the walkway near the yachts came a horrible shriek. My grandmother was running toward us. Mrs. Kim raced back to protect me and tripped on Annette's shoes, bumping into me and sending me forward. When I put out my hands to break my fall, I landed on Annette's leg.

For the fourth time in my young life, a dead body released energy into me. Annette's voice simply howled through my mind as her spirit gift transferred to me. "NOOO!" I pushed off her and was about to stand when Jennifer pushed me so hard that I landed on my butt at Mrs. Kim's feet. I'd already touched grandma putting on the ankle bracelet, but this was the first time she knew she could get inside my mind.

"Stay away from her," she screamed. She grabbed at Annette, testing for the energy. "Did you take it?" Her eyes and voice filled with rage. Ole Grandma cared about the binding spirit gift more than she seemed concerned that her daughter was dead. Binding people's magic was an ability she wanted, but Annette's body had already released it. Locking up someone's magic without a court ordered bracelet was a part of what made Annette so dangerous. She wanted that power.

Maybe it was shock, but then maybe not. Now that she had touched me, she knew that she could get inside my mind and began sending yellow mixed with black at me in forces I had never felt before. Reinforcing my shields with everything in me was still losing the battle. The element of surprise when attacking is powerful. She wanted to kill me for the gift.

"Jennifer, stand down or I will order your arrest, and this would be a terrible time for you to be locked up," Mrs. Kim demanded from behind me. She cast strong magic to restrain her. Mrs. Teufel collapsed on the dock, putting her head on Annette's chest, and wailed. It all played out as a terrible act of suffering. It came off as phony. Mrs. Kim took pity on her and lifted the restraint.

My hand felt lighter. When looking down, I noticed the yellow diamond was gone except for a few tiny shards. It must have shattered when the bullet hit my shield. Mrs. Teufel recovered enough to come over and forcefully tear what was left of the ring off my thumb. She looked at the inside band of the ring, then glared at me. "I gave this to Annette for her thirtieth birthday to protect her. How did you get it?" She demanded, invading my thoughts at the same time. I didn't bother to answer. She could see my thoughts. So, the ring that was intended to protect Annette saved my life. Magic was connected to family, possibly stronger than blood.

Still in shock, my head was pounding, and my magic was drained or weakened because it wasn't self-soothing me. A part of me was relieved that I no longer had to worry about Annette killing me, but now Grandma was pissed.

Ticking off a mama bear with her powers was nothing to dismiss.

Several people had called for emergency help. The police force arrived first, driving right up to the dock. They secured the scene and made everyone clear the area. We were ordered to stay a good distance away.

Everyone was surprised to see a gun here in Nokuland. They all were trying to get a look, but most backed away when they saw what was left of Annette's face.

Mrs. Teufel insisted on getting her dog from the yacht. An officer escorted her to get Dotty. By the time she walked back, Annette's body was covered.

When the ambulance arrived, they didn't even try to heal Annette, it was much too late. Mrs. Kim, Jae, and Gi all stood around me for support when the officer took my statement.

Mrs. Kim gave her statement. "Annette raised the pistol and shot Sera right in the back," she told the officer questioning us.

"How is it that she's unharmed?" The officer asked puzzled.

"From what I can figure, she was wearing a protective ring that shattered from the impact and ricocheted the bullet back at Annette. Mrs. Teufel has the band."

This felt a bit like déjà vu to me, except hopefully I was now out of danger.

"Well, if she fired the bullet that killed her, this will most likely be labeled as a suicide."

"It was suicide, but it happened just the way I told you. Annette fired the pistol intending that the bullet would kill Sera. She tried something similar earlier this summer." Mrs. Kim also told them to link the investigation to that earlier attack.

This was all so insane. Me trying to correct a social injustice led to Annette and Mr. Horton wanting me dead. Exposing their horrific behavior made them want to annihilate me. It really does seem like the more powerful they are, the harder the fall, and the more vengeful they become.

IN THE CARDS

FREYA, ALEX, AND Caly came out to comfort me. They took me back to the house as soon as I was allowed to leave. I took a long shower and was going to lie down when Caly told me Mrs. Kim wanted to have a talk.

Pulling on my typical summer outfit, I then headed out to the patio to meet her, but she wasn't there.

"She's in the library," Caly told me when I stepped outside. This conversation must need some measure of privacy.

Mrs. Kim was sitting on a small sofa. She motioned for me to come sit beside her, and I did.

"How are you feeling dear," she asked, patting my knee.

"Drained."

"I'll make this short then. I won't go into all the complex laws, but due to Annette trying to kill you, you are entitled to compensation."

"I don't want anything from her," I protested.

She continued, ignoring my words, "I have petitioned the court on your behalf for the house, everything in it, the yacht, and living expenses for one hundred years. I had the officers escort Mrs. Teufel while she collected her bags. All Annette's servants are still at the house for now. I would like you to come meet them. Before you turn this down, I want you to know that her help is completely damaged from working for her. We can try to rehabilitate them, but under the court psychiatrist's advice, they should be left in the house, it's their comfort zone."

"You've already consulted a psychiatrist?" I asked astonished.

"It was an emergency. I made a mistake telling them they were free to go, and some broke down crying. They're calm now and ready to meet you."

"Shouldn't we wait until the courts have made their ruling?" I asked.

"Annette's properties and assets are massive. Most of it will be sold for reparations. This request is a tiny piece of her possessions, and it has a humanitarian angle, considering the servants. With my name on the petition, I have no doubt it will be approved."

Mrs. Kim walked with me to Annette's house. As soon as we were on the property, I could feel that Mrs. Kim had put up wards and spells.

"Are you worried for the staff's safety?" I asked.

"If I know Jennifer, she will be trying to take items from the house that she considers family heirlooms. Part of the property settlement is supposed to hurt and shame the family. So, if there are important items, she is definitely not entitled to remove them."

We found a group of eight servants eating lunch at a kitchen table that could easily seat twelve. The food smelled delicious, and my stomach rumbled.

"Sera, this is Suzy. She was Annette's personal assistant and household manager. Any questions you have, she'll be able to help you find the answers." After Mrs. Kim's introduction we shook hands.

"Can I get you anything to eat?" Suzy pointed to a side buffet.

"I can certainly fill a plate easier than instructing you." I walked over to the stack of clean empty plates. "Mrs. Kim, will you join as well?"

"No, thank you. I've got dinner waiting at home. You eat, get settled, and let me know if you have any questions. I know my way out." Mrs. Kim motioned for Suzy to get back to her meal.

With a few items on my plate that I probably wouldn't eat due to the residual emotional trauma from someone firing a bullet at me and a glass of iced tea, I joined them at the table. Suzy remained standing until I sat down.

"Let's start by having everyone introduce themselves and tell you what our typical duties are." Suzy broke the silence.

At the table were the chef, a driver, a gardener, and five all-purpose staff. The all-purpose staff was trained in several areas so that they could assist anywhere help was needed. They each had individual responsibilities. When we'd finished eating, Suzy gave me a tour.

The art pieces in this house could fill a fine art museum. That didn't mean the house was stuffy. It was bright and airy. Many of the paintings were of beach scenes and ballet dancers. There were statues of ballet dancers, as well. The library had a horse theme and leather furniture. Annette was pictured with several different racehorses, each in the winner's circle. She had bronze statues of the winners, each about a foot tall. The garage had a very luxurious limousine, a sedan, and two cars built for speed that were beyond anything I had ever seen. The driver accompanied us to the garage, and he told us that each of the sports cars would resale for over a million dollars. The gardens were immaculate.

When I was alone with Suzy in Annette's bedroom suite, I asked, "Are there any safes in the house?" I was hoping to find out more about my Teufel side of the family and nothing from the tour explained anything.

"At least two. One in the library behind a horse painting, and one here in her closet."

"Can you open them?" I asked.

"Yes, ma'am." She walked into a closet that was larger than my bedroom. Net worth of this room's contents could probably buy this mansion. There were a couple long shelves of purses. I'd seen similar ones in fashion advertisements, but some looked far more exclusive, possibly commissioned just for her. Rows and rows of clothes filled the shelves and drawers. Some of her shoes had actual precious gems on them.

Suzy easily accessed the safe. It was amazing how much control Annette had over their lives, to the point that she could entrust a staff member with safe combinations.

This safe had a stack of cards, several boxes of what looked like expensive jewelry, and a small velvet bag that had a drawstring.

"Do you know what the cards are for?" I asked, picking them up.

"They contain DNA and magical identity coding in case she wanted to order death bombs," she said so matter-of-factly that I had to close my eyes a few times to process that I'd heard correctly. "The ones with a black X are dead.

The ones with red circles around the X she tortured to death. Red circles without the X she just liked to torture."

Dividing them into four piles on a dresser in her closet, the only two with just the X were my parents. Every member of the Nokuland Council had a card, including the auditors. Many cards were for lower court judges. She had one on Dr. Gobel and Dean Harrison. She had an incomplete one for me, nothing but my name and picture. Several were unknown to me. There was so much power in having these cards. Part of me wanted them destroyed right now, and the other part didn't want me to make a hasty decision.

Returning the cards to the safe, Suzy handed me the bag. I dumped the contents into my hand and was surprised to see two miniatures of the flower of my mom's pendant. There was a ring and one earring. The ring fit on my middle finger, and it glowed for just a second the moment it touched my skin. Clipping on the earring, it responded the same as the ring. My skin was tingling from the jewelry. It was a mild humming but not unpleasant like the dark magic.

"Do you know anything about these pieces?" I asked Suzy.

"Annette received them from her mom. Her younger sister also has the same, one ring and one earring. They have been in the family for years. They once held great power, or so the story goes, but Annette didn't believe a word of it. Jennifer insisted she keep the jewelry in a safe. I believe her grandmother kept a tiara and her mother the bracelets, but I've never seen them."

"Do you know their history?" I prompted her.

"Well, it's a fable or fairy tale about a princess or a goddess, it varies depending on who tells the story."

"How would you tell the story?" I asked.

"Oh, the condensed version is something like: A long time ago the seven immortals made Amaku. To commemorate their achievement, each commissioned a set of jewelry. The set for the god of healing was blue sapphires, nature was green emeralds, and force was red rubies. A yellow diamond set for the mind, black star sapphire set for control, and white diamond for blending. The seventh immortal, the story goes, made a set from all the colors in the shape of a flower with clear andalusite for the center. She could use all powers."

She continued, "The gods still live on but only as spirits. They're very picky about merging with people. Choosing only those they deem worthy. Some say it drives people mad and most end up hermits. When they all gather again, there will be one thousand years of kindness, or so the fable predicts.

"Having all the pieces of jewelry is supposed to provide great power. Jennifer Teufel could never get any of the pieces to work, so she divided some of them up among her children. How did you get the necklace?" she asked, staring at my neck.

"A neighbor found it and gave it to me," I said, telling only part of the story.

She didn't look convinced but was too well conditioned to push the issue.

Leaving the safe as I had found it seemed right. None of this was really mine to make any decisions, at least not yet.

"Do you know what's in the library safe?" I asked Suzy.

"Papers. Her will, titles, deeds, and contracts."

I didn't have any desire to read legal documents.

"Suzy, I have some healing powers. Would you like me to see if I can help undo some of the work Annette did to your brain?" I was thinking of Mandy.

"I guess it would be all right, but I don't think of myself as sick. I'm just a loyal person. If you do try, please do so while wearing the jewelry."

"Why?" I asked.

"You radiated a soothing feeling when you were wearing them."

"It seems a little odd wearing one earring, but sure, just for the healing process," I agreed reluctantly. She reopened the safe and brought me the jewelry.

"Let's go to the spa," I directed her. It was a room off the bedroom suite.

She laid faceup on the massage table. I sat near her head, like I did with Mandy, and with the jewelry in place, I put my hands over her ears. First sending in relaxation vibes, then scanning her body and her brain for any damage. One area in her brain was like tiny, melted wires.

This is what Annette had tried to do to me with the lasers. How many people had she damaged with that equipment? Using Dr. Corona's anatomy model, the psychiatrist's knowledge of the brain, and my copying skills, I reshaped the area to look like my brain. It was slow work. It was like pulling a wire out of wax and then cleaning it, but there were thousands of very thin strands in the waxiness. This whole clump was smaller than a pin head. After working on her for over an hour, only five strands were cleared.

When I pulled my hands away, she opened her eyes. "It feels better, now," she said.

"There are a lot of gunked-up strands in there, it's going to take a while to undo unless I can learn some better techniques. Since you're already on the table, would you like a back massage?" I asked. This time would be used to ask her questions without her being aware.

"Do you know how to give one?" she asked.

"I've only read about it," I replied honestly.

"I'm super good at them, I can talk you through it," she offered.

"Sure, get comfortable."

Suzy showed me how to adjust the table. She set the room up with low lights, warm oil, soft sounds, a pleasant smell, and she stripped down to her panties. This time she laid down on her stomach putting her face in a hole in the bed. She explained that massage therapists usually provided a sheet for the customer's modesty. She had me rub the oil on my hands and then on her back.

At this point, I froze her and copied her massage training. While rubbing her back, I picked through her mind. She had a Ph.D. in mathematics, Annette used her for bookkeeping. Nothing like over qualifications. The massage training was part of Annette's all-purpose rule. Suzy oversaw the household staff, so I gave her instruction that they should stay on at the house if they wanted. They were free to come and go as they pleased. They could contact whoever they wanted. If they decided they wanted to stay on, they would be given proper pay. All would get a service bonus whether they chose to stay or not. The amount depended on how long they had already worked here. She had worked for Annette for more than twelve years, never once was she allowed to contact her family, not one vacation day, and never received a salary. Amaku was a better place with Annette dead.

It was hard to understand her magic. She had some, but it wasn't reacting to mine, and she wasn't even using most of it. Just grasping at straws, I asked, "Why aren't you using your magic."

"It's been bound."

"I don't see a bracelet."

"Annette's magic could do it, no objects needed."

I now had Annette's spirit gift. I'd had all of her magic at one point, and nothing was different about it. There must be a way to undo the binding. Pulling her magic as if to take it. It moved normally. It compacted easily. Trying a releasing spell I'd gotten from Mrs. Kim, I uncovered the binding so that it was visible. Letting the spirit gift work on the binding was much the same as untying a hard knot. After about ten minutes, it worked loose. It was the work of an evil genius. Annette used Suzy's own magic to make the bind. I studied the magic, untying it and retying it several times until it was as simple as tying my shoelaces. Leaving her loosely bound, it would work itself free in time, but it wouldn't be associated with me.

Finishing up, I instructed Suzy's brain to release all the feel-good chemicals and to believe the whole session was just about the massage. Unfreezing her, she was allowed to get up at her own pace.

"I feel absolutely amazing," she said, when she was up and dressed. "You have insightful hands." Then her face got somber, and she asked, "Annette's dead and now you are in charge, right?"

"That's the way Mrs. Kim has petitioned it, but it's not official yet. Until this is all figured out, please make sure you take care of yourself and that the other staff members take care of themselves. Hopefully, you can all help and support each other through this. All the household expenses will continue to be paid. Like Mrs. Kim said, feel free to contact us if you need anything."

"Are we allowed to take the yacht out for a day," she asked.

"Sure, but isn't that work for you?" I asked.

"With all of us helping, it will be more fun than work, especially if Annette isn't on board."

"How about this coming Saturday, everyone from Nana's house could join. You guys could teach us what to do. We'll bring our own food and drink," I offered.

"Meet us on the dock at sunrise?" Suzy questioned, with a smile.

"Great, we'll see you then."

I left the house still wearing the extra jewelry, it wasn't intentional, but I didn't go back to return it. Instead, they were added to the pouch with my leaves and seeds.

What a day! My body was exhausted from all the emotions. We ended up having a movie night at the Kims'. All of us snuggled together on the huge sectional couch. Jae on one side of me and Caly on the other. I felt safe enough to let my guard down and let my magic just pour into them. When Mrs. Kim came to check up on us, she saw us as one huge lump of happy.

GANG ACTIVITY

SATURDAY AT SUNRISE, we all met on the dock with our coolers and beach bags. After introductions, Suzy gave out assignments to start the day, Alex was to help in the kitchen, Dion on the helm, Raine at the bar, and the rest of us were to rotate to give everyone breaks. No one was to talk about the Hortons or the Teufels. We were here to enjoy life. Most of the time, we relaxed while breathing the salty ocean air. We stayed out all night, and of course, I slept out under the stars. We docked about nine o'clock Sunday morning. Everyone pitched in to clean up, so we didn't get back to the house right away.

Jae was waiting for me. Today was his last day of summer with his grandparents and he wanted us to spend it together. We were running kites along the beach when we saw the Horton crowd arrive, and minutes later, the druggie group showed up. Jae stopped and stared.

"I wonder who invited them?" Jae asked, his mouth gaped in surprise.

"Probably Max. I'd be too embarrassed to show up this soon," I muttered.

"You think Max is going to have them sell drugs for him?" Jae tilted his head toward Tifton following Max around like a puppy.

"Nothing would amaze me at this point."

Sharlyn and Brooklyn were in their regular cabana looking like they still owned the place. Without a word, we both reeled in our kites and headed to our end of the beach. Caly went over to be with Brent. The only nice thing about seeing everyone again was they started up the volleyball games. Jae and I watched from a distance.

Both households had supper together with cake and ice cream to celebrate our goodbyes. Jae and I gave each other a long hug and kissed on both cheeks. We promised to keep in touch. I was really going to miss him. Without his friendship this summer, I probably would've joined Nana on the ranch much sooner. This was my last week on the beach.

Feeling lonely and sad at Jae's departure, I decided to lie in the cabana and wait for the stars when Caly came to join me. She had two drinks and handed me one.

"What's this?" I asked.

"The guys were able to break into a yacht and grab some good whiskey, Tifton thought you might like some." My suspicions went on high alert, and I didn't reach out to take a glass. He thought I liked whiskey when I supposedly had such a reaction to it before? Aaron must have told him the real reason I left the yacht.

"Oh, don't be silly, I watched him pour them, they didn't do anything stupid," and she took a drink from both glasses to show me. "I'm so happy Brent came back today. I was worried I wouldn't see him for the rest of the summer."

"Are they gone then?" I asked, even though the partying sounds were ongoing.

"No, I just came to bring you the drink, I'm going to stay just long enough so you know they aren't drugged." Taking a small sip was convincing that it was only whiskey and cola. Caly's mind completely assured me they were clean. She wanted to take the empty glasses back with her, so we dumped out my water and poured the drink into the empty tumbler. When she left, I went into the house to use the restroom and change into pajamas.

Before stepping back out to the cabana, I gulped the last of the drink forgetting it wasn't water. It tasted awful after just having brushed my teeth. Oh well, it wasn't much, and my body wouldn't react to it anyway. No patio lights were on, and this side of the house was dark to better see the stars.

I'd just got situated on the bed when Tifton came strolling up.

"Aren't you going to hug and kiss me goodbye, too," he asked, with a pout that he thought made him look sexy, but my skin tingled alerting me of danger. It was creepy that he'd watched our goodbyes earlier. He climbed right up beside me and propped his head up on his elbow. I had absolutely no feelings for him except fear.

My magic certainly didn't reach out to him. His eyes were a bit mesmerizing. They were exactly like Glenn's. No stargazing was worth being alone with him. As I started to roll to the opposite side to get off the bed and go inside, three things stopped me. My mind and stomach felt woozy, and a powerful restraining ward surrounded me. Apparently, Tifton put something in the drink while I was inside.

He grabbed my arm and pulled me back. I tried to order him to let me go, but my voice was blocked by the restraint. My self-healing was busy trying to isolate the drug, but the ward hampering my magic was even making that nearly impossible. I was in full panic when he shoved me down on my back. He had my breasts exposed and my panties off in a few short moments. He didn't even have to hold me down because my limbs were not responding to my commands. No seduction magic was being used. He had no care for my willingness. He dropped his swim trunks and knelt between my thighs. He then pulled my legs over his shoulders. This idiot was going to rape me and take my virginity.

I called on every combination of my magic, but nothing was getting through the ward. A few drops of purple truffle liquid would come in handy right now. Out of options, desperation had me calling on the dark magic. Starting with blue, then adding black to painfully squeeze his erection. That only seemed to heighten his excitement. Thankfully the pressure slowed the blood flow to his penis and the erection collapsed.

When his brain registered his inactivity, he raged and back handed me across the face so hard that my nose broke causing blood to gush. He didn't even know that my magic caused it, still he blamed it on me. With my self-healing holding down the drugs, no healing rushed to my nose. Oh crap, this hurt. Having been cushioned from pain for so long, this pain felt enhanced, and tears of pain rolled out of both eyes.

He collapsed on me, breathing hard and smelling of alcohol. His thoughts were so derogatory toward me and still self-entitled. What a man he was, how much better he was than me, that I was amazed by his good looks and his big penis. After some time, he rolled off and turned me over, positioning my hips on some pillows. OH NO! He wasn't finished with me. He squeezed some lubricant between my cheeks and started to move in. I reached for the same dark magic again but this time combining it with the freeze. Fortune was with me, and he stopped mid motion.

Reaching for his memory of raping Jae, I did the opposite of a smudge by replaying the event as if it was happening now. Him being drunk helped with the illusion. He finished without penetrating, pulled his swimming trunks up, and headed back to meet his friends, leaving me with my butt still propped up in the air.

When he was out of sight, I was finally able to concentrate enough to break his restraint. The distance must have weakened the hold. Rolling off the cabana bed, I automatically grabbed my panties as I went stumbling to the nearest bushes, my stomach emptied its contents.

The stupid asshole had not even used condoms. I was sticky and slimy.

I was wiping my mouth with the back of my hand and using the panties to soak up some of the stickiness when Tifton returned. I scrunched into the bushes to hide, avoiding the puke. The smell was burning my sore nose.

"My present for you tonight is you each get to have a turn with Sera; I'm in the sharing mood," I heard Tifton say. He approached the bed with Brent, Aaron, and Jacob following him. This imbecile was going to have his friends rape me, too. It didn't seem possible. I had to reach inside each of his friend's minds to convince myself that they wouldn't have followed through with the rape. In utter disbelief, every one of them was looking forward to the act and they already had a pecking order. It went in order of their red magic levels, highest to lowest. Brent was going to be next.

Right now, in this horrific situation with these complete idiots, my dignity demanded they be punished. I hexed all four of them. Their balls would swell to an excruciating size if ever they tried to have sex with anyone that wasn't old enough or without full expressed consent. The swelling would last two weeks, renewable with each attempt. This hex would last their entire lives. Only a spell-breaker could remove it. The spell included that their minds resist any suggestion that someone had used a hex on them.

Tifton deserved extra punishment. I wanted to use dark blue to cut and melt the ducts that would allow sperm to reach the semen so that he would never have children. Uncertain where my restraint came from, I didn't do it. I also wanted to weaken his erectile muscles, but it would be too easily linked to tonight.

"Dude, what the fuck, you didn't put a strong enough ward on her," Brent said as he approached the bed. Each had to check the bed for themselves. Surely the powerful Horton couldn't have made such an elementary security mistake.

"No way, I definitely put a high-security ward on her; she couldn't move," Tifton said defensively.

As they argued about their lost opportunity, I did add more punishment, binding twenty percent of their red magic. This light binding would probably last about three months. Definitely enough time to get their butts kicked in training, and if I understood the academy system correctly, it would affect their after-graduation job selections.

When they finally returned to the party, I gathered the bed sheets and scurried inside. First stop was the washing machine. After pretreating the blood stains, I turned to go to my room, bumping into Freya.

"Is everything all right?" she asked with concern.

"Lady problems," I answered, putting my hands over my lower stomach.

"Take a long soak in the tub, and I'll bring you an herbal tea that will knock you out for the night."

"That would be great, no hurry though, it is going to be a long bath."

I chewed a seed to get rid of the goo, but it wasn't near as bad as it could've been using that much dark magic. Maybe it didn't build up as much if you were protecting yourself. My stomach was empty. My mind and body were in shock. I showered, scrubbing several times with soap. I added a fizz bomb to the bath and soaked for a long time. I drained the water a couple times and refilled the tub. There didn't seem to be enough water to wash away the anger and disgust. When I finally got out and had put on a robe, I heard Freya say, "I've left the tea near the sink. If you need to talk, I'll be in my room."

When I opened the door that separated the bathtub and toilet from the sink and vanity area, it surprised me to see Freya still there. One look at my face, and she gave me a big bear hug. When I let her go, she patted my hand and left. She seemed to know something serious had happened but didn't want to probe. I downed the tea in one long swallow. Caly was sitting on my bed hugging her knees.

"Are you okay?" I asked.

She just shook her head and buried her face in her knees. I climbed on the bed and put my arms around her. We stretched out on the bed, her cheek resting on my shoulder. Her whole chest was heaving in and out. I wiped her tears with my robe sleeve while pulsing comfort and healing into her. We fell asleep in that position without her ever telling me what happened. Of course, everything played out in detail for me to see.

After the boys didn't have their fun with me, they went back to have fun with Caly. They restrained her on one of the yacht's beds. Brent pulled her clothes off and went to rape her with the other three watching. He stopped before penetrating. The same thing happened with the other three. Each howling and holding their cold drinks to their crotches, after they tried to mount her. Sadly, they blamed her for their pain, calling her a witch and sending shocks at her that might have done some serious damage if I hadn't bound some of their magic. Thankfully, Aaron canceled the restraint as they left. As soon as she got dressed, Caly ran here to me.

When I woke, Caly was spooned against my back, just like Jae had done on their patio. I was beginning to wonder if my magic was like snuggling up to someone warm on a chilly night. All of us humans had so many insecurities. My vibrations seemed to calm them. Caly woke when I moved off the bed.

"Thank you for not having me talk last night, it was too embarrassing," Caly said sleepily.

"No worries, some things are just too hard to talk about."

"Brent and those guys are total jerks. I convinced myself Brent thought I was special and that he would protect me."

"I'm sorry for whatever you went through last night," I told her.

In the kitchen, eating cereal at the counter in my robe, I announced, "I'm going back to the ranch by train tomorrow." Everyone stopped what they were doing and looked at me.

"Alex and I were going to drive you in three days, what's the rush," Dion asked.

"I'm homesick."

"Come on, you can wait a few days. Caly will come with us. Right Caly?" Alex asked.

"Sure, I'd love to see the ranch, nothing here at the beach now that summer is ending," she said, and everyone looked surprised.

"What, you won't miss Brent?" Raine asked, trying to hide a smile.

"I really won't," Caly said, looking into her bowl and shaking her head slightly.

Raine gave Alex a surprised but happy look.

"Well, if Caly is coming with, I can wait a few days. I don't see why you need me along."

"Who would point out all the sights?" Alex asked.

"Umm like what, the majestic fruit stands?" I asked with an eyebrow raised.

"Exactly," Alex said.

For the remaining days, we stayed in or near the house. We spent time packing and helping clean. Caly and I both had more luggage than what we'd brought from school. Dion had found a luggage rack to put on the roof of the car. The four of us had way too much luggage to just fit in the trunk.

Freya and Raine were staying here and going to thoroughly clean the house to get it ready for summer's end.

They'd found a small house to rent with Dion and Alex, but they would wait until the guys got back to move.

The day before we left, I stopped over at the house to check in with Suzy. The house was still immaculate, but everyone was much friendlier and happier. Each servant popped to attention when I came near.

"They don't need to do that," I told Suzy.

"It's in their comfort zone to have a boss to please."

"Make sure they get out on the yacht again soon," was my only instruction. I heard a muffled shriek of delight coming from another room. I did another healing session with Suzy, and her magic was fully unbound. I sent Annette's blue magic into her to work on the damage Annette had done, not just for this session but until the threads were cleaned. Then she would heal the damage in others.

"Would you be willing to assist other victims if they came for help?"

"Extremely willing. I'm already involved with the Organization to Help the Victims of Magical Abuse," she informed me. "In the therapy sessions, they told us that helping others might speed our recovery."

On our last sunset walk, I asked Mrs. Kim, "Will you keep an eye out for Suzy and staff in case they're too proud to ask for help?"

"Yes. No need for you to ask. That is my intention," she assured me. "And I already introduced Suzy to the newly appointed board members of the help organization."

Mr. Kim surprised me by giving me a hug goodbye, and I finally got to copy his diving skills. He had won several championships in his youth. I copied his SCUBA skills as well.

HOME ON THE RANCH

WHILE WAITING IN the car for everyone to get settled, I stretched my yellow magic across all the beach houses, sending the message that it was illegal to be bound into servitude and that all were free to leave. If they needed assistance, the Organization to Help the Victims of Magical Abuse would aid them. In addition, Mrs. Kim and Suzy would aid in lining up transportation to their office. Instantly, some of the help walked out of the houses. They were not carrying anything, no suitcases, or purses. These were the staff that had families ready to welcome them home. As satisfying as it was to finally do something substantial, I regretted being too scared to do something sooner. With Annette and Mr. Horton both wanting me dead, it had been too dangerous to call too much attention to myself.

We pulled away from the beach house around nine o'clock. We had about an eight-hour drive to get to Nana's.

But with Alex's detailed itinerary, it was going to take much longer. Caly had her headphones on to listen to music.

"Say, why didn't you use your headset on the beach this summer?" I asked.

"It was rescued from the Hortons' trash when Mom was working there. I didn't want Sharlyn to see. Just one more thing she could mock." It was strange to see how much Sera wanted to be accepted by the elite crowd. Sharlyn's altered clothes didn't embarrass her, but this did. In a way, it was natural to want to be a part of those you thought were better than you. But from my way of thinking, it would cheapen her if she was close friends with them.

Alex and Dion were chatting together and listening to good music in the front seat. I stared out the window at the passing landscapes, thinking about seeing Glenn again. The Red Territory was the most populated, so for a while, it was city and suburbs. However, we were taking scenic routes whenever possible.

We stopped to stretch at scenic overlooks. The first one was a lighthouse that overlooked the ocean and Redding. It was breathtaking. We even saw a pod of dolphins. Lunch was at a dive diner that had rave reviews, and the food was excellent.

It was easy to tell when we crossed into Green Territory. We began passing orchards, fields, and ranches. Alex had us stop at a few of the orchards, he didn't want to arrive at Nana's empty handed. To make it cheaper, we picked what we bought. I paid for refueling the car.

It was near sunset when we arrived. I had them park at the Bensons'. Nana wouldn't like the smell of the car near her house, and Alex and Dion were staying in the Bensons' guest room, while Caly would sleep with me.

Nana was there to introduced them to Mrs. Benson, and she welcomed them like family. She hugged them and showed them the room. Nana and I bear hugged tight and long. Then we settled at the table for some homemade apple pie. Mr. Benson and Neal joined as well. The pie reminded Alex to bring in some fruit for the Bensons.

Before he went back into the house, he helped get Caly's and my luggage off the roof of the car. He handed us Nana's fruit, and it was a struggle to carry everything. We had to walk over grass to get to Nana's, so we had to carry our suitcases, as well. We left the fruit bags on the kitchen table and dumped our suitcases on my bed. It was nice to see Nana had kept my bedroom plants alive.

We hadn't seen Chris or Glenn yet, so I took Caly out to the barn in search of them. Since Chris was out shoveling in the corral, Glenn was probably in the barn, so I went in there first. Excitement at seeing Glenn had me tingling all over. Caly had decided to go pet the horses, most likely to give us some privacy.

Entering the open barn door sent me into shock. I couldn't process what I was seeing. Lysa was leaning back against a stall, with her knee slightly bent, and her head tilted sideways while she looked adoringly at Glenn with an inviting smile. Glenn's hand was on the stall, just above her shoulder, and he was leaning in, looking like he was going to kiss her. My stomach lurched, and I spun around. My foot hit a metal bucket that was on the ground near the doorway. It clanged loudly as it knocked down a pitchfork from the wall. I didn't even stop to straighten it back up. I sprinted toward the lake. My energy was bursting out of me. My eyes were filling with tears. It was silly to be upset. I was too young for Glenn, but logic wasn't always a part of matters of the heart.

Tackled from behind, I landed face-first in the grass. Glenn had used physical force to get me to stop running. His weight was making it hard to breathe. My red started to build to blast him off of me when he rolled over and got to his feet.

"What's the matter?" Lysa shouted from the barn door.

"Give us a minute," Glenn called back. I got to my feet and looked at her. She didn't want to leave us alone, but she reluctantly went toward Caly and the horses. "What happened back there?" Glenn asked me, motioning toward the barn.

"Nothing," I said defensively. My magic was still leaking out and tears had started to fall. Ever since leaving the beach house, I had not been putting up my shields, leaving me with a lot of unspent magic. My magic, my brain, and body were all erratic, making it hard to stay in the moment. My mind was filling with everything that went wrong this summer. My sister being an elitist snob that didn't remember me, Annette trying to kill me, the trials, a grandmother who hated me, Tifton, and now this.

Glenn let out a small chuckle and gave me a big hug. Mostly, to help me control myself. "You don't look fine." He poured his control into me, and I calmed down. We stayed in the hug while he reviewed all the summer events bubbling in my thoughts. While he was doing that, I searched for his relationship with Lysa and was pleased to find out that I interrupted what was going to be their first kiss. He broke off the hug when he realized I was in his head.

"Dang, you slowed Annette's bleeding, possibly saving her life even though you knew what she was up to. I have to say, you're my hero for not letting her bleed out. I'm glad you punished Tifton and his friends. I would probably have killed him if I was there." He was looking at me in amazement. "I was wrong. I do trust and admire you. It was wrong of me to say that I have the same magic as you. You're in a league of your own. Getting a glimpse of how you handled all you've been though, makes me want to be a better person."

I reached into his brain to smudge his memory, and he blocked me. "You don't have to do that. I can't tell anyone about your magic without them wondering how I know."

I turned to look at the lake, scanning the waters to burn off some the surplus energy and to calm me more. Glenn tugged on a lock of my hair, when I looked at him, he said, "Too bad you're only a kid," he gave me a rueful smile.

A frustrated hiss burst out of me. "I don't feel like a kid."

"Oh, isn't this cozy," Lysa said sneering.

Oh great, jealous Lysa has showed up. All the petty stuff she did to me when her friends came to visit rushed through my thoughts. She treated me fine until she had other friends around. I could read Glenn's thoughts as he read mine. Her simple comment just dropped her in his esteem.

Caly came walking over, she grabbed my wrist and pulled my arm around her. We walked arm and arm back to the horses while Glenn walked Lysa to her house. When I looked over my shoulder at them, I was glad to see they were not touching. Looking at the Benson house, I saw Mr. Benson, Alex, and Dion visiting on the porch, so there wasn't going to be a good night kiss either. But it was embarrassing to think that they saw me run out of the barn and that Glenn had to comfort me.

"Tomorrow, we'll ride." I promised Caly to get her to leave the horse corral.

"I've never even sat on one. You shouldn't have told me that, now I'm going to be too excited to sleep."

"No worries, this fresh air will knock you out," I assured her.

"Fresh air? I wouldn't call this fresh."

"Well, we are next to the corrals. Chris actually keeps this quite clean."

"Don't let me be here when it's dirty," Caly said, holding her nose. She could only smell manure, but I could smell horse, leather, and grain.

Chris stopped by to say hi, which was a big deal considering he was shy. Caly loved the dogs, too.

"I can't wait to see this in daylight," Caly said, looking around.

I showed Caly the pellet production process, I was hanging around the barn hoping Glenn would come back. He slept in the barn's upstairs apartment, in Chris's spare room. Even after showing her all the animals and Chris's whiskey still, there was no sign of Glenn. We headed back to the house and saw Glenn had joined the guys on the Benson porch.

At sunrise the following morning, Caly went riding on our gentlest horse, but only inside the fence. Sending her my riding skills bolstered her confidence. We got her out of the gate and going from a trot to a gallop. Her smile and laughter made my summer seem much brighter. As we loped, our hair flowed in sync with our horses' manes. Glenn watching us, and a pleasant rippling went down my spine. We only rode about an hour, but Caly was sore when we walked out of the corral.

In the afternoon, the weather was perfect for windsurfing, so Neal, Caly, and I went out on the lake. We borrowed Lysa's equipment to set up Caly. Sharing my skills with Caly got her going right away, but we still started her on a smaller board. Caly got tired first and went to watch us from the shore. Neal had a crush on Caly, and he was showing off his skills. He challenged me to a race that he won. He'd been windsurfing all summer.

Glenn stopped to watch us from the barn door. We hadn't been near enough to talk all day. He was avoiding me. At supper, I did get close enough to see his eyes, they made my knees weak. The steel blue pinned me, and I froze like prey. He kept his body casual and relaxed even though he was holding his magic tight. He might not want to be interested in me yet, but his magic had a will of its own.

The next day, we all rode the horses up the creek to our favorite fly-fishing spot. The scenery to the fishing hole was breathtaking. We rode between two mountains, following the rushing water upstream. This was easily my favorite ride and activity on the ranch.

Chris brought a pack horse to carry supplies. When we stopped, Chris tied the horses so they could eat the lush green grass. We enjoyed fishing and grilling. One at a time, we shook the fish in a bag of herbs and spices and Chris grilled them. Alex cooked the vegetables.

"You can't get trout better than this. It's fresh caught from clean waters and cooked over an open flame," Neal bragged.

"Plus, Chris's herbs and spices are amazing, too," I added.

When we were done eating, mostly just skin and the bones were left. We took the dishes and grill to the stream to rinse them. We laid them out on the rocks to dry before repacking them.

We all ate a few huckleberries straight from nearby bushes. When we saw a rare Amaku black bear doing the same, we all backed away quietly, except Chris. He was too close to move without having the bear give chase. When the bear spotted him, it reared on its hind legs and roared. Even though our bears were among the world's smallest, it was still dangerous. Chris, with a gentle, careful air, slid his pistol from its holster. This type of dart pistol was allowed to farmers and ranchers. It would probably take a minute or two for the tranquilizer to put the animal to sleep. My red magic started building in case I had to help defend him. Chris never let his eyes stray from the living teddy bear.

When the bear started on his second rear, Chris said in a stone-cold, booming voice, "I'll be your huckleberry." That bear never finished his stance and turned to speed away.

"I guess that bear has seen some old Western movies," Neal said with a smirk. Chris gave him a rare smile in return.

Packing up, we made sure not to leave anything behind, and we watered down the firepit. My pent-up red energy was released into the wind behind us.

We were all sore after the long ride. That evening at supper, I was doubly surprised. First, Glenn was going back to Redding in the morning with Alex and Dion. Second, Caly was staying with us until school started.

Glenn needed to go back early to find a sponsorship so he could attend law school in Senaland. He had been accepted by the university, but for him to attend, he needed someone high up in the Nokuland government to approve. He would have to be screened and sign a contract of intent to become a liaison between the two countries' governments. Most likely becoming an ambassador. It was quite an ambitious undertaking, and he'd be a perfect candidate. I asked Dion and Alex to introduce him to Mrs. Kim when they got back. She would know the correct process to gain permission.

When Nana mentioned that tuition would be expensive, I asked, "Were you able to sell the extra plants?"

"Yes, Glenn was very instrumental in getting a very good price." He used yellow to find out what the buyer was willing to pay, it was most likely the reason for his success.

"Do you have plans for the money?" I asked.

"None, except to deposit it in your account."

"Please, just use it to give Glenn a summer's end bonus."

"It's a nice chunk of money, are you sure?" Nana asked.

"Absolutely." She gave me a quick hug of approval.

"You're wish is my command," Nana said with a smile. "Senaland's university system doesn't have summer breaks. At least not a long one. We probably won't see him back next summer," Nana said a little sad. That made me a little sad, too.

Our goodbyes were quick the morning they left, and my magic felt damp like a wet blanket.

I was glad Caly stayed on, otherwise it would've been miserable because Lysa wasn't talking to me. She was still upset that Glenn ran after me and never picked up the relationship again. Neal wouldn't have spent as much time with me, but with Caly there, he hung around almost nonstop. Neal also insisted that we watch an old Western movie titled *Tombstone*. Chris joined us for the viewing.

Caly received notice from the Healing Arts Institute that she had done so well as a first-year student that not only was her scholarship renewed with a bump in funds, but she would be in the most prestigious dormitory room. The corner room with a view of the mountains, and she could have her pick of suite mates. She selected me as her roommate. Jamyla and Kya would share our bathroom for another year. Starting our second year was going to be much more interesting, especially with Freya's talented alterations to both our wardrobes.

In a way, Caly was becoming a surrogate sister ever since being disappointed at finding Tatiana was Audrey, the elite golden child. Getting to know more about Audrey seemed like a pursuit of folly. Spoiled, entitled upper class was what was wrong with this island. Plus, Caly understood that learning about family could be more traumatic and less fairytale.

As excited as we were for a new school year, my emotions were tempered with dread of having more people wanting revenge on me. Jennifer and the Hortons' rage at me was nothing to dismiss. If or when Caly realized how much of my power was hidden, she'd hate me. Audrey would eventually despise me. The only thing for certain was that being blessed beyond measure wasn't all chocolate and sunshine.

ACKNOWLEDGMENTS

To my neighbor Geany, and my sister Barb for being my encouraging first readers. Many thanks to my editor, George Verongos, for his patience and encouraging words.

Made in United States
North Haven, CT
09 November 2022

26492504R00202